ANDREW
GRANT

DIE TWICE

PAN BOOKS

First published in the US 2010 as a Thomas Dunne Book for Minotaur Books
an imprint of St Martin's Publishing Group, New York, U.S.A.

First published in the UK 2010 by Macmillan

This edition first published 2022 by Pan Books
an imprint of Pan Macmillan
The Smithson, 6 Briset Street, London EC1M 5NR
EU representative: Macmillan Publishers Ireland Ltd, 1st Floor,
The Liffey Trust Centre, 117–126 Sheriff Street Upper,
Dublin 1, D01 YC43
Associated companies throughout the world
www.panmacmillan.com

ISBN 978-1-5290-9283-7

1 3 5 7 9 8 6 4 2

A CIP catalogue record for this book is available from the British Library.

Printed and bound by CPI Group (UK) Ltd, Croydon, CR0 4YY

For Tasha

My sun, my moon, and my stars – only brighter
and more beautiful

DIE TWICE

He had two guns, as I expected. His service weapon, and a backup. A factory-fresh Beretta M9/92F, and an ancient, scratched Walther PPK. One under his left arm, the other strapped to his left ankle.

Both still in their holsters.

There's a strict protocol for bringing the career of a fellow professional to a premature end. It demanded that I take out the Beretta. Place it in his right hand. Curl his index finger through the trigger guard. Release the safety. Discharge at least one round. Give him the final dignity of appearing to whoever found his body that he'd at least gone down fighting.

I'd always followed those rules before. With an Armenian. Two Iranians. A Peruvian. A Ukrainian. Even a Frenchman, on one bizarre occasion. But that evening, I left the guns where they were. I didn't even loosen the straps that held them in place. I just left him lying facedown on the strip of coarse office carpet, picked up the green metal flask he'd been so desperate to take, and walked away.

He was from Royal Navy Intelligence, just like me.

The insult I'd paid him was deliberate. Calculated. Unmistakable, to anyone from our world.

And only ever paid to a traitor.

ONE

I come from a small family. My mother was an only child. My father had one sister, but they weren't close. We didn't see much of her even when I was a kid. Partly because she still lived in Ireland, and my parents found it a nuisance to get over there. But mostly because the two of them didn't get on. My dad is very practical and down-to-earth. If he can't see or touch or taste something, it doesn't exist. My aunt was the absolute opposite. Her life was barely her own. She abdicated all personal responsibility and just drifted happily along, governed by an endless stream of signs and omens and portents and premonitions.

The premonitions in particular drove a wedge between the two of them. He thought she was some kind of crazy, half-pagan simpleton. She thought he was too stiff and stubborn to see the world in front of his nose. And so any-time the family was together, they fought. Relentlessly. Not physically, obviously. It was more subtle than that. At some point, soon after we arrived, she would announce a prediction. We would be waiting for it. He would denounce it. Then the duel would begin. There'd be endless, pointed looks. Barbed comments. Contrived, cynical observations. The level of sarcasm would ratchet higher and higher until one was proved right and the other descended into days of impenetrable sulking.

Believe me, those visits were always fun.

My own view falls somewhere between the two. I certainly don't believe the future is already set. We're not helpless. Our destiny is ultimately in our own hands. But take some time to think, mix that with a little experience, and it's not too hard to see what's waiting around the corner.

In some circumstances, at least.

Mainly the ones involving bosses and their stupid plans.

I knew no one was following me, but I still had the cab from Midway drop me half a mile from my destination. But this was no random paranoia. Old habits die hard. The first thing you always do when you're sent somewhere new is tap into the service grapevine. To find out how the land lies in your next city. It's quicker and more efficient than any corporate intranet I've ever come across. And from what I'd been hearing about the current state of play, a little extra caution would not be out of place.

The ride in from the airport felt strangely flat. I had no idea why I'd been sent to Chicago, but that wasn't unusual. You begin lots of assignments without the slightest clue what you're going to be asked to do. And the way a mission looks on paper is generally a million miles from how it plays out in the field. For me, that's part of the excitement. Like being handed a Polaroid photograph, fresh from the camera, and watching as the image gradually takes shape on the warm, shiny paper. But the familiar feeling of promise and anticipation was completely missing that morning. Normally I love the first glimpse of a new place, but as I watched the cityscape morphing out of the traffic haze, it left me absolutely cold. Because I knew I wasn't going to have anything meaningful to do, there. I was just passing through. Quickly, I hoped. I should have been called straight back to London. This detour had the feeling of a wrong turn about it. The sense that the fallout from my last mission—or the debacle that followed it—had knocked me off the freeway and shunted my career onto an obscure backstreet. I needed to get back into the thick of things, to put the record straight. And to find some real work to do. Something to keep me from dwelling too long on absent friends.

My orders were simple. Report to a liaison officer called Richard Fothergill. I'd never worked with the guy, but I'd heard him talked about often enough over the years. The prospect of meeting him was the one ray of sunshine cutting through the heavy, swirling clouds that had filled the sky since dawn. And not because he was supposed to be nice. His reputation made him out to be pretty much the opposite. Which actually seemed like a good thing, that morning. Recent events had left me with no wish to add to my circle of friends.

In my profession there's a line that's better not crossed when it comes to building friendships. The rationale is pretty obvious. And the line is even more pronounced when it comes to closer, more personal relationships. This rule was made clear to me when I first started out, and back then I'd never have dreamed of breaking it. Assignment after assignment came and went, and I never wavered. I never came close. I never thought I would. And then, three years ago, something happened to change that. Or rather, someone. My liaison officer on a job in Madrid. Tanya Wilson. The most spectacular human who ever lived.

Tanya and I both knew the conventions. We were aware of the protocols. We'd heard all the wise words and sensible advice from the senior ranks. But despite everything, the line that divided us evaporated before our eyes. I felt like it had never existed. Without it, we started to fall. And we'd have fallen all the way—there's no doubt—if it hadn't been for two things. A spell in the hospital for me. And a transfer order for her.

The hours after Tanya left turned into days and then weeks, but she was never far from my thoughts. And even after the months had become years, no one ever took her place. I often wondered whether things would be the same if our paths ever crossed again. I'd almost lost hope of that happening, though, when she did suddenly resurface. It was at the end of the case I'd just closed. And her presence showed me two things.

The flame had not burned out during our time apart.

And the line that should have separated us had been drawn for a reason.

So, with both the personal and professional sides of my life needing a shot in the arm, it's fair to say I was looking for a short-term distraction. Richard Fothergill sounded like he could fit the bill. He was a very unusual person. Because although he worked in liaison now, he'd started his service life in the field. He'd made a transition that most observers would tell you is impossible. Which statistically, it is. I've checked. And from what I've been told, only sixteen people have ever managed it.

I figured the Hancock Center was a suitably innocuous location, so I bailed out and found a good spot, near the flags and the fountains. I paused there for five minutes, watching the shoppers and tourists and office workers bracing themselves against the wind. I waited until I was certain that no one was paying me any undue attention. Then I walked north for another block, crossed the street, and made my way back up the opposite side of Michigan Avenue.

It took me twelve minutes to reach the Wrigley Building. The public entrance to the British Consulate is on the thirteenth floor, but I took the elevator to the fourteenth, to an office marked with our usual cover name—UK Trade & Investment. The receptionist was expecting me. She checked my ID and then came out from behind her desk and led me to a row of doors on the right of the lobby area, away from the main corridor. There were four. They looked like closets from the outside, but when she opened the nearest one I saw it led to a clear cylinder, about seven feet tall and three feet across. The segment facing me slid open, and she gestured for me to step inside. It was unusual for people to make me bother with this kind of thing, but after what had apparently happened here in the last couple of days I supposed a bit of stable-door bolting was inevitable. I complied, and immediately the curved glass slotted back into place behind me. I heard a gentle hiss and dry, bottled air swirled around me for fully twenty seconds. The sound died away. I waited while the machine sniffed for incriminating particles. Then an indicator light above my head turned from red to green and the panel ahead of me swung aside, releasing me into the narrow gray corridor on the other side.

The office I wanted was at the far end, on the left. The door was standing open, so I gave a cursory knock and stepped straight inside. The room was larger than I was expecting. Around twenty feet by thirty. Not a bad size for a liaison guy. In fact, the biggest I'd ever seen. There was a glass desk to my left, completely bare, with a high-tech chrome and black mesh chair behind it. A round glass coffee table to my right, covered with newspapers, and surrounded by four black leather chairs. A densely woven Oriental rug filling most of the floor space between the two areas. And another man, directly ahead of me on the far side of the room. He was on his feet, his back toward me, gazing out at the river from the central one of three large windows. He was around five feet eleven with thick, glossy gray hair clipped neatly above the collar of his blue pin-striped jacket. When he turned to greet me I saw that his lined face looked somber and dignified, like a statesman or a judge. I put him in his late fifties. He was smart. Imposing. The kind of person a corporation or government department would put on TV to break the worst kind of news. The only thing that jarred was his left arm. It was in a sling. But it wasn't the injury that struck me. I'd already heard the rumor about his recent brush with a 9 mm bullet. Fired by a fellow officer. In that very room. No. It was the material he'd used to support it that caught my eye. It was fine, blue, pin-striped wool. Exactly the same kind of cloth as his suit. A haute couture bandage. I couldn't see this guy cutting it easily in the field, anymore. He must be spending too much time behind his desk. Or in front of a mirror.

"Commander Trevellyan?" he said, offering me his hand. "David?"

"In the flesh," I said, as we shook.

"Delighted to meet you," he said, taking my arm and guiding me toward the easy chairs. "Shall we sit? My name's Fothergill, by the way. But please, call me Richard."

"Any chance of a coffee around here, Richard?"

"I'm sure we could round some up for you," Fothergill said. "Be pleased to. We've heard a lot about you. Word spreads quickly. Especially from New York. The Big Apple's a very leaky place, you know. You should remember that. Though I doubt you'll be rushing back there, anytime soon."

I didn't reply.

"No trouble en route, I hope?" he said.

"None," I said. "Why? Should there be? It's hardly an arduous journey."

"Nothing untoward at La Guardia?"

"Nothing. I used the Marine Terminal. It's small. Quiet.

There was no problem at all. I wish all airports were like that."

"Well, that's good. It's a relief, actually. I'm just glad we were able to pull the right strings. Get the NYPD to back off for long enough to get you out."

"We?"

"Well, the New York people did the actual string pulling, obviously. But I'm happy we're here to offer you a port in a storm, as it were. No use them getting you out if you had nowhere safe to go."

"Are you confusing me with someone else? No one got me out of anything. I'd finished what I was doing over there. And the police had no reason to be sniffing around me."

"Of course," Fothergill said, pulling a newspaper from the bottom of the pile and placing it in front of me. "Whatever works for you. I completely understand."

The paper was a copy of yesterday's *New York Times*. It was folded to emphasize the story beneath a double-width photograph. The picture showed a house festooned with crime-scene tape. The headline read BUTCHERED IN THE BRONX: WOMAN, MEN MASSACRED IN UNEXPLAINED, SAVAGE ATTACK. I didn't need to read the report. I knew they wouldn't have got the details right. And what happened in that house didn't strike me as unduly savage, given the circumstances. So instead I took a moment to glance around the room, checking the walls and furniture for signs of bullet damage. I wanted to know if the story about how he'd been injured was true. Being shot in your own office by a colleague did seem a little unusual. Not to mention embarrassing. But then, I'd known this guy less than two minutes and already I was beginning to understand how it could happen. Only if it had been me pulling the trigger, he'd have been left needing more than a fancy sling.

"Interesting story," I said, thinking of the last time I'd seen Tanya. "Someone must have had a pretty good reason to do all that."

"A very good reason," he said. "I hear the first officer to respond lost his breakfast, the scene was so brutal. Which is something, for a cop used to working the Bronx."

"Really?" I said. "I wouldn't know. I've never been there."

Well, I'd been there once, actually. To one house. To take care of one piece of business.

"Of course you haven't," he said, tapping the side of his nose. "Of course, the NYPD think otherwise."

"They've been wrong before," I said.

"Not this time. I understand they're very confident."

"How so? I hear there were no survivors. No witnesses. No usable forensics."

I knew there were none. I'd gone out of my way to make sure.

"But they do have the victim's identity," he said. "And that tells them a lot."

"Which victim?" I said. "Weren't there several?"

I remembered each one's face. Their clothes. Their smell. What they'd been doing as I tracked them through the house. How they looked as I lowered them, lifeless, to the ground and moved on to the next one in line.

"There were eight or nine, they think," he said.

"I'd say more like seven," I said. "From what I heard."

Only four of them had been any good, though. The others should have found another line of work.

"It's the woman they're focusing on," he said.

And why not? That's exactly what I'd done. Though for an entirely different reason.

"How chivalrous," I said.

"No," he said. "Just practical. A lot of things stand out about her."

"I'm sure they do."

"I'm serious. The way she was singled out, for example. She was the last to go, you know."

I did know. Because I'd planned it that way. I hadn't wanted any interruptions.

"Are they sure about that?" I said.

"Yes," he said. "They're certain."

"Then maybe she was hiding when, whatever it was, all kicked off. Maybe the others were trying to protect her."

They didn't try very hard. But it wouldn't have mattered if they had. Nothing and no one could have saved her that night.

"That's what the NYPD think," he said. "That the men were her bodyguards."

"They didn't do such a good job, then," I said. "They hardly put up a fight. By the sound of it. She should have hired more carefully."

I remembered the misplaced sense of peace in the house, when the final guard was dead. The stillness. The silence. The inevitability, once the last obstacle had been removed.

"The police don't think it was the guards' fault," he said. "They're not blaming them at all."

"Why not?" I said.

I felt like I was back there, moving from room to room, feeling her presence, knowing the end was near.

"They were all ex-military," he said. "Well trained. Heavily armed. No trace of drink or drugs. None of them had been sleeping on the job. They were just overwhelmed."

"Implying a number of attackers, then, surely?" I said.

I'd had her in my sights once before, and then stood aside to let the authorities take their shot. I wasn't going to make that mistake again. And she knew it.

"No," he said. "Just one. A professional. Someone who does this kind of thing for a living."

I had warned her. She knew I'd be coming.

"They don't know that," I said. "The police are just fishing."

"No," he said. "Look. These guards were killed one at a time. Silently, so as not to alarm the others. Or the neighbors. Some had their necks broken. Others were stabbed, neatly, between the ribs. One was suffocated. They were picked off methodically to give . . . someone . . . access to this woman."

He was right. It had been methodical. A means to an end. Collateral damage. Nothing more. And no worse than you can expect, if you sign up for the wrong side.

"That proves nothing," I said.

"And there's the way she was killed," he said. "Someone physically dragged her out of her panic room. Then shot her in the head. Twice. From close range."

I hadn't wanted to touch her, but there'd been no choice. She wasn't dignified enough to come out on her own.

"Probably a mob hit," I said.

"No," he said. "The police think not. She wasn't on her knees when she was shot, for a start. Mob guys always make their victims kneel, apparently. Whoever did this wanted to look her in the eye when they pulled the trigger."

He had it backward, this time. I didn't want to look at her, particularly. I wanted her to look at me. To know who was pulling the trigger. And to have no doubt as to who was being avenged.

"Maybe this guy took more pride in his work," I said.

"Maybe, but it wasn't brutal enough," he said. "There was no sadism. If one outfit was moving in on another, they would have wanted to send a message. Something depraved. Crazy. Psychotic, even. It's the same the world over. But whoever did this was cold. Calculating. Deliberate. Like a surgeon chopping out something malignant."

Now he was back on the money. The woman had been malignant. Like a virulent tumor, corrupting everything she touched. There was no way, in all good conscience, I could have let her survive.

"Well, we could speculate all day," I said. "But whoever killed her, I expect she deserved it."

"I'm sure she did," he said. "But the point is, this was personal. This woman was executed. This specific woman. Who you just happened to know. Very well, I understand."

"I did?"

I knew her only too well. And I wish with all my heart that the day I met her had never dawned.

"You were a recent houseguest of hers, apparently," he said.

"Really?" I said. "Who was she? I didn't see any names in that report."

"The police withheld it. My sources could only give me a first name."

"Which was?"

"Lesley. Although I think you knew that."

Lesley. An ordinary name before I met her. Now a name I'll never forget.

"Lesley?" I said. "That's pretty common sounding. There must be lots of Lesleys in a city the size of New York."

"Come on, David," he said. "I've played along with this for long enough. We all know what you did. And you're with friends, here."

"Nice try. But I'm admitting nothing."

"Of course not. That's the first rule. But you wouldn't be worthy of the uniform if you'd just stood back, after what this woman did."

I didn't reply.

"I understand, David," he said. "I do. Working here isn't that different from life in the field. The liaison community, well, we're a pretty tight bunch. I heard about what this Lesley did to Tanya. And I heard you two were close."

I wasn't happy that we'd become fodder for the navy gossip machine. And I had no idea what he'd heard about us. But whatever it was, I could guarantee it fell a long way short of the truth.

"Besides, Tanya had a lot of friends," he said. "We'd all have done the same thing. Given the chance."

I bit my tongue.

"Look, David, even London approves," he said. "Unofficially, of course. That's why the NYPD were kept at arm's length for so long. But there's a limit to what they'll turn a blind eye to. They were straining at the leash. You dump the worst horror show anyone's ever seen in the middle of their patch and leave them looking like they can't catch the perpetrator. The press are slaughtering them ten ways till Christmas. They're humiliated."

"They'll get over it," I said, "or they'll just frame someone. Some lowlife they've been trying to rid themselves of for years. It's happened before. Whoever's behind this probably did them a favor."

"They don't see it like that. Seriously, we needed you out of there. Pronto. I was genuinely worried we'd left it too late."

"I left because I was ready. Nothing else. My only question is, why am I here? I should be back in London. It's time to get back to work."

"It is. And that's exactly why you're here. Your next job is here."

"It can't be. You never work the same country twice. It's a rule. You know that."

"Technically, it's a convention. But that doesn't matter. The point is, you're still off the books. Officially, you don't exist. And that's what's important right now."

"Why?"

Fothergill took a moment to reply. He licked his lips, and I saw his eyes track across to a point on the wall in the shadow of the radiator below the left-hand window. To a patch of paint that was slightly lighter than the rest. A recent repair. Around an inch and a half square. The kind of area a bullet could still make a mess of, even after passing through someone's arm.

Immediately, that second, I knew what was coming my way. Housecleaning. Again. The most distasteful task there is. And I realized something else at the same moment. That there was another difference between my aunt and me.

It gives me no pleasure when my premonitions turn out to be right.

None at all.

TWO

Back in the far-off days of basic training, I remember the various exercises we took part in always started with a full, formal briefing.

In the early days of the course, the administrators made a point of giving us plenty of notice. They gave out printed timetables, and posted any amendments on the huge notice board that dominated the training school foyer. That way, if something went wrong with someone's performance, the instructors knew the person's underlying skills were to blame, rather than wondering if they'd just misunderstood their instructions. As time went on, though, things became less reliable. We'd find ourselves being dragged into a conference room at the end of a run or hauled out of bed in the middle of the night, when we were too tired to concentrate properly. We were given less time to absorb the information. And details that were always bang-on accurate at the start became increasingly vague and unreliable with each passing week.

At the time I thought this was all done to boost our powers of initiative and self-reliance. It certainly did that.

And whether this was an intended consequence or not, it taught us something else.

That however bleak things look at the outset, there's a pretty high chance they're going to get a whole lot worse.

Fothergill fetched some coffee, closed the door behind him, and told me how a man he'd known for ten years had tried to kill him.

"So who is this guy?" I said.

"His name's Tony McIntyre," he said. "He's Scottish. A lieutenant commander, just like you. Five years' less service, but a good man all the same. Or so I thought."

"You worked with him in the past?"

"Four times. On four different continents. Plus another stint when we were instructors together. It's funny how people's paths keep crossing like that."

"And he was recently posted here?"

"No. He was AWOL. Made it here under his own steam. Sought me out. Told me he'd gone off the rails—blamed some other people for it, of course—but said that he wanted to come clean."

"Really? He just came out and told you that?"

"Yes. You've got to understand something. I've been around a while. People hear about me. And they're only human. Sometimes they slip. This wasn't the first time I'd been asked to help someone get back on his feet."

"So what was it that tripped him up?"

"Weapons. The urge to steal them. Then sell them. To

all sorts of shady characters, he said. For large sums of money."

"That's not good."

"Actually, it was worse than just weapons. He'd got his hands on something really filthy. A canister of some kind of poison gas. Awful stuff, apparently."

"Only one?"

"That's more than enough."

"Above the counter? Or below?"

"What do you think?"

"How did he come across it?"

"Goodness knows. But he'd been in Afghanistan for more than two years. Have you ever been there?"

"I can't recall."

"Well, I've been. Twice. And I can tell you—it's crazy there. Absolute insanity. I'm not surprised by anything that finds its way over there. Or back out again."

"So what was he planning to do with this stuff?"

"Ha. Here's where everything went pear-shaped. He told me he was scared of it. He'd found out what it can do. Realized it was too dangerous to put in the hands of random terrorists. So, he wanted some kind of a deal. He wanted me to broker one for him. Because of our history. Said I was the only person he could trust. He thought he could just hand in the gas and squeal on his buyers in return for immunity."

"And you went along with this? Were you smoking crack, at the time?"

"Look, I liked him. I knew him. I thought I could trust him."

"But you found out the hard way?"

"I saw through him. Do you know what he was trying to do?"

"Let me guess. Sell the gas. Collect the money. Leave you to take the fall."

"Right, right, and right. Unfortunately."

"And?"

"He realized that I was onto him. We both drew down. We both took a round. I got a new rug to hide the bloodstains. He got out of the building and vanished. London tore me a new one for my troubles. Then sent you, to dig us all out of the mire. Now that you're the blue-eyed boy again."

"I doubt that'll last—but anyway. Where's the gas now?"

"He told me he'd brought it with him, to Chicago. To sell. We think it's still in the city somewhere. Only we don't know where."

"Excellent. You can't beat solid intelligence. And the guy? McIntyre?"

"Better news, there. We have a firm lead on him. We know where he went to get patched up."

"Where?"

"To a cosmetic surgery clinic, of all places."

"No chance. That's too obvious. He wouldn't go anywhere listed in the yellow pages. He'd find some other way. However badly hurt he was."

"No. The police recovered surgical instruments from the place. The blood matched the samples he left behind on my floor. He was definitely there. And because of the way they organize things for hygiene, we even know which doctor treated him."

"It's got to be a setup. It's got red herring written all over it."

"Normally, I'd agree. But we didn't stumble on this clinic by chance. It's part of a chain. Here and in Europe. Remember McIntyre blamed other people for turning him dirty? Well, one of them runs mercenaries out of Prague. A bloke called Gary Young. He's ex–Royal Marines, just like McIntyre. We've been watching him for years. And he uses these clinics whenever one of his men needs attention, away from the public eye. He may even own a slice of them."

"I'm still not convinced."

"It flies, David. We've checked. It was definitely McIntyre's blood. And based on what the police recovered from the place, we know he had surgery. That means his wounds were serious. So his options were limited. He couldn't wander the city indefinitely, leaking everywhere. He'd have been spotted."

"OK. Maybe he was there. But how does that help?"

"Our doctors say he'll need follow-up treatment. He'll have to come back. Probably tomorrow. Possibly the day after. London want you to be there. To lift him when he appears."

"That's ridiculous."

"Why?"

"One, he won't show. Even if he risked it before, no way will he go to the same place twice. And two, even if he does appear, you don't need me to nick him. The local plod's already on board. They can pick him up."

"We can't let the police any further into this, David. We have to close it down in-house."

"Why?"

"Two reasons. First, there's the gas. The bottom line is, it has to be recovered."

"I'm sure it does. But not by me. This has nothing to do with embassy or consulate security."

"McIntyre tried to kill me, remember."

"That's a shame. And it's something for Internal Security to sort out. Not me."

"These are London's orders, David. I'm not calling the shots, here."

"Then you should have challenged them. Because whether it's me you're talking about or someone else, giving it to an individual is crazy. They should put a team on a job like this."

"For what it's worth, I agree. I asked for a team, in fact. But London said no. They're adamant. They want things taken care of discreetly. Too many cooks can cause a scene, and no civilians can hear anything about this. And no one from the U.S. authorities, either. One of our people has left lethal chemical agents lying around in our major ally's second city, for goodness sake. And the prospective buyers may be here, too. Think of the consequences."

"Think of the consequences if the job goes wrong, because we're shorthanded. This better not be a budget thing."

"I understand your concern, David. But you're looking at things from the wrong angle. After New York, it's fair to say you're not flavor of the month, back home. Yes? So this is your chance to put that right. Get your career back on track. The situation's serious. It's on the verge of humiliating several senior people. Taking care of it will buy you a lot of forgiveness. Moaning about resources? That'll do the opposite."

I didn't respond.

"Something else to think about," he said. "I'm still pretty well plugged in. Make this go away with the minimum of fuss, and I can put in a good word for you. Directly into some very influential ears."

"That's an interesting angle," I said, sensing the inevitable. "Suppose I give it a shot. Is there anyone in-house who could help? Specialists, to handle the chemicals, at least?"

"Don't worry about the gas. It's completely safe. As long as it stays in its container."

"Sounds like a big if to me. And the second thing?"

"London want a hard arrest. And you know those are always carried out solo."

A hard arrest. The kind that involves body bags rather than handcuffs. They're usually reserved for known terrorists and hostage takers who somehow slip every other kind of net. But they're also applied to our own people, gone bad. Cases like that were rare. Which was lucky, because carrying them out was never straightforward. They put you up against a highly motivated individual with the same background and training as yourself, but generally with an added dose of craziness. They're not easy. And they're not fun.

"Hard?" I said. "Is that definite?"

"Yes," he said. "I'm sorry. I triple-checked. But it shouldn't be a problem for a guy like you, surely?"

"I'll need secondary confirmation, before I even consider it. I need to hear the words."

"Understood. I thought you'd say that. I've got a call already set up, with my control."

"And McIntyre's mug shot. The most up-to-date we've got."

"Already prepared."

"Details of this gas. And whatever kind of container it's kept in."

"I've got pictures of the canister. It's fairly standard, apparently. But information on the gas itself is a bit thin on the ground. That might take a little longer."

"What about the doctor? Do we know his name? What he looks like?"

"We do. He's called Alvin Rollins. His picture's all over the clinic's Web site. I've printed you a copy. Anything else?"

"A cell phone."

"You don't have one?"

"No."

"Well, we'll have to put that right. I'm going to need regular updates from you, David, whenever you're outside this building. I can't help you if I don't know where you are. Luckily I have a couple of spare handsets right here. Personally, I think staying close and tight is key. You can't overestimate the importance of communication on an operation like this."

"Don't worry. I'll keep you posted. But on top of the phone, I'll need a weapon. Something clean. The old one accidentally fell into the East River."

"We've got the usual to pick from, downstairs."

"I'm fine with a Beretta."

"That's easy, then. I'll get them sent up. Anything else? Or does that wrap things up?"

"One other thing. Transport. I'll need a car."

"I'll call the motor pool. It's over near O'Hare. They should have something available."

"Thanks. But I don't think that's going to work. I've got something fairly specific in mind. And I doubt it's in our usual stable."

THREE

Ten years is a key milestone in Royal Navy Intelligence. Reach it, and you get an extra week's annual leave. Enhanced death in service benefits. And you find that all kinds of alternative career paths can start to open up. If you last that long. And you want them to.

One of the most popular options is to become an IOR, or instructor on rotation. The accreditation process isn't all that arduous, and once you're certified, you keep one foot in the field and one in the classroom. It averages out to around an eighty/twenty split in terms of time throughout a whole year, and there are many advantages to this way of working. It adds some variety to your everyday life. Takes you away from the sharp end for a few weeks at a time, like another kind of paid vacation. And ensures that the new recruits are taught by people with up-to-date, real-world skills.

For all the advantages, though, it's not an idea that's ever appealed to me. I like life at the sharp end. And I think I'd have trouble cooperating with the course assessors. Because in my experience, they're not always looking for what's important after you've left the classroom behind.

In training, what they look for is the ability to follow your brief.

In the field, the only thing that matters is getting the job done.

I didn't care what Fothergill said. He'd been out of the field for far too long. He wasn't anticipating how McIntyre would think. If the guy could make his way from Afghanistan to the United States with a canister of illegal military gas under his coat and not get caught, he must be halfway competent. There was no chance he'd be stupid enough to set foot anywhere near the clinic a second time. The best we could hope for was that he'd rely on the same doctor. So I changed London's plan a little. I didn't go inside and find a pretext to hang around there for hours, the next day, as they suggested. I only stayed long enough to verify that Rollins—the surgeon identified by the Chicago police—had showed up for work. I located his silver BMW in the basement garage. Made sure I had sight of where both fire exits emerged onto the street, as well as the main entrance. Then I dropped back out of sight. And waited.

The officer who'd delivered the Police Interceptor to my hotel that morning was refreshingly enthusiastic about his work. He briefed me at length about the vehicle's V8 engine. Its heavy-duty transmission and brakes. Up-rated springs and shock absorbers. Special shielding around the fuel tank. Kevlar linings in the front doors. Stab plates in the front seats. But strangely, he didn't mention the one feature I actually cared about. The exterior appearance. The car had been done up to look exactly like a taxi. And since ninety percent of the city's cabs are also Crown Victorias, that gave it a critical advantage. Tucked into the mouth of an alley between the buildings opposite the clinic, it was effectively invisible.

I'd been dubious about whether McIntyre would risk using any kind of mainstream medical facility after his confrontation with Fothergill, but when I found the building I saw it did have a couple of points in its favor. For a start, its location. It was on the corner of Illinois and State. Less than four blocks from the consulate. Not too far for him to go, even carrying an injury. Then there was its clientele. A constant stream of people entering and leaving, offering him plenty of cover. Many of them were also covered in bandages, so he wouldn't stand out. Add to that its layout, and I was prepared to change my mind. It had multiple exit points, to lessen the chances of being cornered. And if he could acquire a vehicle, there was easy access to escape routes north, south, east, or west.

I knew there was a chance that McIntyre would break the chain at that point. Skip the follow-up altogether, or find another medic to carry it out. And if he did summon Dr. Rollins, he could send a cab to fetch him. Or a car, with a professional driver. Neither of which would be the end of the world. They would just make it harder for me to follow without being spotted. But in the end, after two and a half hours—just before eleven o'clock—I saw the nose of the silver BMW edging out of the clinic's garage. The doctor was at the wheel. Alone. He turned left, heading east, toward the lake. I let two other cars move between us, then eased out into the traffic behind him.

Rollins drove smoothly, making no late turns or unexpected maneuvers. He was making no attempt to disguise where he was heading, which made me think he didn't know where his final destination would be. He was probably going to collect instructions from McIntyre along the way. Most likely several times. That's the way I'd have done it in McIntyre's shoes—injured, gone to ground, with no backup, in a strange city.

We continued down Illinois Street, followed underneath Michigan Avenue, swung right onto Columbus, and eventually merged with Lake Shore Drive. We passed the Field Museum and Soldier Field on our left. Then through the centre of McCormick Place, pale on the right, dark and mysterious on the left. Rollins cruised sedately in the middle lane. I stayed with him—sometimes two cars behind, sometimes three—until I was sure where he was headed. Midway Airport. Satisfied, I dropped back another six car lengths. Rollins was an amateur. There was nothing to suggest he was even looking for a tail, but it never hurts to be careful.

The main reason for McIntyre to send Rollins to an airport would be to neutralize any aerial surveillance the Chicago police might have put up. Even police helicopters aren't allowed to operate near major commercial flight paths. But there were two other possibilities. One was to give Rollins a safe place to make his first call for directions.

There were plenty of pay phones in the large, public concourses. McIntyre would know he couldn't risk letting Rollins use a cell phone. Or even to e-mail from a BlackBerry. Anyone doing that is just asking to be tracked. I'd give a pound to a penny that Rollins had been told to leave them locked in his office, in case the temptation proved too much. The other explanation was to give him the chance to change cars. With time to prepare, McIntyre would have left a replacement vehicle, keys hidden nearby, in one of the parking lots. In these circumstances, though, he'd have to rely on a rental car. I knew from the notices I'd seen yesterday when I was passing through that eight rental companies operate from Midway. All have their collection points in the same parking garage. And that was the garage I saw Rollins pull into, twenty-one minutes after leaving the clinic.

The garage exit is relatively wide. There are seven tollbooths. Four were out of service that morning, so I found a spot behind a group of maintenance vehicles where I could keep an eye on the other three. One hundred and ninety-eight cars emerged during the next thirty-three minutes. Seven were silver BMWs. Four were the right age and model. But none belonged to Rollins. His must have been left inside. Because he had switched cars. To a white Ford Taurus. I saw him sneaking out through the center booth, crouched low in his seat, the light reflecting off his bulbous Rolex as he showed the rental company exit pass to the parking attendant.

Rollins stopped at four pay phones on his way back

from the airport. One was at a gas station. One outside a McDonald's. One near a Starbucks. And one inside a tattoo parlor, which clearly made him uncomfortable. After each phone call we looped back on ourselves, re-covering old ground and switching direction apparently on a whim. And each time he got back behind the wheel, his driving became a little jerkier and more erratic. He was clearly getting nervous, jumping a light on Clybourn and nearly colliding with a minivan at a weird six-way junction between Halsted, Fullerton, and Lincoln. Then finally, after we'd covered just short of forty-eight apparently aimless miles, Rollins slowed down. He took a right from Orchard onto Arlington Place. There was a gap in a line of cars parked outside an old, stone-fronted apartment building. Rollins spotted it late and swung the Taurus wildly into the space, stopping abruptly with his front wheel jammed up against the curb and the car rocking drunkenly on its springs. I dumped the Crown Vic half a block farther down and made my way back along the opposite side of the street, on foot. Rollins stayed in his car for exactly ten minutes. He was sitting bolt upright, his eyes alternating anxiously between his watch and his rearview mirror. I guessed he was following instructions. Probably McIntyre's idea of Anti-Surveillance 101.

They both should have saved their time.

Rollins took one last anxious look behind him, then shuffled out awkwardly onto the sidewalk, dragging a battered black leather medical bag after him. He started walking slowly, almost inviting me to come after him. I watched him stroll halfway back to Orchard Street, then suddenly turn on his heel and head back quickly toward his car, blatantly staring at everyone who approached him. I smiled, and stayed in the lee of a UPS van until he was well past me, almost to the junction with Geneva Terrace. Then I followed. He turned right, still hurrying, spending so much time looking backward that he almost got run over by a blond woman in a white Toyota who was pulling out of a narrow driveway. He waved apologetically and immediately crossed the street, still heading for Fullerton. But before he got to the intersection he turned left, into an alleyway. It was clean. Straight. About five hundred feet long. I could see the service entrance for a modern apartment building at the far end. And the alley was broad. There was enough space for two cars to pass, if they took it easy. Which made it wider than the streets in some cities I'd been to. Many of the houses it served had garages or spaces to park. But one thing it didn't have was house numbers. Rollins slowed down, appearing to count the gates. He stopped outside the tenth from the end, took a moment to gather himself, then disappeared from sight.

I reached the gate in time to see Rollins standing at the side of a large building. It was built of red brick. Three stories high, with ornate stone set all around the deep bay windows that overlooked the rear yard. Originally a single residence I'd guess, but now converted into apartments, judging by the iron fire escape that ran its full height, filling the gap between it and its neighbor. Apartments that were now vacant, judging by the weeds that filled the yard and the empty rooms I could see through the grimy rear windows.

It was perfect. McIntyre was lucky to have found it.

The side door opened, and Rollins stepped inside. He moved stiffly, as if he were reluctant to enter. I waited a moment to make sure he didn't reappear. Promising as things looked, there was always a chance he was only there to pick up more instructions. But the door stayed closed, so I called Fothergill and brought him up to date. I hadn't given him a situation report all day. After my last conversation with Tanya in New York I was feeling pretty disinclined to use the phone, and he did nothing to encourage me to communicate more. He'd turned into a typical desk jockey, all questions and queries and worries and second guesses, so I fobbed him off with the bare minimum of information and got back to work. I switched my phone to vibrate. Then I slipped through next-door's gate and made my way silently toward the buildings, hugging the fence for cover.

I'd guess that this house had also been divided into apartments, based on the size of the two Dumpsters that were lined up against its rear wall. The left-hand one was only a foot away from the fence so I tested its lid, then climbed on top. From there I could reach across the boundary and get a grip on the lowest horizontal platform of McIntyre's fire escape. The fence looked too flimsy to take my weight so I braced one foot against the wall and vaulted over to the other side. I hung by my hands for a moment then dropped to the ground, making sure to avoid the lowest metal step. I didn't know where in the building

McIntyre would be holed up, so I couldn't afford to make any sound.

Thick clods of dark red paint were peeling from the beams that supported the fire escape, and the whole structure was rusting badly, but when I tested the bottom step it didn't creak or squeal. The next one up was the same. I crept up to the first platform without making a sound. It ran the whole width of the house. An emergency door served it from each end, and four windows overlooked it. I tried both doors. Both were locked. The windows were all closed. But two had frosted glass. That meant they would lead to bathrooms. Which was good. Bathrooms are less likely to be permanently occupied than bedrooms or kitchens or living rooms. And anyone who did happen to be inside would be in less of a position to resist.

I picked the window on the left, because it was closer. I worked my fingers between the casement and the soft, rotting wooden frame. Then forced them up toward the center, where I guessed the catch would be. And pulled.

The window gave way with no more than a soggy tearing sound, like ripping open a damp cardboard package, and I caught the remains of the lock before it hit the iron platform. But still I ducked down, out of sight. I waited for two minutes. Nothing stirred from inside, so I climbed into the room. I balanced on the end of the bathtub. Stepped down and crossed to the doorway. Checked the landing. And headed down the stairs.

Normally I would have expected McIntyre to favor one of the upstairs rooms. It would give him a better view of anyone approaching from outside. Separate him from any random trespassers, snooping around for anything easy to steal. And give him a tactical advantage, if it should become necessary to defend his position. But today I wasn't interested in finding him straight away. It was more important to intercept Dr. Rollins on his way back out of the building. He could fill me in on McIntyre's condition. Whether he was armed. The location and layout of his bolt-hole. And possibly provide a way to persuade McIntyre to open his door without me having to break it down.

At first I thought there were two apartments on the first floor, because there was an entrance at right angles on either side of the glass door that led to the large, square entrance lobby. One was locked. But the other door swung open as soon as I touched the handle. It led to a wide space with a tiled floor, fluorescent lights, and rough whitewashed walls. It was empty, but from the marks on the tiles and the remnants of pipe work strewn everywhere I'd say it had been a laundry room. No doubt useful for the people who'd lived in the building when it was still occupied. And certainly convenient for me, now.

I was still rooting around in the debris on the floor, looking for a length of abandoned pipe to use as a backup weapon, when I heard footsteps in the hallway above me. I moved quickly, sliding into place behind the open door and checking the view through the gap beneath the hinges. The footsteps moved to the stairs. They started to come down. There was only one set. The person was in a hurry. They reached the ground. Then I saw a figure reflected in the glass entrance door. It was Dr. Rollins. He scampered across the corridor and reached out, his hand shaking almost uncontrollably as he scrabbled for the latch. It wouldn't turn. He wrestled with it, focusing entirely on the lock and paying no attention at all to his surroundings. A ten-year-old could have strolled up and tapped him on the back without him noticing. So it was no challenge at all to clamp my left hand over his mouth, grab his collar with my right, and march him back into the laundry, out of sight.

I closed the door behind me with my foot and led Rollins into the center of the room, under the light, where it was bright and spacious. His quivering was getting worse by the second, and I didn't want him completely losing control. Not yet, anyway.

"Can you hear me?" I said. "Can you understand what I'm saying?"

I felt the muscles in his neck stiffen a little, but he didn't answer.

"Dr. Rollins, can you hear me?" I said. "I don't want you to worry. I'm here to help you. Now, if I let go, will you make a noise?"

His head twitched slightly.

"This is important, Doctor," I said. "I need to be sure. Personal safety is on the line here, for both of us. So, if I let go, will you scream?"

This time he went to the opposite extreme, jerking his head wildly from side to side.

I removed my left hand from his mouth, and when

twenty seconds passed without him squealing, I let go of his collar.

"Excellent," I said. "Thank you. Now, turn around. Let's talk."

Rollins didn't move.

"What's wrong with your feet?" I said.

He didn't answer.

"Are they stuck to the floor?" I said.

He stayed silent.

"Did you tread in wet cement?" I said. "Shall I call the fire department?"

Still nothing.

"Let's simplify this," I said. "Turn around. Answer my questions. Or I walk out of here and let the Chicago police come in and collect you."

Rollins groaned softly and started to sway, but he still didn't turn.

"The guy upstairs—he's no choirboy," I said. "You've been aiding and abetting a wanted felon. You've been caught red-handed. The police want to throw you in jail. And you know what will happen to a guy like you in jail, don't you, Doctor?"

Rollins was silent again.

"You know what they'll do to you?" I said. "Let's just agree, it won't be you giving the injections."

"You're disgusting," he said.

"Maybe," I said. "But do you want that, Doctor? Night after night?"

"No," he said, eventually. "Of course not—but—please. I had no choice."

"You have now," I said. "Go to jail, or talk to me. Choose wisely. I'm the only one who can help you."

"How? How can you help?"

"Turn around and we'll talk."

"Who are you? What can you do?"

"Turn around. Now."

He stayed still.

"There are police officers outside," I said. "Twelve. If you're lucky, they might just shoot you. You could die in this room. In about thirty seconds. Unless you show me your face."

Rollins shuffled around in a tight circle, taking tiny, slow steps like an arthritic old man. He was staring at the floor. I said nothing. His eyes crept up as far as my knees. I waited. They reached my waist. My chest. He faltered. Got a grip on himself. Wiped his eyes. And finally, awkwardly, managed to look me half in the face.

"My name is David Trevellyan," I said. "I'm from the British Consulate. The man you've been helping is a friend of mine. Was a friend, anyway. That's why I'm prepared to give you a break."

"He's your friend?" Rollins said. "He's a psycho. He's insane."

"No, he's a soldier. A veteran, from Afghanistan. He has PTSD. Very badly, I'm told."

"So what's he doing in Chicago? Running me all around the city? And threatening my family? He did that, you know. That's why I helped him. There was no money involved."

"It's a long story. He doesn't know what he's doing. He may not even recognize me, he's so far gone. But if I don't talk him down, the police will shoot him. Half the officers they have out there are snipers. Six of them. All top-of-the-line experts. I have one chance to save him. Only one."

"That's not my problem. I've done my part. Why won't you just let me go?"

"I will. But I need your help, first."

"All I did was to give a sick man vital treatment. I'm a doctor. It's my sworn duty. And now I want to go. Right now."

"Did you report it? The gunshot wound? To the police?"

He didn't answer.

"Talking of your duty," I said. "Did you report it?"

"I guess not," he said. "I was too busy saving his life. Why? Does it even matter?"

"It does. Because that's a felony, right there. As a physician, you're obliged under several laws—state and federal—to report all gunshot wounds. Immediately. Before the patient even leaves your care. If you don't do that, you're screwed."

"Wait. I didn't know. I'm a cosmetic surgeon, for goodness' sake. I'm not used to criminals. Or crazy soldiers, or whatever he is."

"That doesn't matter. It's an absolute offense. There's no way to mitigate it. If I hand you to the police, you're toast. And that's what I'm going to do. Right now. Unless . . ."

"Unless what? What do you want?"

"Information. I want to know everything about the guy's situation, upstairs."

"No problem. I'll tell you. I'll draw you diagrams, if you want."

"Just tell me. That'll be fine. Oh, and one other thing."

"What?"

"I'm going to make a call to my office. Then I want you to go back up there with me."

"Why?"

"I thought you might like to knock on his door, one more time."

FOUR

When I was a kid I loved watching movies. All different kinds. Cops and robbers. Spies. World War II. Disaster films. Comedies. Anything that could transport me to another world. Looking back, I'd sit through pretty much everything I could find on the box.

Except musicals, obviously.

There were fewer channels on TV in those days, and no video or DVD, but I still seemed to have plenty of choice. The BBC showed at least one movie every Saturday, for example. Early in the evening. Often Westerns, for some reason. They must have been cheap. But I didn't mind. I enjoyed them. There was bound to be a gallant hero to cheer for. A cruel villain to despise. A beautiful girl to rescue. Plenty of fighting to act out in the playground at school the next week. The knowledge that good would always overcome evil.

And however dicey things became, there was no need to worry.

Because, when the chips were down, you could always rely on the cavalry to arrive.

*

I stopped Rollins midway up the second flight of stairs. I'd made him describe the entrance to the apartment McIntyre was holed up in four times, but I still wanted to see it for myself. I didn't trust amateurs. Especially not ones who gave me the feeling they'd say just about anything to save their skins. The mirror I'd taken from his medical kit was small, but it gave me a good enough view to suggest that his account was reasonably accurate. There was nothing obvious to derail the plan I'd just briefed Fothergill on. So, I took out my cell phone, turned the ringer volume up to one notch above silent, set its alarm for four minutes' time, and handed it to Rollins.

"OK, Doctor," I said. "Where will you wait?"

"Here," he said. "Right where I am now."

"Will you move?"

"No. Not a muscle."

"How much noise will you make?"

"No noise. None at all."

"The alarm on the phone will sound. What will you do?"

"Silence it. Immediately."

"And?"

"Go up to the door. Knock three times, then pause, then knock three times again. Just like he told me to when he summoned me before."

"Good. And when you hear footsteps inside the apartment?"

"Run. Fast. And don't look back."

*

It wasn't the world's greatest plan, but I didn't have many options. Normally, once I had a confirmed target securely squared away, I could stand back and hand the reins to a snatch team. From the SAS. Or SBS. Or the host country's police or special forces, if we trusted them or had told them in advance what we were doing. But whoever took it over, they'd take care of the rest. Forcing an entry. Avoiding booby traps. Cleaning up afterward. It was a very satisfactory division of labor. But this time, London hadn't sent anyone to help. And they'd ruled out involving the Chicago police any further. I was sorry the twelve officers outside were fictitious because that left me with just Dr. Rollins at my disposal to create a diversion. Not a very promising position. And not very much time. Four minutes wasn't long to get myself into position. I'd have liked more, but I knew I couldn't risk it.

A drawback of being a new recruit in the navy is that you're used for all kinds of psychological studies. The results are fed to us during training, so I knew I was seriously pushing the limit of how long a frightened person would remain compliant. Give him much longer and his brain would start to reboot itself. He'd start to question everything I'd told him. See that some things weren't quite the way I'd painted them. Begin to doubt everything else. And most likely run for the hills. So the moment I left him I headed back down one flight of stairs and into the apartment I'd gained access through. I climbed back out through the window. Then I crept along the fire escape and made my way up one story, testing each footstep carefully before trusting my full weight to the grimy, corroded metal.

Rollins had confirmed that the apartment McIntyre was squatting in had the same basic layout as the one below, so I edged along to the bathroom window and checked my watch. There were eighteen seconds to go. I pried the frame away from its mounting and wriggled my fingers into the narrow space. The wood around this window was drier and less decayed, and as I waited for the time to pass I could feel the points of several splinters slowly burrowing into my skin. A thin trace of blood had just reached my palm when the second hand finally reached the twelve. I knew the alarm on the phone should be starting to sound. I pictured Rollins switching it off. Standing up. Climbing the final few stairs. Approaching the door. Raising his hand. Knocking. McIntyre hearing it. Focusing on it. Recognizing the agreed pattern. Moving to investigate. And leaving his back momentarily unguarded.

I took a deep breath and heaved sharply backward.

McIntyre had left nothing in the bathroom that would reveal the apartment was occupied. But a few sheets of dusty newspaper were lying on the floor beneath the window, artistically off-center, where an intruder's foot would naturally land. The positioning was too perfect to be a coincidence. So I stretched to the side, got my right foot on the rim of the tub, and bypassed them. Then I checked underneath. Something was hidden there. A strip of bubble wrap. I don't know where he got it from, but it made a half-decent perimeter alarm—for something improvised out of scrap. The guy was certainly thorough. It was just a shame he hadn't put his skills and training to their proper use. We'd both have been spared a whole lot of trouble if he had.

There were no further obstacles between me and the door so I crossed the room and paused for a moment, to listen. At first I heard nothing. I was beginning to think that Rollins must have bottled and run away when I picked up a slight sound. It was coming from my left. From the far end of the corridor, where the main living room would be. Maybe a chair leg scraping lightly over a wooden floor. And it was followed by footsteps. One set. They were cautious. Coming my way. They reached the door in front of me, but I let them pass. Even with him injured, I saw no reason to get into a fight with McIntyre if I could reasonably avoid it. So I gave him another couple of seconds to make up some ground on the front door. Then I stepped into the corridor and raised my Beretta so it was pointing at the back of his head.

"Commander McIntyre," I said. "Stop. Blue on blue."

He stopped, arms by his sides, a Beretta matching mine in his right hand.

"Bend down," I said. "Put the gun on the floor. Gently."

He bent his knees so he could reach the ground, but kept his waist completely straight. The move looked awkward. Rollins had told me he'd been injured in the lower abdomen during the shoot-out with Fothergill. I guess he was still feeling the effects of the surgery. Or at least, that he wanted me to think so.

"Stand up," I said. "Raise your hands. And kick the gun away, behind you."

So far, so good. Stopping him had been perfectly straightforward. And I was still wondering whether he would give up the gas canister just as easily when the front door was ripped off its hinges. Something had sent it hurtling down the corridor toward us, cannoning off the floor and walls and finally biting into the wooden boards at McIntyre's feet.

It seems that the movies had a point about the inevitable sound of hooves in the distance. But there's one thing those old Westerns never warned you about.

The cavalry might always arrive. But it isn't always on your side.

FIVE

Civilians were mentioned a lot during our first couple of weeks of training. The instructors never missed an opportunity to remind us that members of the public always came first. Everything we were taught was ultimately aimed at preserving their safety and well-being. Because although our job was very specialized, when you boiled it down to the bare bones, it was actually extremely simple. We were there for one thing. To look after those who couldn't look after themselves.

I didn't have a problem with that. In fact, it made perfect sense. On the whole, I welcomed it. My only reservation was about the people who were capable, but wouldn't look after themselves. Who chose not to. Who thought they were entitled to have someone else do all the hard work on their behalf. But in the end I didn't have much time to waste thinking about them. As our exercises became more complex, mention of the wider population dropped off dramatically. Soon they were hardly part of our thinking at all. Not much more than a background presence. We were too focused on the job in hand.

Until one Saturday when we were sent out, on our own, to major cities around the country.

We were told that a fringe terrorist group was planning to activate a device that would release clouds of fumes into the crowd at a Premier League football match, later that day. The vapor was thought to be highly acidic. It was capable of causing horrific burns wherever it came into contact with bare skin. Possibly permanent blindness, if it got into the eyes. And even death, if enough was breathed in to destroy a victim's lungs.

The attack was to be part of a protest against the working conditions the group alleged were forced on workers in clothing factories in the third world. The ones who made the replica shirts the supporters were so keen on wearing. It would be carried out by four people. All would be women. Our job was to help the police spot them, so they could be arrested before any damage was done. We had their pictures. We believed they would be arriving by train. But still, picking them out of a crowd of tens of thousands of people wasn't going to be easy.

We were given our destinations as soon as the morning briefing was over. Mine turned out to be Birmingham. I made good time up the motorways, dumped my unmarked car on some waste ground near the spot where the Aston Expressway crosses Trinity Road, and started to make my way toward the railway station. This part was slow going, pushing my way through the unbroken river of people. Then, when I was nearly at the stadium, we stopped moving completely. Some sort of disturbance had broken out just ahead of me. I shouldered my way through the onlookers to find out what was going on. A knot of people had formed outside a pub. Two were supporters of the visiting team, and five were home fans. It was a dangerous combination, but still at the pushing and shoving stage. There was still time for it to be defused. I looked around for the police. There were none to be seen. I called it in, but was told that somehow, inexplicably, there was no cover in that sector. The nearest officers were ten minutes away. An eternity, in the circumstances. Punches started to be thrown. One guy went down. He took a kick to the head. A knife appeared. Then another. I scanned the crowd. People were sickened. Excited. Fascinated. Horrified. Delighted. But none of them was ready or able to intervene. The situation was out of control. It was on the verge of becoming a bloodbath.

Unless I stopped it.

I did step forward. But not to break up the fight. Instead I just eased around the edge of the mob and continued on my way. I had a job to do. The next ten minutes were difficult, pushing visions of the guy on the ground out of my head and trying to focus on the pictures of the terrorists I'd memorized that morning. Comparing them against the swarms of happy, smiling supporters. And trying to conceal my surprise when I finally spotted a face I did recognize.

One of my instructors.

The whole episode had been staged. There was no plot to release acid into the crowd. The point of the exercise was completely different. To see if you had the presence of mind to put the needs of the many ahead of the few. Even in the heat of the moment. Even when you had to get blood on your shoes to do it. Because that put the place of civilians in its full context. You don't involve yourself with them on purpose, but occasionally they get caught up anyway. Sometimes by accident. Sometimes through their own greed. Sometimes because of stupidity. And sometimes, plain bad luck.

But whatever the cause, it wasn't your problem.

You couldn't allow anything to stand in the way of your objective.

When they saw the remains of the shattered apartment, the fire department wanted to take me to hospital. The police wanted to take me to jail. And Fothergill wanted to take me somewhere secluded so he could shoot me.

Fothergill came closest. He got the first half of his wish, at least.

After we'd disentangled ourselves from the authorities, I got him to stop at my hotel so I could change my clothes. The look on his face as we drove told me not to expect much hospitality once we reached the consulate, so I made him stop again at the nearest Starbucks. I was in need of a major dose of caffeine. And then, when I was well enough supplied, I let him drag me back to his office.

"Are you fit?" he said, glaring at me from behind his desk. "Can you at least continue?"

"Of course," I said, dragging one of the visitors' chairs across the room and sitting down.

"What did the paramedics say?"

"Not much."

"They seemed to be worried."

"They're paid to be worried. It's nothing."

"Your head's OK? They spent a long time looking at it."

"I took a knock in New York, last time out. They saw where I'd been sewn up."

"That's all?"

All? Twelve stitches. Neatly done. Barely a scar left, now. Small beer, in the scheme of things. But it had caused way more than its share of trouble. Nothing good had happened since that incident. Looking back, it seemed more like a curse than a wound. I wondered if it would ever stop haunting me.

"Yes," I said. "That's all."

"Well, that's something, I suppose," he said. "Saves having to call for a replacement. The last thing I need to be doing right now is talking to London. Not till I've figured a way to explain this latest fiasco. How the hell did it happen?"

"Looks like McIntyre had a couple of friends in town we didn't know about."

"You're sure they were friends?"

"They blew his door off its hinges and tried to haul him out of there. Who else could they be?"

"If they were friends, why break down the door? Why not just knock and wait to be let in?"

"'Cause of Rollins. He'd already knocked. I told him to do that and then run away. They must have bumped into him on the stairs."

"You think he'd have alerted them?"

"In a heartbeat. He was a flake. He'd have spilled everything, immediately."

"I guess. Fat lot of good it did him, though."

"Shame he couldn't have kept it buttoned a little longer."

"Shame you got him involved at all."

"I didn't. He got himself involved."

"You could have let him go. He may not have asked for any of it. He may have been coerced."

"How? Was someone threatening to bludgeon him with a sack of cash?"

Fothergill stood up slowly and moved over to the central window, keeping his back to me for a few moments.

"You should see the paperwork I'll have to do on him," he said. "Mountains of it. It'll take weeks. And if we can avoid making his widow a millionaire, it'll be a miracle."

"She's probably already a millionaire," I said. "Forget about her. McIntyre's the problem. I can't deal with him if we don't know where he is. So what are you doing about finding him?"

"Not much, right now. And certainly a lot less than if we could talk to either of those guys who raided the apartment. If you'd just shown a little restraint . . ."

"Interesting idea. I suppose I could have. I knew someone who showed some restraint, once. A policeman, in Holland. He was up against guys with MP5s, too. And do you know what he got for his trouble?"

"No. What?"

"A bronze star. Set into the wall in the foyer of their HQ."

"Really?"

"Really. They put one there for every officer who buys the farm."

Fothergill was silent for a moment, and then came back to the desk.

"OK," he said. "We can't talk to them. So let's draw a line under that. But what else can we figure out about them? Every contact yields some kind of intelligence. And what we really need to know is, where did McIntyre go when he got out of the building?"

"No idea."

"Was he hurt?"

"Not by me. And I'd say he wasn't in too bad shape generally, by the way he dived through the gap between his mates. And he was on his feet again pretty quickly, too. He was out of the door before the others hit the ground."

"Did anyone help him? Someone waiting outside?"

"I didn't see anyone. But I can't rule it out."

"So he could be on his own again. Or being sheltered by others?"

"Right."

"We don't know which?"

"No."

"Then we need to find out. That has to be our first priority."

"Agreed."

"What about the two you took care of? Did you hear them say anything?"

"No."

"What accents did they have?"

"Neither of them spoke at all."

"We don't even know what language?"

"No."

"So we don't know where they're from? What country, even?"

"No."

"Could you tell anything from their clothes?"

"Not without some work. Everything looked new. Jeans, trainers, hoodies. Innocuous stuff. Standard chain-store issue, probably bought specially. What you'd expect from people who know how to look anonymous."

"That kind of thing is safe to ask the police to follow up. But it does make sense. Shows a level of professionalism. And it ties in with the arms-dealing angle. Just like the weapons. MP5s are expensive pieces of kit."

"They are. But you can never be sure. I saw one on a council estate in Leeds, once."

"You're not being a lot of help here, David."

"Then maybe the autopsies will reveal something."

"How? You shot both guys. Multiple times. Pretty straightforward, no?"

"Forget cause of death. Think stomach contents. That might tell us where they're from, if they followed McIntyre to the States in the last couple of days."

"Oh. Good thinking. I'll talk to the PD about that, too. Try to get the medical examiner to put a rush on it."

"And what about their identities? If they entered the country legally, there should be a record somewhere."

A muffled soprano started singing an aria from *The Magic Flute* somewhere inside Fothergill's jacket. It was his phone. He pulled it out and placed it on the desk between us. Then he must have caught the look on my face.

"I love Mozart," he said. "Don't you?"

"Are you going to answer that?" I said.

"No. Whoever it is, they can wait. We need to get some kind of plan worked out, first. We should draw up a list of actions. Then we can decide what's reasonable to pass on to the police, in terms of security and logistics. And whatever's left, we'll deal with ourselves."

I heard a sharp knock behind me, the door swung open, and Fothergill's assistant appeared. Sadly he wasn't bringing refreshments.

"Did your mobile not ring?" he said, glancing down at the cell phone on the desk.

"It did, actually," Fothergill said. "Didn't quite manage to answer it in time, though. Anything important?"

"It was London," he said. "Word has spread. They gave me two minutes to find you. Sounds like it's time to break out the asbestos underwear."

"Damn," Fothergill said. "One minute they refuse the resources I need. The next, they're moaning when the job goes pear-shaped. I can't win."

I began to think there was a little more field agent left in him than I'd given credit for. His assistant just shrugged.

"David, I'm sorry," Fothergill said. "I'm going to have to make this call. How about you head back to your hotel? Catch your breath a little? And as soon as I can get anything concrete pulled together I'll have it biked straight over to you. Then you can review it in peace."

I figured that between fending off his bosses in London and calling in favors in the States, Fothergill was going to have his hands full for quite a while. My hotel was only twenty minutes from the consulate. There was no chance he'd have anything for me to see in that length of time. Which meant I could turn my attention to more important matters. Such as food. I hadn't eaten a thing since breakfast. That was the best part of nine hours ago, and I was starving.

On the plane yesterday I heard a couple arguing about which was their favorite restaurant in Chicago. The debate was intense. It lasted nearly an hour. At first I thought a Spanish place was certain to come out on top. Then a Mexican, with a choice of bars. But ultimately, the winner was French. I remembered the name. And the location. It was convenient—on Hubbard, not much farther away than the clinic. The menu sounded good. The prices, reasonable. The service, not too intrusive. The decor, not too fussy. Which left me with only one problem. The restaurant where I was supposed to meet Tanya for our final, ill-fated dinner had been French. Part of me never wanted to go into one again. I was on the verge of heading for the Mexican instead, but I realized that was ridiculous. I couldn't let my life be ruled by ghosts. So I decided to give it a try. The only thing I hadn't considered was their hours of business. I arrived at the door on the stroke of four thirty. But they didn't open till five. And that left me with a dilemma.

I decided to wait. Not on the doorstep, obviously. But in the general vicinity. In the nearby maze of backstreets and alleyways. Where you can get right under the skin of the city. Or lose yourself in the genuine, unadorned areas that the guidebooks don't tell you about. Away from the shop windows and neon signs and office facades, and into the parts where real people get their hands dirty making deliveries and emptying Dumpsters and busying themselves with their ordinary, everyday lives.

Places that people like Fothergill might have gone to, once. But I couldn't picture him there now.

Most of the buildings on that street seemed to be offices, but the place on the left of the restaurant looked like some sort of shop. I couldn't tell what kind. It was closed. There were no signs, and the door and windows were obscured by heavy, gray blinds. A passageway led down the side, separating the two businesses. It was paved with cracked, square slabs. They were shiny and well worn. Obviously in frequent use. Almost calling for me to follow them. It seemed like an interesting enough place to start.

The passage led straight to the back of the buildings. There were no lights. No doors or windows opened onto it, and it was too narrow for anything to be stored there. I made my way to the far end, then paused to check the lie of the land. I could see I'd reached a kind of grubby, cobbled courtyard. It was about twenty feet square. To my left was the back of the shop. It had a single window—lined with cardboard and heavily barred—and one exit. The outside of a fire door. Neither showed any name or number. The buildings on the far side were much deeper, reaching almost to the ones from the next street, leaving just enough room for another narrow passageway. That was handy. It would be a second way out of the place, if needed. And a third possible route stretched away to my right, beyond the back of the restaurant, where the space remained wide enough for a medium-sized vehicle to pass through.

It was the restaurant side of the courtyard that caught my attention. Orange plastic packing crates had been arranged in a horseshoe shape outside the double kitchen door, like seats. There were six. Cigarette butts lay scattered all around them. Maybe two hundred altogether. Around a quarter had lipstick marks on them, and I could see at least four different brands. The doors themselves were standing open a couple of inches, and I could hear the murmur of voices and the clash of metallic items banging together from inside. But it wasn't the sights or the sounds that grabbed me. It was the smell. Frying meat. Onions. Garlic. Carried straight at me by the clouds of steam that were pouring relentlessly from four stainless-steel vents, lined up in the back wall at head height. It made me think that the couple on the plane had been right. Which again reminded me of Tanya. And made me fear that the next few minutes were going to pass very slowly.

There was nothing else of interest in the courtyard so I crossed behind the restaurant and started down the broader alley on the far side. I was planning to outwalk my memories and kill the rest of my waiting time by making a broad loop back around to the main entrance on the street. But I'd only gone about nine feet when I heard a noise behind me. A loud crash. Something heavy had connected with the brickwork. I stopped in the shadows and turned to look. It was the fire door at the back of the shop. Someone had thrown it open, all the way, so that it banged into the wall. A woman staggered through the opening. Her arms were flailing and she was teetering wildly on transparent plastic stilettos. They were at least four inches high. She finally caught her balance after another half-dozen steps, ending up with her knees pointing inward as the heels slid awkwardly into the cracks between the cobbles. She wobbled again, then quickly ran her hands over her lace-up leather bodice, around her tiny velvet miniskirt, and even down the seams at the back of her sheer black stockings.

A man followed her out. I'd put him in his midforties. His clothes—gray stonewashed jeans and a plain white sleeveless T-shirt—were an extremely tight fit. I guessed he wore them that way to emphasize his pumped-up thighs, torso, and arms. He was only about six feet tall, but that still gave him a good eight inches over the woman, even allowing for her ridiculous shoes. He stepped toward her. She held her ground, glaring up into his face. Then three more guys emerged from the store, moving forward and half surrounding her. The original one gestured for her to go back inside. She shook her head. He raised his hand, palm open. She flinched, as if anticipating the blow. But she didn't back down.

The left-hand restaurant kitchen door swung open and a man stepped halfway out, then froze. He was dressed in chef's whites, maybe in his late teens, scruffy and unshaven. The guys from the store turned as one and stared at him. He held their gaze, hypnotized, for twenty seconds. Then he hunched over, reversed his direction, and withdrew from sight. I was relieved. It seemed like the ideal solution. I'd seen a pair of chefs going after each other in the kitchen of an Italian restaurant in London, once. One had a cleaver. The other, a carving knife. The fight didn't last long. But it did have a decisive ending. Something like that would be welcome right now. I didn't know what the woman had done, but I couldn't help feeling like the four men could use a more challenging opponent. I figured the young guy would be fetching some of his colleagues. That they'd come charging out, any second, brandishing all kinds of cooking implements. Sharp ones. Hopefully, lethal ones.

Nothing happened. Thirty seconds crawled past. Then a minute. The store guys relaxed. They returned their attention to the woman. She took a step back. All four followed, pressing in close. The first man raised his arm again. He leveled it with her face and pulled it back farther, twitching, like a snake all set to strike.

"Jaime?" I said, stepping out of the shadows.

The four guys snapped around simultaneously to face me, but none of them spoke.

"It is you, right?" I said, cutting into the distance between us. "Where have you been, all these years? We missed you."

The main guy lowered his arm.

"Who the hell's Jaime?" he said.

"She is," I said. "Jaime Sommers. The Bionic Woman."

"The hell are you talking about?"

"I mean, she must be bionic, right? Otherwise, why would it take all four of you to chase her around this yard?"

I was close enough by now to see a vein throbbing above his left temple. He glared at me, his mouth dropped open, but he didn't manage any words.

"Seriously, I'm interested," I said. "How many of you does it take to persuade one girl to walk through a doorway?"

The guy nearest me slipped his right hand into the back pocket of his jeans.

"But don't let me interrupt," I said. "Go ahead. Do what you need to do."

He pulled something out, concealing it behind his leg and shifting his weight onto his front foot.

"Looked like you were going to hit her just now, when I arrived," I said to the main guy. "So go on. Take your shot."

He didn't move.

"What are you waiting for?" I said. "Twenty dollars says you can't take her down with one slap."

The next guy in line broke ranks and moved to block my path.

"No?" I said. "OK. So here's another idea. Why not try it with me?"

All four were facing me now, their backs to the woman. She started moving smoothly away, reversing, never taking her eyes off them for a second.

"What's the problem?" I said. "There are four of you. And only one of—"

Without breaking stride I drove the heel of my right hand into the jaw of the guy who'd ended up in front of me. The impact knocked him off his feet, leaving him sprawling on the exact spot where the woman had been standing a moment earlier. His limbs followed a second behind his body, slapping limply onto the ground as I drew my forearm back and smashed my elbow into the side of the next guy's head. He went down too, pivoting sharply around so that his face was the first part of him to crack against the cobblestones. A wooden-handled switchblade slipped from his fingers. I kicked it away and brought my fist across the opposite way, my first two knuckles connecting with either side of the third guy's nose. I felt his bone and cartilage crack, and saw that blood was already spurting from his face as his legs buckled under him and he flopped down onto his back.

I checked the kitchen door. There was no activity. I looked for the woman. She was safe, ten feet away, backing up against the wall. I watched as she disappeared from sight. Then I scanned the surrounding buildings. Confirmed there were no other windows overlooking us. No security cameras. In fact, no one watching us at all. It was just like Fothergill had said. As far as anyone could tell, I didn't exist.

"Did I say, four of you against me?" I said to the remaining guy. "Sorry about that. I should have said, one. For another few seconds, anyway."

The lesson I'd learned from that football ground exercise was still valid. I hadn't forgotten about it. And I still didn't choose to get involved with civilians.

But sometimes, it seemed, they chose to get involved with me.

SIX

Theoretically, the classroom elements of our training should have been the most popular. There was no danger of freezing to death. No maladjusted members of the Parachute Regiment lying in wait, itching to kick great big chunks out of us. No heavy equipment to carry. It didn't rain, indoors. You always had food to eat and a bed to sleep in. But even so, given a choice, we'd always have voted for the practical courses. We loved to be out of barracks, even if it was just for an afternoon. For a change of scene. A breath of fresh air. A new challenge.

Even if the task we ended up with was rarely what we'd been told to expect.

Whatever kind of exercise we were sent on, though, the routine was always the same. We were briefed. Given our stores. Deployed. Retrieved. And debriefed. At the beginning, we were always given everything we were likely to need. The process seemed like the model of efficiency. But as we continued, I noticed that the odd essential item was missing from our kit. The first time, it was an ax. The next, a paper clip. Then a length of chain. And because the activities were new to us, we didn't know what we'd need until we actually got started. There was no way to anticipate or take relevant spares, just in case. The shortages started to occur more and more frequently. Some people started to complain. Eventually, we were being sent out with little more than the clothes we were wearing. Only by then, those of us who were left had woken up to the underlying point.

Success doesn't depend on what you're given by others.

It's about what you can find for yourself.

At the restaurant, I started with the mussels. Then I had steak, cooked extra rare, with mustard butter. Both were sublime. Simple. Elegant. And perfectly executed. The only slight off-note came when I was waiting for my espresso. Two police officers arrived. They appeared from the kitchen and started wandering around between the tables, asking questions about an alleged disturbance in the vicinity, earlier in the evening.

They came to me first.

I had nothing for them.

The streets were still swarming with people when I left the restaurant, just before six thirty. There were office workers, leaving the city. Drinkers and theatergoers, pushing their way back in. Shoppers, rushing for their final few purchases. A repair crew, trying to pump the water out of a leak in some foundations they were digging next to the river. But none of that caused me a problem. I had no need to hurry anywhere. There was no sign of the guys from the courtyard. Or the woman. And still no word from Fothergill.

A courier arrived at the hotel twenty-five minutes after I got to my room. She brought two packages for me, secured with official consulate seals. I asked her to wait while I opened them. And the first one, I gave straight back. It contained photographs, courtesy of the INS. Portraits of travelers. Everyone who'd arrived in Illinois from overseas in the last week. Followed by the records from all the surrounding states. The stack was five inches thick. And even without the note confirming that there were no matches for the dead men's fingerprints, I knew it wouldn't tell me anything. It was pointless having sent it. A typical example of a desk guy trying to give the impression of productivity. One of the skills you had to master, to be a success on Fothergill's adopted side of the fence?

The second envelope wasn't much more useful. It was from the police lab. There was an initial analysis of the men's clothes. A breakdown of their last meals. Details of their physical condition, before they were shot. And a sketchy inventory of McIntyre's apartment, where they'd died. Every aspect came up blank. There was nothing to tell me where the dead guys had come from. What they'd been doing. Or where McIntyre was likely to be, now. None of which was a surprise. It was par for the course at this stage of a job. There was little to do besides settling down and waiting for more information. I was used to it. And at least I was in a hotel. I had a bed. A bathroom. A TV. And room service.

I guess my feelings about the quality of the intelligence he'd gathered didn't reach Fothergill until the morning because I didn't hear from him until past eight o'clock, when I was still contemplating the need to leave the comfort of my duvet. And even then, he only sent me a text message.

qqo?

Questions, queries, or observations? That was standard protocol following a remote briefing, and no more than I was expecting.

natt, I sent back. Nothing at this time.

I knew what his reply would be without looking at the phone.

hypafo.

The inevitable, *Hold your position—await further orders.*

In other words, sit and wait. The bane of service life. There was no telling how long the machine would take to churn out something useful, so I decided to get started with some breakfast. I ordered room service. A full English, with extra coffee. It was a good choice. I followed it up with a shave and a shower. And then crossed to the window to sketch out my own plans for the day.

The sky was a radiant, unbroken blue. It reminded me of deep, clear water. I thought about strolling over to the lake. Maybe carrying on along the shore for a while. Seeing how the city looked, floating above the waves. But I wouldn't be able to go far. I needed to stay in touch in case we got a lead on McIntyre. Somewhere closer at hand would be better. Somewhere central. Something unique to Chicago, since I wasn't planning on being here long. I moved to the window on the other side of the room, and straight away my eyes settled on a pair of massive antennas that rose above the surrounding buildings like white devil horns. They were on the roof of the Sears Tower. Or whatever it was called now. The tallest building in the world for more than twenty years. Still the tallest in America. And now, there it was, calling to me.

I pulled the tourist information folder out of the desk drawer and checked the address. Read up on the building's history. Glanced at extracts from its original blueprints. Skimmed through photographs of it being built. Studied a table of key facts. Looked for details of its observation deck. And found a leaflet tucked inside the back cover saying it was closed. The whole floor was out of commission. It had been shut down for some kind of emergency repair work, reading between the lines. So people were expected to settle for an alternative vantage point they were offering, on a lower floor.

Or find somewhere else to go.

The guidebook gave plenty of alternatives. It showed pictures of animals in the zoo. Paintings, at the Art Institute. Models of ancient Mexican cities in the Field Museum. Various exhibitions about planes. Trains. Cars. Ships. Body parts. And a submarine. A German U-boat. A genuine World War II relic. It had been captured off the coast of Africa, brought back to the States—complete with its pair of fully functional Enigma machines—then transported to Chicago in the fifties. Recently moved underground, into a reproduction concrete wolf-pen. Still loaded with torpedoes. And the sort of icon that no one from any navy would willingly ignore.

My coat was on and I was halfway down the corridor when I started to wonder about what kind of state the sub would be in. It was more than sixty years old. It had stood outside in the rain for maybe forty years. That would have called for some degree of restoration. Even German steel would be unable to weather that kind of neglect, unscathed. Plus, it must have been adapted somewhat to allow museum visitors to wander safely around inside. And with all those feet passing through, it would need regular cleaning. Which means its original character would have been changed. The marks and scratches and pieces of everyday detritus left behind by the original crew—dozens of guys crammed into the tiny space for weeks on end, like sweaty sardines—would have gone. They'd have been painted over. Swept aside. Or rusted away and replaced with fiberglass.

I was disappointed. I considered just staying in my room. But then thoughts of the U-Boat triggered off another realization. I'd also been disappointed with the Chicago police report that Fothergill had sent me. In particular, the file on McIntyre's apartment. It had been little more than a list of contents. There'd been no serious attempt to interpret or analyze. And now it hit me why not. McIntyre wasn't the kind of individual they were used to dealing with. He wasn't an ordinary criminal. They weren't on the same wavelength as him. In the same way as you'd need to be in the navy to fully appreciate the submarine, you'd need to be in the same line of work as McIntyre to look at where he'd been hiding and see any sort of significance. And the only other person around here in that line of work was me.

So I did still leave the hotel. But I changed my destination.

I told the guy at the front desk I needed a cab to O'Hare, but once we were under way I told the driver we had a new heading. Lincoln Park Zoo. I'd seen a sign for it yesterday when I was zigzagging around the city behind Rollins, so I knew it was in the right general area. The guy took it well at first. He was happy as long as I let him talk. But he was less impressed when I pulled him up short on Clark, just shy of Fullerton. I got out of the taxi, turned the corner and walked past the building McIntyre had been using, staying on the opposite side of the street. There were cars parked on both sides. I checked carefully, but none of them were occupied. I suppose the city's budget didn't run to stakeouts in the way ours did. Either that, or they were less thorough. But either way, I didn't risk approaching the place from the front. I followed round to Geneva Terrace and made my way back down the alley at the rear. Only this time I didn't have to worry about gates or fences. I guess the police had taken care of those, when they responded to the "shots fired" call yesterday. There were splintered remains lying around everywhere, so I just picked my way through the debris and walked up to the side door.

Three lengths of police crime-scene tape were hanging from the frame, flapping limply in the breeze. They'd been cut. Not with a knife, though. At least, not a sharp one.

From the ragged edges I'd say more likely with the edge of a key. I peered through the dusty glass, and right away I saw someone. Some legs, anyway. They were on the far side of the inner door. Lying down. Nothing was visible above the knee. The rest of the body was hidden by the internal wall. It must have been stretched out, toward the abandoned laundry room. All I could see was the lower half of a pair of stained, ripped jeans and two shabby shoes. One was brown. One was black. It wasn't a promising outfit. And not a place you'd usually choose to sleep, either.

The door opened as soon as I applied the slightest pressure. The lock had been broken. Forced, from the outside. The same had happened to the inner door. I eased that one open more carefully and squeezed through the gap, keeping well clear of the body. Or actually, bodies. A second one was sprawled out farther down the corridor, out of sight of the entrance. Both were male. I'd guess the first was in his thirties. The other was maybe twenty years older. The state they were in made it hard to be sure. Their clothes were ruined and filthy and torn. Their skin was blotchy and riddled with scabs. Their hair was unwashed, uncut, and plastered to their scalps. They were unshaven. And definitely unwashed.

The only question was whether they were still alive.

The younger one's problem was with the side of his head. Something had made a real mess of it, just above his right cheekbone. The skin wasn't broken, though, so I was thinking maybe an elbow had been used. Delivered hard enough to knock him out cold, if not more. I checked his breathing. It was shallow, but definitely present. The other guy hadn't been so lucky. He'd taken a blow to the throat. It looked like his airway had been crushed. I guessed he'd suffocated, but I wasn't about to put my fingers down his windpipe to make sure. There was no point. His days of receiving help were clearly over.

The floor was much dirtier than yesterday. I could make out at least nine sets of dried, muddy footprints leading from the door to the stairs. They'd be from the emergency crews I'd seen swarming all over the grass, I guessed. Two more sets—darker in color, with less well defined sole patterns—were smeared over the top of these. They led toward the window. Which had been broken. From the inside, out, judging by the pattern of glass fragments. That suggested two people escaping, presumably from whoever had set upon the other homeless guys. I thought that was all there was to find, but when I looked really carefully I picked up one final set, on top of all the others, also heading for the stairs. Someone had gone up there. Recently.

And there was no sign of them having come back down.

Logic told me that whoever had arrived there before me could have gone anywhere in the building. But I didn't believe in coincidences. And I didn't have much time. It would be stretching credulity to be found there with another dead body. So I gambled. I headed straight for the apartment that McIntyre had been hiding in. I still had the mirror I'd borrowed from Rollins, so I used it to check the entrance.

The door had been replaced with a new one. It was made of rough, unfinished wood. Industrial ply. I could see Chinese emblems stamped into the surface with red dye. A flimsy plastic handle had been attached above a roughly cut, not quite circular keyhole. Off cuts of the wood someone had used to build the temporary frame had been left lying on the floor near the bannister rail. And next to the timber was a wad of discarded crime-scene tape.

I took out the replacement cell phone Fothergill had pressed on me and checked that it was set to vibrate as well as make a sound. I scanned the list of ringtones and selected the one that looked the most annoying. Made sure the volume was set to maximum. Then fired off a text to the duty receptionist at the consulate.

call back. this no. 2 mins.

Most of the pieces of leftover wood were too short to be of any use—five or six inches, at the most—but I did manage to uncover one chunk that interested me. It was a hair short of three feet long. I extracted it from the pile and picked my way toward the apartment door, moving carefully to avoid the worst of the ill-fitting floorboards. I took my time, arriving silently with twenty seconds to spare. Just long enough to wedge the phone between the handle and the frame—tight, so its vibrations wouldn't shake it loose—step to the side, and line up with my makeshift club.

The phone rang, dead on cue. "Ride of the Valkyries" grated electronically from its tiny speaker. It was surprisingly loud. The hollow door buzzed and rattled in time with the vibrations. I tightened my grip on the wood. But no one emerged for me to hit.

The snippet of music played for a second time. And a third. Until finally I heard movement from inside the apartment. Rapid footsteps. They approached the door. Stopped. Then bullets started to rip through the plywood surface.

Three were at head height. Three at chest level. And three low down, skimming the ground.

I heard a thud. Metal on wood. A magazine being changed. Then nothing for twenty seconds. Thirty. The person inside was patient. Armed. And with a choice of exits. I wanted to be sure they came out of mine. So I switched my grip on the wood and tossed it down the stairs, spinning it around and sending it cartwheeling off the treads.

The footsteps started moving again. Faster than before. The door flew open. I dropped down to the floor, took all my weight on my hands and whipped my legs around in a wide arc, catching the guy emerging from the apartment just above his ankles. He went down, hard, losing his grip on his gun. I was up first, kicking it away and closing on him before he could get to his feet. He rolled onto his side, keeping his head off the ground, jabbing with his right leg, effectively fending me off. They were controlled kicks. Well aimed. Economical. Certainly not desperate lunges. He clearly knew what he was doing. Overpowering him was going to take a while. It would be tiring, and hard to guarantee he'd be in a position to talk at the end of it. So I pulled out my Beretta and put a round through the floor on either side of his head. To warn him. I didn't want him dead. I just had no desire to waste all my energy.

And after that, he decided not to waste any more of his.

In training, we'd learned to look for items that could be useful to us.

In the field, we found the same thing applied to people.

SEVEN

There are lots of ways to teach a person to navigate.

The way our instructors did it was to show you a map. Give you an hour to memorize it. Make sure you didn't have a compass. Then send you out into the Welsh countryside to find a specific place where they said another agent would be waiting.

The exercise was designed to be realistic. The idea was to simulate your part in an emergency covert rendezvous. And it seemed simple enough, at the outset. You didn't have far to travel. There was nothing heavy to carry. You didn't have to steal anything or trick your way into anywhere secure. It was daylight. They even gave you a packed meal.

Get there on time, you pass. If not, you fail.

The truck dropped you off exactly where they promised. But that was the last thing to go as advertised. First, they changed the meeting point. Four times. Each time you reached what you thought was the correct spot, all you found was a concealed note containing new coordinates. Each set was harder to find than the previous one. And on the third occasion, they added an extra piece of information. The "agent" had been delayed. She could be anything up to two hours late. And despite the sheets of icy rain that had begun to fall, you had no choice. You had to stay. You couldn't abandon your contact.

My final map reference turned out to be the location of a telephone box. One of the old-fashioned red ones that you don't usually see anymore, except in the tourist hot spots around London. I guess it was too remote for the phone company to bother with a replacement. It really was isolated. Scrubby, barren fields stretched out on both sides. A narrow, winding country lane led back to the nearest village. The lights of a single farmhouse glowed in the distance. And nowhere in sight offered any kind of adequate shelter.

I slid under a stretch of thin, weedy hedgerow and settled down to wait. The rain cascaded onto me from above. My clothes absorbed more water from the ground. I was thoroughly soaked within seconds. Daylight started to fade. The temperature was dropping steadily. The wind picked up and started to make the sharp strands of bramble dance and scratch at my face. My head filled with reminders of why I've never felt at home in the country, but I kept my eyes on the phone booth the whole time. And saw that no one approached it. Not a single person passed it on the road. Even a pair of stray dogs gave it a wide berth. It was like a magnet with the wrong polarity, designed to repel people and animals.

An hour and a half crawled by. The daylight had drained

almost completely away. Another half hour passed, and I realized I was shivering more or less uncontrollably. I'd been there for the designated two hours. There was no sign of the agent. She'd technically missed her contact. I would have been entitled to return to base. Officially it was time to call it a day but I gave her an extra fifteen agonizing minutes, just in case. And because I hated the idea of not having met my objective. But still, she didn't show up. So I slid out from my hiding place. Crouched at the edge of the rough grass verge. Checked both ways along the road. Scanned the fields. Saw nothing. Started to move. And heard the sound of a shotgun cartridge crunching into place behind me.

At that moment I thought I'd blown it, but the exercise turned out to have been a success after all. The scope was just a little wider than I'd been led to believe. As well as our people, the army was involved. Their challenge was to capture the operator I was supposed to be meeting. It was a kind of contest. Pride was at stake, so our instructors were taking no chances. They suspected that details of the final rendezvous would have been leaked, since the army was handling the communications. So, to find out, I was sent to the place alone. The theory was that if the army was staking it out, they wouldn't react as soon as they saw me. They'd wait for my contact to show herself and snatch both of us. And if she didn't show up, they'd snatch me hoping that I'd know about some backup plans, rather than let the trail go cold. So my role had been to flush them out. With that achieved, the other operator was successfully retrieved. The navy won. And an important lesson was learned.

In an operation, everyone has a role to play.
It just may not be the one you're expecting.

Everyone knows that interrogating a suspect is A PEST. To make it work, you need:

Access control, so that word of his capture doesn't have the chance to spread.

Privacy, to make sure nothing he reveals is overheard.

Efficiency, to milk every last drop of useful intelligence out of him.

Security, so that no one can silence him before he spills the beans.

And a way to judge the . . .

Truth of what he says before you commit any resources on the strength of it.

So, all things considered, the third-floor landing of an insecure building would not be top of your list of favorable locations for the job. If the guy was a big enough fish, you'd take him somewhere specially designed for the task. A place where he couldn't escape, and no one else could get at him. Where the physical environment itself would help to demoralize him. And where experts were on hand to harvest and validate his information. The snag was, in the middle of

Chicago, in daylight, without a vehicle outside, and with no one to assist, I had no way of moving him. Not without attracting unwanted attention. There was nowhere locally to take him. And no one qualified to handle the questioning. So that left me only one option. If I couldn't move him physically, I'd have to take him somewhere else inside his head.

It was obvious that the guy knew how to handle himself, so there was no point in trying to beat any information out of him or scare him with threats of arrest or jail. Instead, I'd have to rely on a technique I'd picked up a few years ago. Or at least a variation of one. Something I'd seen a Danish anarchist cell use. I'd been sent to Copenhagen to penetrate them after the eavesdroppers at GCHQ sniffed out a plot to blackmail one of the ambassador's assistants. As missions go, it was pretty much a damp squib. Two months of work to confirm the threat they posed was negligible. They were more interested in raising beer money than stealing state secrets. The shadow they cast just turned out to be larger than they were because they were so good at manipulating hostages. And that was down to one of their leaders. He prided himself on controlling people. Not through violence, though. Or bribery. Or empty threats. He had a much more effective technique. He turned his victims' minds against themselves. Led them to accept they were about to die. To really, truly embrace the fact that their lives were over. And when they reached that place, they were like putty in his hands.

I took a step back, scooped up the discarded gun and waited in silence. The guy from McIntyre's room lay as still as the wooden floorboards beneath him. He stayed that way for just over a minute. Then, very slightly, beginning with his left foot, he started to fidget.

"Take out your phone," I said.

My plan was to offer him one last call. I didn't care who to. His wife, maybe. His girlfriend. Or a significant other of whatever kind. Because whoever he spoke to, if I could get him to say good-bye to them, to hear his own voice announcing out loud that he only had moments left to live, I knew he'd be on the verge of believing it himself.

Things didn't start out very promisingly. The guy glanced to his left and his eyes settled on the shattered remains of the Nokia that Fothergill had given me. One of his bullets must have caught it when he shot up the door. The corners of his mouth curled into a tiny smile, but other than that, he didn't move. Then confusion spread across his face, followed by a tinge of hope.

"Wait a minute," he said, in a faded Newcastle accent. "You're English?"

Nothing like that ever happened to the Danish anarchist. No one had shown the slightest interest in his dialect, and I'd seen him use the same trick four times in two months.

"Get your phone, Einstein," I said. "It's not for me. It's for you."

"Are you from the Wrigley Building?" he said. "You know, UK Trade, et cetera?"

An intriguing question, from a civilian.

"Get the phone," I said. "Do it now."

"Oh, I get it," he said. "I know who you are. You're Green Slime."

That was even more intriguing. Green Slime is generic British Army slang for military intelligence, but I hadn't heard it used in years.

"I'm right, aren't I?" he said. "But I know you won't admit it. So let's stop talking about the phone, and start talking about how I can help you."

Maybe things would work out after all. People always ended up helping Kaspar the anarchist, but even with him they didn't usually volunteer so readily.

"You think you can help me?" I said. "With what?"

"Can I sit up?" he said. "This is getting uncomfortable."

"No. Help me with what?"

"Finding Tony."

"Who's Tony? And why would I want to find him?"

"Tony McIntyre."

"Doesn't ring a bell."

"Look. Three people in the world knew Tony was in the United States. Me. Richard Fothergill, Tony's old mate in the Slime, who's now here in Chicago. And one other guy."

"So?"

"Well, I didn't tell you. And the other guy didn't tell you."

"How do you know the other guy didn't tell me? How do you know I'm not the other guy?"

"He's a government employee. A government that only employs people from its own country. And that country isn't England."

"What country is it?"

"Some tiny one, in Africa. The name escapes me."

"I can wait. Or I could help you remember, if you're struggling."

"Don't worry. It'll come back to me. But the point is, it must have been Fothergill who told you. About Tony."

I didn't answer.

"Don't try telling me that you showing up here, outside his door, is some kind of coincidence," he said. "I'm not new."

"How did you know he was here?" I said.

"It was me who told him to come here. I gave him the address."

"When?"

"Twelve days ago."

"Why?"

"We served together, in another life. Stayed in touch. I help out once in a while, when Tony needs something done on the q.t. Everyone in the Slime has a back-door man, don't they?"

"How did this other guy know?"

"He's got lots of fingers in lots of pies. Like a giant octopus. Found out Tony was coming here. Then followed him."

"How did he find out?"

"I don't know."

"Why did he follow?"

"Tony had something he wanted."

"Something Tony was selling?"

"No. Tony wasn't selling anything. The thing he had, he wanted to destroy."

Or at least, he didn't want to sell till he had a scapegoat lined up, I thought. People don't destroy big heaps of their own money. Maybe this was big enough to be his pension fund. He could sell it, deflect the attention, and disappear into the sunset.

"What is this thing he had?" I said.

"I don't know, exactly," he said. "But Tony thought it was bad shit. He wanted to get rid of it. Safely."

"Why weren't you here, taking care of things, if you've got Tony's back?"

The guy shrugged.

"I got here as quick as I could," he said.

"Where does Fothergill fit into it?" I said.

"Tony needed help. Fothergill was his last hope."

"What kind of help?"

"Getting rid of this thing—whatever it was—and getting the other guy off his back."

"Sounds straightforward. What went wrong?"

"I don't know. Something came off the rails. Fothergill was on board. He'd agreed to help. Tony was on his way to see him. I guess he never got there."

"Really?"

"No. But where are you going with this? You've been briefed, right?"

"You know bureaucrats. Fothergill plays his cards pretty close. He only paints in the broad strokes. So, McIntyre never made it to the rendezvous, do you think?"

"Right. He got hurt. Wound up with a slug in his side."

"How?"

The guy shrugged.

"Someone pulled a trigger on him," he said. "Don't know who. Don't know why. I just know he needed surgery."

"Where?"

"At a place I know."

"What place?"

"A clinic. In the center of the city. Does cosmetic work, normally."

"Why there?"

"I own it. Or a piece of it. I told Tony about it ahead of time, just in case. That's standard planning, for us."

"What's your name?"

"It doesn't matter what my name is."

Something creaked downstairs. I raised my gun, lining up on the bridge of the guy's nose, and held my breath until I was sure no one was coming. His eyes locked onto the muzzle. He swallowed. Twice. Rapidly, like his Adam's apple was trying to break through his skin.

"It matters to me," I said, when I was satisfied we were still on our own.

"Young," he said, after a couple of seconds. "Gary Young."

That tallied with what Fothergill had told me in his office, two days ago. Gary Young was the person McIntyre had blamed for corrupting him, so I slowly lowered the Beretta. Some of the way. Using a recognizable name was a good start, but it didn't explain everything.

"McIntyre's accident with the 9mm was nearly a week ago," I said. "Why are you just looking for him now?"

"I have my reasons," he said.

"Could they include, now, let's see—you not really being his friend, for example?"

He didn't answer.

"Or that really you're here to buy this evil stuff he had, but you're a little off the pace?"

"Look," he said, "I had to get into the country. That takes time. See, the authorities would prefer I stayed out. There's no welcome mat for me. Then, 'cause I hadn't spoken to Tony since he got hurt, I didn't know which safe house he'd be using to recover in. He wasn't answering his phone. I couldn't find out from his doctor—the one from the clinic—'cause he's disappeared, too. So, I had to start at the first location and work my way down."

"How many safe houses have you got?"

"Five."

"That's not possible. McIntyre wasn't here long enough to scope out that many."

"He didn't have to. They're located in advance. By me. Or by my people, anyway. That's how we work."

"What number safe house is this?"

"Four."

"So there's one more you haven't checked yet?"

"Yes. Not far from here."

"Then get on your feet," I said. "We're leaving."

*

Young gave McIntyre's cell phone one more try as we left the building and walked east on Fullerton. There was no reply, so I took his phone and called Fothergill instead. His lust for detail turned to near panic when he realized I was with the sidekick of the guy who'd tried to kill him, and I was still trying to calm him down as we crossed Clark and turned left onto Lakeview. We kept going for another two hundred yards, then Young veered off onto a footpath on the right. It took us away from the apartment buildings and single-family homes on the opposite side of the street, across a stretch of grass, and through a long, narrow tunnel which led under another road. The trees were denser on the far side, lining the route toward a building at the edge of a large pond. It was wide and low, made of wood, like an old-fashioned pavilion, and it had a tall stone-faced chimney at the far end. A row of symmetrical French windows were standing open all down one side, overlooking the water. A sign on the wall said it was a restaurant. The door was to our right, but Young went left and led the way around the corner of the building. He started to pick his way through the trees, and I soon realized what he was aiming for. A rough wooden fence, about forty yards from the restaurant. It was the boundary of some kind of compound, eight feet high and twenty-five feet long. Young was heading straight for a gate in the center, but when we'd closed to within ten feet of it I held back and listened.

"What's the matter?" he said. "I thought you were in a hurry."

"Dogs," I said.

"Don't worry. There are no dogs, here. No precautions at all. Just storage for the café. Spare furniture, old machines, Christmas decorations. Nothing worth a bag of bones."

The gate was locked shut with a padlock. One that used a combination, not a key. Young fiddled with the barrels for less than two seconds before the hasp sprang open. I saw the code he'd used. 1—2—3—4. On that evidence, maybe he was right about the level of security.

There were six sheds inside the compound. All were an identical size and shape. Rectangular, eight feet by six. They were arranged in two lines of three. All had wooden walls, shingle roofs, and no windows. And all were padlocked from the outside.

"Doesn't look hopeful," I said.

"Don't judge a book by its cover," Young said. "And I want my SIG back, please."

"That won't be necessary."

"It will. I need it. I'm not going in that shed unarmed."

"Why not? You said McIntyre was your old mate."

"He is."

"Old enough that he's senile?"

"No."

"So he remembers what you look like?"

Young didn't answer.

"You think he'd recognize you, and shoot you anyway?" I said.

"No," Young said.

"So you need a lethal weapon because . . . ?"

Young scowled at me, then made his way around to the

back of the last shed on the left. He counted seven panels in from the far corner, pushed gently to check they were loose, then knocked rapidly four times.

"Terry?" he called.

"Wait a minute," I said. "Who d'you think we're looking for, here?"

"Tony," he said. "Obviously. But we only use real names if we're in trouble. As a warning. Makes sense, if you think about it."

We turned back to the shed. There was nothing but silence from inside.

"Terry?" he called, again. "It's Graham. It's OK. Are you there? Are you hurt?"

Still no reply.

"Looks like you could be right," he said. "Not hopeful at all."

"We need to be sure," I said. "In you go."

Young sighed, swung the loose panels out of the way, and wriggled through the gap he'd made. I took out my Beretta and followed him in. If McIntyre was there it would be a safe bet he'd remember what I looked like, too, and I'd be hard-pressed to call myself an old friend.

There wasn't room to stand up straight inside the shed other than in the very center, due to the pitch of the roof. The air was heavy with damp, rotting wood pulp, and even with the narrow beam of light that followed us through the hole in the wall it was clear that the place hadn't been used for years. Except maybe by woodworm. The interior was completely empty, and the entire floor was shrouded in fine sawdust. It was everywhere, apart from the places where Young and I had stepped. If anyone else had been there recently, it would have been immediately obvious.

"Not much of a safe house," I said, as Young reluctantly replaced the panels from the outside.

"A long shot, at best," he said. "I knew it was the worst place. That's why I left it till last."

"So where else could McIntyre be? What about an emergency rendezvous?"

"Didn't think we needed one, with five safe houses. And I'm starting to worry. Something had obviously happened at that last place. The crime-scene tape wasn't there for decoration. And the door was gone, so someone must have busted in uninvited at some point."

"True."

"And what about the bloodstains? There were three. Two inside, and one outside. On the stairs. Did you see those?"

"Yes."

"So, who could it have been? I was thinking, a bunch of random idiots? They tried something, and Tony dealt with it? Then I figured he moved on to the next place, since I'd tried all the others. Your people would know if he'd wound up in the hospital, right? Or if the police had arrested him for something?"

"They would."

"Then we should head back up there. Try to find some more scrotes to talk to. Those last two were useless. They gave me nothing. But there were a couple more hanging around. They got away. We could find them. Maybe they know something."

"Looks like you asked some pretty hard questions."

"There's a lot at stake. If Tony's in the wrong hands, we've got huge problems."

"Well, Tony does, anyway. I'm not so sure I care at this point. And I doubt the guys you killed did, either."

"Forget them. They should have been more cooperative. But believe me, you should care."

"Why?"

"Because of the stuff Tony had. If it's gone, there'll be a huge piece of Africa with a population of zero, very soon. Or stuck with a government full of ruthless, corrupt assholes with their snouts permanently welded to the trough."

"What, you mean politicians?"

"This is serious."

"OK. So, Africa? Why a piece of there?"

"That's where the guy's from. The Republic of Equatorial Myene. The other person who knew Tony was here. He works for that government. And there are elections coming. Elections they're going to lose, otherwise."

"Maybe Tony was happy to sell to these guys. Or maybe they offered him a job, in lieu. Minister of ethical integrity, perhaps."

"You don't understand. Tony's not like that. He's completely ethical."

"He sounds it."

"He is. He isn't here to sell. And specially not to them."

"Really."

"Trust me. He wouldn't piss in their mouths if their teeth were on fire."

"Well, if he wasn't helping them with their election strategy, how did they know his address? It's one thing knowing he was in the States. It's another knowing which city. Which street. Which building. Which floor. Which room."

Young didn't reply.

"What, you think they just guessed?"

He stayed silent.

"Fothergill didn't even know," I said. "So you told them. Or Tony did. Or you're just generally full of shit."

"We don't know it was them," he said. "Not for sure."

"We do. Your idiot theory? Forget it."

"Why?"

"I saw the guys who disagreed with the door. And they were no idiots. Trust me."

"How would you know? You weren't there."

"Oh, but I was. Right there. In the room. With Tony."

"Doing what?"

"Following up after the rendezvous problem. Fothergill was concerned. Like you said, he wanted to help. He asked me to track Tony down."

"What did Tony say? Did you speak?"

"No. I was about to broach the subject when the door imploded."

"How many gatecrashers?"

"Two."

"The two bloodstains?"

I nodded.

"Dead?" he said.

"That's what happens when you bust in uninvited," I said.

"Tony killed them?"

I didn't reply.

"Was it Tony? Did he take care of business?"

I shrugged.

"Oh. That was your work, then?" he said. "Hypocrite."

"Someone had to deal with them," I said. "Tony was more concerned with leaving."

"Can't blame him for that. He was hurt. Stop. Wait. The stain on the stairs? That couldn't have been . . . ?"

"No. It was the doctor. From the clinic."

"Oh. Was he dead?"

"Apparently so."

"What was he doing? How come he was there?"

"It's a long story. But forget him. The point is, I didn't see where Tony went. And I need to know where else he could be. I guess we both do."

Young didn't answer.

"Wake up," I said. "People are trying to kill your friend. I can't help him if I don't know where he is. The shed was a blank. So think. Where else would he have gone?"

"How many guys busted in?" he said. "Two?"

"You know him. What was his MO.? Back against the wall, what would he do?"

"'Cause if there were two guys, we're screwed. Were there two?"

"Where would he run to?"

"I don't know. But please. How many? You said two?"

"Two. Obviously. Else there'd have been more bloodstains."

Young didn't reply.

"Don't go all coy on me, now," I said. "And why are you so bothered with the head count?"

"Because you don't know how these guys work," he said. "They're not like us. They don't have budgets to worry about. I'm talking unlimited resources. What weapons were they carrying? Nothing cheap, right?"

"MP5s."

"Right. New clothes?"

"Yes."

"I could go on. And I can guarantee, they never just travel in pairs. There'd have been six of them, on a job like this. Minimum. You burned two, so that's four more outside. Tony's good, but there's no way he's getting past four guys, while he's wounded. It's time to face facts. They've got him."

"OK. Supposing you're right, where would they take him?"

"No idea."

"Think."

"No point. I have absolutely no idea."

"And if he did somehow get past them? How could we find him?"

"No idea."

"No? What do you have an idea about?"

Young scowled at me, but said nothing.

"Then wait there a minute," I said. "And keep your mouth shut till you've got something useful to say."

Fothergill answered the phone on the first ring. He was disappointed, but not exactly surprised. He'd never expected my time with Young to turn up anything of value. And he was less than encouraging when it came to sketching out our next steps.

"I'm afraid so," he said. "Young is ex–Royal Marines, after all. So you better get yourself ready. London will be ordering another hard arrest. They're still deliberating, but I can't see another outcome. I'd put money on it coming through."

I looked across at Young. He was skulking next to the compound fence, hands in his pockets, kicking his toes into the dusty ground and trying to avoid catching my eye. I could almost see the tidemarks on his clothes. He was up to his neck in McIntyre's cesspool of a scheme. That's what I'd put my money on.

"Don't worry about it," I said. "Que sera, sera. Let's just not drag things out, eh? McIntyre's in the wind, and I'm not going to find him if I'm bogged down in this other mess."

"Agreed," he said. "I'll confirm directly. In the meantime, take him somewhere safe and sit on him. And I'll keep you posted if anything else breaks, this end."

My first thought was that if I had to waste time on this guy, I might as well do it somewhere with room service. I was tempted to head up to Clark Street, grab us a cab, and stash him away at my hotel for as long as necessary. But the snag with that plan was, if Fothergill's hunch played out and I did have to dispatch Young anytime soon, there'd be nowhere convenient to do it. I needed somewhere with more privacy. Somewhere with disposal facilities. And certainly somewhere with no housekeepers who could stumble across the body.

A picture of the tramp he'd just killed floated into my head. McIntyre's building was close. I knew I'd spent too much time in it recently, but I couldn't think of a more appropriate place to run down the clock on Young. And because I'd been outside, chasing after his red herring, I still needed to have a thorough look for any traces the police had missed.

Young seemed tense and distant as we made our way back along Fullerton. He stared at the ground as we walked and made no attempt to speak, which was fine by me. He grew more anxious the closer we got to the building, but didn't break his silence till the moment we entered the apartment.

"When he left, he must have been in one hell of a hurry, yes?" he said.

I pushed past him and kept going toward the end of the corridor. I wanted to see the room where McIntyre had been waiting before going to answer the door.

"What I mean is, was he carrying anything?" he said. "McIntyre? Did he have time to stop and collect anything?"

Three items of furniture had been left in the living room. An air mattress, slashed, gaping, and discarded in the far corner. A mountaineering-style sleeping bag, dull and green, three feet from it on the floor. And a bentwood chair, battered but still standing, in the center of the room.

"No," I said. "His hands were empty."

"So if Tony wasn't carrying the stuff when he ran, it might still be here," he said, following me through the door. "We should look for it."

"Do you think?"

"Wait. Something's changed. The Maggot. It's moved."

Green Maggot was army slang for sleeping bag, as far as I could recall. But I wished he'd just speak in plain English.

"You sure?" I said.

"Certain," he said. "I was here earlier. Just before you turned up. I looked in all the rooms. The bag was on the mattress. I guarantee it. Hobos must have got in. Trying to steal it, I guess."

"Go and check," I said, pulling back to the corridor. "See if there's any other reason."

Young walked all the way round the sleeping bag. Twice. Slowly. He pulled back the top layer and peered inside. Then he rolled the whole thing over, looked underneath, and called me over to see what he'd found.

"Run your finger over that," he said, pointing to the join between two floorboards.

It wasn't certain by eye, but you could feel that one of the boards was definitely proud of its neighbor. I traced the raised joint along and around, and found that it formed a rectangular section about two feet square.

"Open it," I said, stepping backward again.

"Empty," he said, after scrabbling at the edges of the trapdoor for a few seconds. "Oh, no, wait a minute. Come and look at this."

Young was right. There was nothing hidden under the floor. But something had been roughly scratched on the underneath of the removable panel. Two numbers. One above the other, like a fraction. A four. And a five.

"They must have brought Tony back here," Young said. "To pick up the stuff. He must have had it stashed."

"If anyone even has him," I said. "He could have come back on his own. After you'd conveniently made sure the place was deserted with all that shed bullshit."

"No. If he was alone, he'd have just answered his phone. I called him enough times. Or he'd have texted me. Or got a new phone, if the old one was unserviceable."

"I'm not convinced."

"Think about it. This is the fourth place out of five. On the list that I wrote. No one else knew about that. The message was for me. It tells me he was back here, and he's in trouble."

"Maybe."

"And think about where he wrote it. That was no accident. It was to show me the people who have him, have the stuff too. They won't need him anymore. Which means next time your phone rings, it'll be someone telling you where his body's been found."

"I seriously doubt that."

"And then we're going to be reading about the worst civilian massacre of the twenty-first century, soon after. The worst to date, anyway. Unless we can stop them from taking the stuff out of the country."

"You think so?"

"You can count on it."

"Then it's time to stop talking, and start looking. Just in case you're right. 'Cause we're going to need more than a pair of numbers to tell us where to find them."

We started in the main room, and as I worked my way back toward the corridor I tried to piece together what must have happened in there. Young believed McIntyre had been dragged back to collect the canister of gas. He'd taken quite a risk, leaving a message. I admired him for that. But the more I thought about it, the less it made sense to me.

"Young?" I said. "Tell me something. McIntyre's message. Why didn't he say who'd taken him?"

"No idea," he said.

"Or how many of them? Their disposition? Or location?"

"He probably didn't have time."

"See, here's the thing. If I was risking everything to leave a message, I'd make sure it said something really important. Like where the bad guys were holding me, or how you could find them."

"It's a miracle he left anything at all. And it's churlish to start criticizing now."

"I think there's another reason for skipping the critical part. The person he left the message for already knew."

Young was silent for a moment too long before replying.

"That's crazy," he said. "He was leaving the message for me."

"Exactly," I said. "Because you already know who these guys are. And you know how to contact them. Don't you?"

"No."

"OK, it's time to turn your cards face up. All of them. I'm not looking to cause you any trouble over this. We can keep everything unofficial. But your friend's life is on the line here. And, if you're right, a load of innocent Africans, too."

Young didn't answer

"I'm going to find McIntyre," I said. "That's the job I've been given. One way or another, I'm going to do it. The only question is, will I be bringing back a person? Or a corpse? And here's the thing. If it turns out a coffin's needed, it'll be down to you. And I'll make sure it says so on his gravestone."

Fothergill didn't believe Young's claims of innocence any more than I did when I called him. He was happy to know I had a phone number for the people who'd snatched McIntyre. But annoyingly, he didn't see eye to eye about how we should use it.

"It's easy," I said. "I'll get Young to call the buyers. He can set up a meeting. And I'll go to it with him."

"On what grounds?" Fothergill said. "Why would they see you?"

"To buy more of this gas."

"There isn't any more."

"I know that. But they don't."

"What if they want a sample?"

"You know what the containers look like. You could get a mock-up made for me."

"What if they rumble you?"

"How? What are they going to do? Open the lid and take a sniff?"

"No. But still, it's too risky."

"Letting them take the stuff out of the country is what's risky."

"OK. Suppose you met these guys. What would you do?"

"Let them lead me to McIntyre. Retrieve the canister. And him too, if he's still alive at that point."

"How?"

"No idea. It's too early to say. But I'll find a way. I do this for a living, remember."

"The plan's too vague. Too complicated. There's too much to go wrong."

"Have you got a better idea?"

Fothergill didn't reply.

"I'm telling Young to make the call," I said.

"Not yet," Fothergill said. "Please. Wait. Young's got quite a past behind him. At least let me run some more background. See how far we can trust him. You can't build a mission around untested intel. That would be suicide."

I agreed, and this time I did head back to the hotel. Young was quieter and more preoccupied than before, not saying a word except to tell me what food he wanted brought up. His mood didn't even improve when Fothergill finally called back, two hours later. The sting was on, but on one condition. We still had no backup, so the meeting with the buyers had to be at a specific bar. The Commissariat, on State and Rush. The owners were friendly, Fothergill said. And very discreet. No one would pay attention to what we were doing there. No one would remember seeing us. No questions would be asked if violence happened to break out. And whether it did or not, a CCTV recording of the whole proceedings could be on Fothergill's desk inside the hour.

Young's contact said he'd be able to find the Commissariat. He was suspicious to start with, but as soon as Young's hints about the availability of additional merchandise had sunk in, he quickly softened up. We agreed to meet at a quarter after four. That only gave us two hours, but the guy was determined. He wouldn't budge. The situation was far from ideal, but we were low on options. It would just have to do.

Fothergill picked us up from the hotel at two forty-five, as agreed. He was using the undercover taxi I'd borrowed from the police yesterday. It was a good choice, blending in perfectly with the traffic as he weaved his way through the city. Fothergill drove with one eye on Young, and the other on the rearview mirror. The route he took was crazy, dodging down an endless variety of alleyways and back-streets, avoiding the worst of the delays and making it hard for any potential tails to latch onto us. It was so effective we hardly stopped until we were within two blocks of the rendezvous. Then Fothergill rolled the car over to the curb. But instead of just letting us out he switched off the engine, pulled his Beretta out of his shoulder holster and began to rapidly check it over.

"Richard?" I said. "What are you doing?"

"Sorry," he said. "Old superstition. Always have to check my weapon one last time. Can't move, otherwise."

"But why? Move where? You're not coming in with us."

"I have to. Who are these guys you're meeting? They're a completely unknown quantity. And they're not the only threat," he said, nodding discreetly at Young. "You need someone in there with you. Someone to watch your back."

"You can watch our backs," I said, handing him both guns, my wallet, and the hotel room key. "But you can't come in. We can't take weapons with us. And I don't want to carry ID. They're bound to search us. So if things go south, we'll need to bail in a hurry. We need you outside, engine running, ready to get us out of Dodge."

Young and I walked past the bar three times before we went inside. Once to identify the alternative exits, and twice to scope out the security. The main entrance was set at an angle at the corner of the two streets. A bloated guy in a dinner suit was standing by the door the first time we strolled by, but he'd moved to perch on a flimsy-looking bar stool in an alcove to the right by the time we returned. Two smaller, lighter guys in similar clothes were loitering just inside the building. One was pressing buttons on his cell phone. And neither of them seemed particularly alert, hardly turning a hair as we pushed past and made our way down a set of carpeted stairs to the main bar area.

We had forty-five minutes to kill before Young's contacts were due to arrive, so we ordered a couple of beers and settled down to wait at a round table near the back of the room. There were seven other people in the place. Three were working. One guy was behind the bar, leaning listlessly against the wall, waiting in vain for someone else to want a drink. Another was halfheartedly clearing martini glasses from a large rectangular table in the center. A girl was jammed into a tiny DJ booth to our left, fiddling with an iPod. And the four customers—all men in their fifties—were huddled over some paperwork in a booth at the foot of the stairs.

Fifty minutes gradually ticked away. We sipped our Peronis. The busboy wandered back and dawdled over wiping the long table. The DJ churned out one dire eighties hit after another. The barman looked like he was asleep. The older guys wrapped up their meeting and left, all together. But no one new came into the bar. I began to feel like we were frozen in time. The gloomy lighting, the lack of movement, the outdated music—they made it feel like the world had forgotten we were there. I had to check my watch to make sure the hands were still moving. I saw them creep around another five minutes. And another. Then there was a pause between songs. And I finally heard footsteps on the stairs.

Four people entered the room. They were all fairly tall—three men between six one and six three, one woman around five nine—and they were wearing identical clothes. Black trainers, with no discernible branding. Stiff, new jeans. Dark blue CHICAGO hoodies, pulled up high to conceal their faces, and baggy enough to give easy access to the obvious bulges on their hips.

The new arrivals fanned out, six feet from the stairs, and scanned the room. Then they strode straight up to our table, spreading out and penning us in against the wall.

"Gentlemen," said the tallest of the group, "I apologize for our timekeeping. I fear our knowledge of this fair city, and its traffic issues in particular, is not as encyclopedic as I would wish it to be. But still, we are here now. As are you. So, shall we get down to business?"

"By all means," Young said. "Let's get started."

"Excellent," the guy said. "However, before we commence, a couple of precautions would be welcome. Would you mind accompanying my associates for a moment? Perhaps the privacy of the restrooms would be appropriate?"

The guys each took a step back, and the one who'd been speaking gestured for us to stand and follow them. I looked across at Young.

"It's OK," he said. "This is standard with these guys. Nothing to worry about. Best to just get it over with."

I nodded, and squeezed out from behind the table. The woman was standing nearest to me so she took my arm and we started to walk. Young slid out from the other side and immediately overtook us, heading toward the toilets. The next guy in line quickly fell into step, grabbing Young's shoulder and steering him left toward the ladies' room. The woman guided me to the right, and into the men's.

The restroom was small and basic. The walls and floor were covered with white tiles. There were three urinals. Three stalls. Two basins. And one hand dryer. The woman motioned for me to stand next to it while she checked that no one else was in the place. Then she shook the hood off her head and turned back to face me.

For a moment she stood in front of me, silently, without moving. Then she raised both hands, palms together, and pressed her fingers against me, just below my collarbone. She looked me in the eye and began to move her hands slowly down my body, crossing my chest, then my stomach. She reached my belt, paused, moved her hands apart slightly, and kept going till she reached my thighs. Then she stepped back, tipped her head to one side, and pursed her lips.

"No," she said. "That just doesn't tell me what I need to know. Give me your shoes."

I leaned down and unzipped my boots.

"Give them to me," she said.

I set them on the floor between us. She rolled her eyes, picked up the boots, examined the insides, then tossed them into the corner of the room.

"Now, your shirt," she said.

I pulled my T-shirt over my head, paused, and dropped it in front of me. She ground it into the tiles with the sole of her foot, then kicked it aside.

"Your pants," she said.

I unfastened my belt, let my jeans fall, and stepped out of them. She pulled the waistband closer with her toe and leaned down to grab them, leaving the back of her neck temporarily exposed. She was only in that position for a fraction of a second, but that would have been all I needed. Still, it wasn't too big a sacrifice to let the chance go begging. Something told me her time was going to come. And soon.

"Now, the rest," she said, letting go of my jeans.

I slipped my shorts off and held them out, level with her face. She stared back, then slowly and deliberately lowered her gaze.

"It's OK," I said. "Go ahead. You can touch."

She let ten seconds pass, then slowly reached toward my groin.

"I meant the underwear," I said. "It was fresh on this morning."

She snorted, snatched the shorts, and crammed them into her pocket.

"Come and see me later," she said, opening the door. "You can get them back, then. If you're still breathing."

The woman was sitting in my place when I came back out into the bar. The men were with her, plus a guy I hadn't seen before, and all five had glasses of sparkling water lined up on the table in front of them. Someone had dragged over one extra chair. I took hold of another one and had started to move it when the man who'd spoken to us before looked up and caught my eye.

"That's very kind," he said. "But we won't be needing it."

"What about Young?" I said.

"Who?"

"The bloke I came here with."

"He doesn't need it. He won't be working with us after all."

"Why not?"

The guy shrugged.

"We're very particular about who we accept as colleagues," he said.

"Where is he?" I said.

"That's an interesting question. I expect it depends on your religious outlook."

I started for the stairs, but changed tack after three steps and headed for the ladies' room instead. None of the men moved from the table. The bartender looked the other way. The woman winked at me. I covered the ground quickly and pushed the door open with my foot. The layout inside was just like the men's, except that two extra stalls took the place of the urinals. They filled in the space all the way to the far corner. My eye was drawn to the last one in line. It was the only one with a closed door. But that wasn't what worried me. I was more concerned about the red stream snaking its way under the side wall and flowing along the joins in the floor tiles.

Fresh blood.

It was already halfway to the basins, and showed no signs of slowing down.

The navigation exercise all those years ago showed that you can use a fake rendezvous to flush out your enemy. You can even use a real one.

But it's only once they're in the open that you see what they're truly capable of.

EIGHT

Ask a sane person to commit suicide, and the answer will be, "No." Every time.

That's not to say people will never give their lives for a cause. Sometimes, things are worth dying for. For parents, their children. For soldiers, their comrades. For some people, a flag. Or a country. Or a concept, such as freedom or honor. For them, it can be a choice. And for others, it can just happen. Rational decision making doesn't stand up well in the heat of the moment. Like for the Battle of Britain pilot my father remembered watching in a dogfight over London. Out of ammunition, desperate not to let the invaders through, he ploughed his Hurricane straight into the side of a Ju88. In a sense, his desperate plan worked. The bomber broke in half and went down in flames. But it was the British pilot's last action, too. 'Cause he went down with the four Germans.

Everyone in the navy knows that lives can be lost. At our level, we accept it. There's no room for soft hearts in our line of work. It's a different equation for the senior ranks, though. To them, it's just another example of cost versus benefit. Operatives are expensive assets. Training takes time and money. Experience is worth even more. If you die while getting the job done, there's a chance the result will be worth the sacrifice. But if you sense that you're falling short, it's better to pull the plug right away. There's no merit in almost. The top brass always take the same view. He who fights and runs away, lives to fight another day. Or more importantly, doesn't have to be replaced at great expense, another day.

That's why you'll never leave an operational briefing without one critical piece of information.

A number to call for emergency exfiltration.

I looked back at the door that led from the bar. No one came through after me. I didn't realistically expect anyone to. If they'd wanted to try anything, their moment would have been in the men's room when I was getting undressed. But still, I was disappointed. A bathroom floor is a poor place to take your last breath. Even Young didn't deserve that. Part of me wanted to settle the score there and then, before his blood so much as had the chance to congeal.

I moved into the adjacent stall, stood on the edge of the bowl, and looked over the dividing wall. Young's body had fallen backward, blocking the door. His throat had been cut. The gash was so deep his neck was almost severed, and the broad crimson arcs that bridged all three walls were already turning brown. His legs were partly covered with a balled-up set of coveralls. The killer must have brought them to protect his clothes. I could see the handle of a butcher's knife peeping out from beneath the splattered fabric. That meant there would be a pair of discarded gloves somewhere, too. There was no point searching for them, though. It didn't take a genius to figure out who'd done the cutting. There were only two suspects. And anyway, as far as I was concerned, all five of the Myenese were in it together. They were equally guilty. And they would all have a price to pay.

I stepped down from the toilet, moved over to the sinks, and pulled out my phone. Fothergill answered on the first ring and listened in silence until I'd given him the basic facts.

"Is there a window in there?" he said. "Or are the stairs clear, at least? I can be outside in two minutes."

"Good," I said. "Get over here. But not to pick me up. Young's contacts will be leaving in a couple of minutes. I need you to follow them. We need to know where they go."

"What about you? What will you do?"

"They might split up," I said, describing each of them in detail. "If they do, stick with the tallest one. He did all the talking. It's pretty clear he's in charge."

"Is that safe?" he said. "Killing Young could just be a warning. What if they come after you?"

"They won't."

"How do you know?"

"Nothing ever works out that neatly, when I'm involved."

The barman was delivering a second round of sparkling water when I got back to the table. I saw that he'd included one for me, this time. I ignored it, took the fresh glass from the woman's place, and sat down in the empty chair.

"Thank you," I said.

"You're welcome," she said. "Help yourself."

"Not you. And not for the drink."

The main guy raised an eyebrow.

"Not many people would thank us," he said. "Not in these circumstances."

"Then there's fresh air between their ears," I said. "You just turned me into Captain Scarlet."

"What are you talking about?"

"You've made me indestructible. I'm the last link to the merchandise. If anything happens to me now, there'll be no nice goodies for you. Which I'm guessing would make you very unhappy, given the distance you've traveled and the trouble you just went to."

"A most undesirable outcome, I agree. For both of us."

"Then let's make sure we avoid it. Shall we say, tomorrow? Same time, same place?"

"That would be satisfactory."

"The fee is unchanged."

"Of course."

"Excellent. And after that, would you be interested in further consignments? If any should find their way into my hands?"

"The situation would be worth exploring, should it come to pass."

"I'll bear that in mind. If you wish to keep that line open, though, there's something I need to know."

"What would that be?"

"About Young. One minute he's a trusted supplier. The next he's surplus to requirements. How did that happen?"

"That's none of your concern."

"Actually, it's very much my concern. Taking Young's place on your payroll is one thing. Finding myself in his spot on the bathroom floor is entirely different. How can I avoid his mistake, if I don't know what it was?"

The guy took a sip of water before replying.

"Perhaps you're right," he said. "You may find the episode illuminating. After all, your association with Mr. Young was itself young, I understand?"

"Droll," I said. "But accurate."

"How did your ill-fated partnership establish itself?"

"Through a mutual friend. He set up the introduction. I work through word of mouth, just like you, I imagine. In our line of work, it pays not to advertise."

"And did this friend explain to you why Mr. Young was seeking a new connection?"

"No."

"You weren't curious?"

"What's the point? Ask no questions—hear no lies."

"A very laissez-faire attitude."

I shrugged.

"Not really," I said. "Just practical. Allegiances shift. People move on. All I care about is finding the opportunities."

"This particular opportunity came at a price," he said. "Mr. Young's previous partner became indisposed."

"An occupational hazard. And this indisposition—it was permanent, I take it?"

"Not yet. But it soon will be."

"Good. Less competition for me. How did it come about?"

"The idiot attempted to defraud me. Some of my people went to collect him, aiming to iron out our little misunderstanding. Something I have, happily, now accomplished. But before this could happen, Mr. Young interfered. His foolishness cost two of my men their lives."

"Sounds like we're well rid of him, then. Both of us. And I can assure you there'll be no such trouble with me. I keep my word. When I say I'll do something, I do it. End of story. I deliver the goods, collect my payment, and stay out of your hair. Unless you decide to do business with me again."

The guy seemed to think for a moment, then nodded and got to his feet. His people stood up with him, a second later, like puppets on long strings.

"That will be satisfactory," he said. "Till tomorrow. For now, stay here. For fifteen minutes. You are being watched. And I think you're developing a sense for what happens to those who cross me."

My phone rang fifteen seconds after the last of the group disappeared up the stairs. It was Fothergill.

"Got them," he said. "They've cleared the premises. They're on the street. Heading for a couple of cars. Two Cadillacs. DTSs. They look new. Both dark blue. Parked at the side of the street. Probably rentals."

"I saw one when I arrived," I said, getting to my feet. "It was already there."

The barman glanced up at me as I drew level with the table in the center of the room. He realized I'd noticed him and quickly looked away. I stopped moving.

"If anyone asks, when did I leave?" I said.

He didn't reply.

"When did I leave?" I said.

"Oh, you're asking me?" he said.

"When did I leave?"

"Don't know."

"When?" I said, taking a step in his direction.

"A few minutes after the others."

"How many minutes?"

"Fifteen."

"Are you sure?"

"Positive. I looked at my watch when the other guys split. Again when you did. There was exactly a quarter of an hour in between."

"Good," I said, holding up my phone, switching to camera mode and taking his picture. "I'm sending this to twelve of my friends. Any confusion about the timing, they'll be paying you a visit. And trust me, you don't want that."

The phone rang again. Fothergill was still outside.

"They're in the vehicles," he said. "The tall guy and the woman in the first. The other three men in the second. OK, they're pulling off. I'm staying with them. Heading north on Rush. Into State. They're sticking together. So far, at least."

"Good," I said. "Leave the line open this time. Keep me posted."

There were four cabs waiting outside the building when I left the club. I took the first one in line. Another ex-police Crown Vic, with a drooping spotlight still attached to the driver's door. It was painted dark red and the bodywork was a little worse for wear, but otherwise it was cosmetically similar to the one Fothergill was using, a couple of blocks away.

I told the driver to start off straight, and that I'd give him directions as we went along.

"Going left on Schiller," Fothergill said. "Right on Clark. Right on North Boulevard. Oh. Right again on Dearborn. They're doubling back. Where are you? Can you cut across on Burton? Maybe jump in ahead of us?"

We did as he suggested, but reached the junction just as the second Cadillac was passing through. Fothergill was holding his distance, two cars astern. I told the cabbie to hang back, join in behind him, then stay on his tail no matter what else happened.

The Cadillacs stayed together through the next two intersections, drifting along innocuously in the steady flow of traffic. They took a left on Division Street, then went left again, taking us back onto State.

"Hey," the cabbie said. "What's going on? We're going in circles here."

I ignored him.

The next junction was State and Goethe. The first Cadillac

turned right, swerving at the last minute without using its signal. The second kept going straight, darting ahead of a delivery truck.

"I'm on the leader," Fothergill said, pausing for a moment to let a bicycle rickshaw through on the inside before accelerating away down the side street. "Good luck with your guy. Don't let him get away."

The second Cadillac moved much faster without its partner. The traffic was building steadily but the driver was relentless, weaving around other vehicles and jumping four red lights in a row. My cabbie had real trouble keeping up, swearing almost continuously and glowering at me in the mirror on the odd occasion when we did stop moving.

We finally came to a complete halt on Pearson, just up from the Hancock Center. The Cadillac swung over to the side of the street and the driver climbed out, tossing the keys at the feet of a smart, uniformed man in his late fifties.

"See that?" the cabbie said. "Asshole. If I was him, that car would be getting parked in the lake."

The passengers emerged from the backseat before the startled valet had even moved. They pushed past him, caught up with the driver, and formed up under the entrance canopy of the Ritz-Carlton. None of them moved again for fully three minutes. They were in a triangle, one looking east, the others west. Then they turned and moved, one at a time, through a wide set of revolving doors.

I paid the cabby and followed the guys from the Cadillac into the hotel. An elevator took me to the lobby level, and I emerged just in time to see them veering away from the long line of reception desks and heading for a second bank of elevators on the far side of an elaborate octagonal fountain. A giant sculpture of waterbirds cavorting in a broad white dish was set high in the center. There were two, rearing up with long necks and outstretched wings, ready to fly away. They could have been swans. But whatever the species, they made for excellent cover. The three guys were constantly scanning the area around them as they walked, but they had no idea I was watching. They paused when they reached the elevators, but still didn't spot me. The driver hit the call button and the doors to the left-hand car slid open almost immediately. Then they stepped quickly inside, standing together in front of the entrance and blocking a gray-haired couple from following them.

I watched as the digits on the floor indicator above their elevator counted steadily upward. They wound all the way to thirty, paused, and began a leisurely descent. I waited to make sure they didn't stop again before the lobby, then made my way around to the nearest customer service desk. The clerk switched on a training-course smile as she saw me approach, but she seemed genuinely pleased when I told her I was interested in a room for the night.

"It has to be something special," I said. "My girlfriend's in town for the first time. From Antwerp. I want to surprise her. So let's think. The best views are up high, right? What have you got on the top floor, right now?"

"We only have rooms as high as the thirtieth," she said. "It's all apartments above that."

"OK. How many rooms do you have on the thirtieth?"

"Three. But they're all suites, not rooms."

So the Myenese guys had themselves a suite. That made sense. Fewer other guests passing by. And plenty of space to keep a prisoner under wraps.

"Even better," I said. "I want something she'll really remember. What kind of suites are they?"

"We have the Executive Suite. The Premier Suite. And the Vivaldi Suite."

"Just one of each?"

"Yes."

"Very exclusive, then. Which one is the best?"

"They're all equally good, sir. And there are none better in Chicago."

"Well, how can I decide between them? I know. What about availability? No point in setting my heart on something I can't have."

The woman took a moment to consult her computer.

"The Premier's available," she said. "And the Executive. But not the Vivaldi."

"Shame," I said. "I liked the sound of that one. But at least it narrows things down. So what about prices?"

She told me the Premier was twice the cost of the Executive.

"OK," I said. "That's great. I'm pretty clear about what I want to do. You've been a huge help. I'll be sure to mention your name to the manager when I make my booking."

"Thank you," she said. "It was my pleasure."

"One other thing, though, before I go. I need to check

a couple of details before I go ahead and book, and I need to get back on the road in a minute. The traffic out to O'Hare's been brutal lately. Any chance you could just jot down the number for reservations for me? That way I can call from the car."

"Of course," the woman said, reaching for a hotel compliments slip.

"You wouldn't have a Post-it note, instead, would you?" I said. "I don't want the paper to slip out of my things at the wrong moment and ruin the surprise."

"Oh, my goodness," she said, opening her drawer. "I'm so sorry. I wasn't thinking. I've got a whole bunch in here. Let me give you one of these."

The elevator lobby on the thirtieth floor opened onto a kind of vestibule, ten feet by fifteen. A pair of Louis XV chairs was lined up against the back wall. One was sitting on either side of a rectangular table. It was made of wood. A decent attempt at French provincial, I'd say. A giant ormolu clock sat in the center. Its gaudy turquoise and gold marquetry was reflected clearly in the polished surface. The little cluster of furniture was flanked by two pairs of doors. There was one for each of the suites. And another which had no visible name or number.

I took the Post-it note the clerk had given me, stuck it over the spy-hole on the Vivaldi Suite's door, and rang the bell. I gave it three long blasts. Twenty seconds passed without a response. I was stretching out to try knocking when I heard footsteps approaching from inside the suite.

They were heavy, but not hurried. Definitely one person. They lumbered closer, and stopped near to the door.

"Who is it?" a man's voice said.

"Valet parking," I said.

"What? Up here? Why?"

"Allow me to explain, sir. My name's Ferguson. I'm the shift supervisor."

"I don't care what your name is. What do you want?"

"I'm afraid there's been a slight problem. Are you the driver of a dark blue Cadillac?"

"You moron. What have you fools done to my car?"

"We parked it, sir."

"Have you damaged it?"

"No, sir. Not at all. In fact, the car's as stunningly immaculate as the day it left the factory, I would imagine."

"Then what's the matter?"

"It's one of our valets, sir. Señor Benitez. It seems he hurt his back in some sort of key-dropping incident. Threw out a disk, in all likelihood. Not a good prognosis, I'm afraid. He may be unable to continue in his job. His future earning potential may be severely curtailed."

"Who cares? Why are you wasting my time with crap about this guy?"

"Because, sir, he doesn't feel the situation that led to his injury came about entirely by accident."

"Why's that my problem?"

"Well, his current recollection is that the driver of the Cadillac dropped the keys on purpose. That would be you, sir. So he's looking for some kind of compensation from you. And if none is forthcoming, he's talking about involving the police."

"What? No way. Nothing happened."

"Señor Benitez has secured CCTV footage of the whole affair, sir. From both of the cameras under the front canopy. They leave no doubt as to what transpired."

"What, maybe. But not who. It wasn't me. And there's no need for any police."

"I'm sure you're right, sir. And I thought you might feel that way. That's why I'm here. To see if we can find some way of discouraging that particular course of action."

"Bring the guy up here. I'll discourage him. Permanently."

"I'm sure you could do that, sir. But I think there might be a simpler way."

"Like what?"

"Perhaps a more transaction-oriented solution, if you see what I mean, sir? One that would draw less unwelcome attention from the authorities."

"You're trying to shake me down? Seriously?"

"Not at all, sir. Just trying to help. That's how we do things in Chicago."

The guy didn't reply.

"Obviously there's no obligation to accept my proposal, sir," I said. "But if you do decide to go with the police option, I have one request. On behalf of the hotel manager, actually. Do you think you could allow yourself to be arrested somewhere else? Handcuffs and nightsticks are not consistent with the image we try to propagate here at the Ritz-Carlton."

Silence.

"Why don't I give you some time to mull things over?" I said. "But not too much. Señor Benitez will be making the call in ten minutes, if we haven't heard anything. I'll be outside, at the valet desk if you need me. Good afternoon, sir."

"Wait," he said. "Give me a second."

I said nothing.

"Are you there?" he said. "Hang on a minute. Let's talk about this."

I heard the security chain rattling against the inside of the frame. The guy must have disengaged it. And before it could stop swinging I reached out and took hold of the handle. Lightly at first, so that he wouldn't realize what I was doing. I let him open the door an inch without resisting. Then I pulled against him, stopping the gap from growing any wider. He grunted and started tugging harder. I matched his efforts, waited till he was heaving like crazy, then suddenly let go. The door gave way instantly and the guy collapsed backward, losing his footing. I followed straight after him into the suite's entrance corridor, getting a good look at him for the first time since he left the Commissariat. He was one of the guys from the club, all right. But not the one who'd ambushed Young. And he was already trying to sit up. His right hand was reaching under his hoodie as he moved. I couldn't allow that, so I crashed the ball of my foot into his jaw. He went down again, this time spinning around and ending up sprawled out on his face, not moving.

I looked down the length of the corridor. No one else had appeared. It was a safe bet that the other two from the Cadillac were in the suite somewhere. And possibly more who hadn't been with them at the club. I couldn't run the risk of the first guy coming around and popping up behind me—or maybe getting to McIntyre before me, if he was being held there—so I leaned down and put my right knee between his shoulder blades. I slid my left arm under his chin and took hold of his right ear. My right hand gripped his other ear. I glanced up once more to check we were still alone. And twisted. Sharply. The guy's neck rotated through a full ninety degrees. Then I rolled him over and took the Browning pistol he'd been hiding in his waistband.

The corridor gave way to four rooms. There were two on each side. The first on the left was a bedroom. I checked behind the door, under both king-sized beds, inside all four wardrobes, and in the en suite bathroom. No one was hiding there. The door opposite led to another, identical bedroom. I found no one there, either. Next on the left was a small kitchen. It held plenty of high-gloss white cabinets and stainless appliances, but no people. Or gas canisters. My options were narrowing. It meant any remaining hostiles would be in the same place, so picking them off one at a time as I preferred would be a little harder than usual.

I took a used wineglass from the sink and moved into the corridor. I positioned myself next to the final door—on the hinge side—and lobbed the glass back into the kitchen.

It spun twice as it sailed through the air, then hit the granite countertop near the far wall and disintegrated into a million tiny fragments.

"Sidney?" a man's voice from the room behind me said. "You OK?"

I kept quiet.

"Sidney?" the man said. "That you?"

I groaned, long and loud.

I heard footsteps. They were running. Again, only one set. The door opened beside me and a man burst through. I recognized him from the Commissariat, as well. He'd been in the group I saw walk in, not the one hiding in the women's bathroom. He headed straight past me, running for the kitchen. For a second that left his back exposed to me. It would have been foolish to try to physically subdue him when he had at least one accomplice only a few feet away, so I did the sensible thing. Raised the 9mm I'd just inherited, and shot him. Twice. In the back of the head. Then I spun around the door, needing to bring the Browning to bear before anyone on the other side could get wind of what was going on.

The final room was a combined sitting and dining area. The nearer half of the floor was finished in wood veneer. It held a large oval table, and was lit by a grotesque triple-tier crystal chandelier. Formal chairs were spaced out evenly all the way around it. There were eight. All were empty. So were three of the brown leather couches that were scattered asymmetrically in the carpeted half of the room. But the fourth, positioned opposite a huge wall-mounted flat-screen

TV, was occupied. By one man. The guy who'd butchered Gary Young. His hand was on the grip of another pistol, which was still only halfway clear of his waistband. And the look on his face told me he knew it was too late to change that.

The guy held my gaze for twenty seconds. Then his eyes peeled away from mine. They moved slowly, as if drawn against his will, and settled on the muzzle of my Browning. I was holding it perfectly steady. I don't know if he was taken with where it was pointing—straight at his head—or whether he recognized it as his friend's.

"Drop your gun," I said. "And kick it toward me."

He did as he was told.

"Good," I said, sitting down on the arm of the nearest couch. "Now, take out your phone . . ."

NINE

For the most part, in my mind at least, assignments seem very linear in nature at the outset.

Looking ahead to what you have to do, one event should lead to another, which should lead to another, until the job is done. Take a task I was given in Germany, last year. The brief was to fly to Berlin. Locate a woman who worked for one of their huge industrial conglomerates. Follow her to the railway station. Get on the same train. And make sure that by the time we reached Düsseldorf, the flash drive she was planning to sell was safely in my pocket and to the rest of the world, it looked like she'd suffered a heart attack in the middle of the packed lunch she'd brought for herself.

The snag is, of course, that real life never runs that smoothly. What starts out as a straight, easy path is soon beset with unscheduled twists and turns. Planes are late. People are sick. Trains are full. And while you can work your way around those kinds of obstacles without any great difficulty, you know that before long something more serious is going to happen. Your route is going to split in two, and you're going to have to make a choice which way to go.

Pick the wrong branch, and you may fall flat.

But wait around for someone else to pick for you, and you're guaranteed to end up on your face.

Fothergill pulled over behind a delivery truck outside the hotel's loading dock. He waited just long enough for me to climb in beside him, then eased the police taxi neatly back into the flow of traffic. I was impatient to see him. He'd been evasive about progress when we spoke on the phone twenty minutes earlier, and the second I saw his face I knew I wasn't going to be happy with his news.

"I couldn't tail them any farther," he said. "It's as simple as that."

"Why not?" I said. "What happened?"

"They crossed the state line. Went into Indiana. A cab with Illinois plates was going to stand out a mile. They were bound to notice me. I had no choice. It was drop out, or get blown out."

I didn't reply.

"I know what I'm talking about, David," he said. "You don't stay in the game as long as me by taking stupid chances."

"They went to Indiana?" I said. "The road they were on. Does it lead to a place called Gary?"

"Gary? Strange name for a place. That was Young's first name, wasn't it?"

"Does it go there?"

"I guess. Probably. I never go out that way, though. Is it important?"

"Could be. It adds weight to something one of the guys told me, upstairs."

"You got them to talk?"

"One of them. He became quite chatty, for a while."

"What did he say?"

"That they have McIntyre, as we thought. And the gas."

"Damn. Where?"

"At some kind of abandoned industrial unit they found."

"In this place, Gary?"

"Yes. So we need to head over there. And fast."

"I don't know. That could be dangerous. Won't the guys from upstairs have warned them by now? To expect us? Or you, at least?"

"No."

"You can't assume that. They're bound to have called. Or texted. Or e-mailed. Or done something to get word through."

"Don't worry. They're in no position to communicate. Not any longer."

"Why not? Where are they?"

"Depends on your religious outlook, I guess."

"What?"

"Well, their bodies are still in the suite."

"Oh. I see. So what happened?"

"Hard to say. You know how confused things can get when three guys hole up together for a while. Especially when they're criminals. Highly strung. Unreliable. All in all, it was a recipe for chaos. Carnage was inevitable."

"How does it look?"

"Like cabin fever set in. Their nerves frayed. They argued. Possibly over a glass that got broken in the kitchen, sometime. Things escalated. Spiraled out of control. Guy one pulled a gun. Guy two snapped his neck and took it. Shot guy three in the back of the head. Then turned the gun on himself. Tragic, really. Such a waste of youth. And bullets."

Fothergill didn't reply for a good thirty seconds.

"Did you make it seem watertight, at least?" he said, eventually.

"That's doubtful," I said. "The police will see through it in a heartbeat, if they have a half-decent look. Some heat could well be coming our way. As soon as someone finds the bodies. That's why I'm giving you the heads-up, now."

"You killed them?"

I didn't reply.

"They're dead?" he said. "All of them?"

"It would appear so," I said.

"Why?"

"Because you told me they couldn't be arrested. Because London wanted this whole thing cleared up, off the books. And because they killed Young."

"Off the books doesn't mean executing people, David. There are other ways. And a couple of hours ago you were ready to kill Young yourself."

"Young's one of ours. His mess is ours to deal with. He crossed a line that we defined. And there's a world of difference between London ordering a hard arrest, and some murderous lowlifes whacking him because they mistook his identity."

"Mistook it for what? Who, I mean?"

"Me."

"What? Why? How do you know?"

"Their boss told me so. He thought it was Young who killed his guys when they went to snatch McIntyre. So actually, it was me they were aiming to kill in that bathroom. Young got his throat cut on my behalf."

"So now what? You feel guilty?"

"Of course not. For what? Young should have been more careful. The rest is just business."

"It smacks of something else to me. They threatened you, so now your knickers are in a twist. You're lashing out, indiscriminately."

"My knickers are in—forget it. Watch the CCTV from the club. I'm just being practical. What happens if McIntyre blabs? Tells them it wasn't Young who stepped in at the apartment?"

He didn't reply.

"And aside from any of that, here's what it all boils down to," I said. "These people came here to buy gas that kills children. I don't see a burning need to keep them alive. Do you?"

Fothergill kept silent and concentrated on the traffic until we were two-thirds of the way up Michigan Avenue. Then he pulled over and turned to face me.

"You look pleased with yourself," I said.

"I am, as it happens," he said. "I've just thought of a

way to turn this situation to our advantage. You have an address in Gary, where these people will be?"

"Not exactly an address. More of a rough description."

"No matter. It's close enough. And it could be all I need to make London change their minds."

"About what?"

"Sending a team. Sounds to me like there's every possibility we'll need to assault the place. And you can't do that on your own, now, can you?"

"I like the way you think."

"Thank you. Now, let's get the wheels in motion. Want to grab a bite on the way to the office? We could be there for a while."

"You could be. I'm not coming to the office."

"What do you mean? I thought we just agreed?"

"You don't need me there to lobby London. Let's face it, I'd just make things worse. So I'm heading out to Gary, Indiana."

"You are? Why? It's no place for sightseeing, you know."

"We need proper intelligence, if we're going to get this wrapped up. The guy from the suite gave me everything he had, but that wasn't a great deal. Not much more than how to get there and sketchy details of the outside of the building where they're holding McIntyre. We need to know how to get in, for a start."

"David, you shouldn't be doing this on your own. It's too dangerous."

"I'll just need my Beretta back, and I'll be out of your hair."

Fothergill took hold of the steering wheel, then let go again and sighed.

"All right, you stubborn mule," he said. "I'll give you your gun. Just don't ask me to drive you all the way out there."

"I won't," I said. "You're more use sitting on the phone, rounding up reinforcements."

The only other thing I wanted Fothergill's help with before he dropped me off was to pull strings at the motor pool. The disguised Crown Vic was unbeatable in Chicago, but as Fothergill had pointed out, it was no use in other states. I didn't want to be hanging around in Indiana using a taxi with Illinois plates any more than he had. Little details like that stand out a mile to people who are naturally suspicious. Or who are trained to look for them. The British Army found that out the hard way, in Northern Ireland. And because I'd likely be spending plenty of time in the car, I wanted something that would give me a high degree of cover. Panel trucks are too obvious. So are minivans, especially when they have tinted windows. I needed something different. Something we'd developed with this particular kind of job in mind. A CURVE—a Covert Urban Reconnaissance VEhicle. Navy engineers take a station wagon—pretty much any sort you like, as long as it's large enough—and conceal a ventilated compartment under a false tonneau cover where the luggage area would usually be. Snipers have their own version where the rear license plate folds down, giving them an aperture to fire through.

With ours, the tailgate is made from a special type of plastic. It acts as a one-way mirror so that we can see out across the full width of the car. Some of the newer ones have built-in cameras for recording, or enabling remote surveillance. But whether video equipment is fitted or not, CURVEs are hard to get hold of. Most consulates only have one. And because they're converted to local specifications, the mechanics tend to be a little touchy about anyone using them.

Fothergill came up trumps, and a disgruntled consulate technical officer met me outside the Tribune Tower to hand over the car. It was a modified Chrysler 300C with hemi badges, black metallic paint, and huge chrome wheels. Not the most discreet vehicle I'd ever seen, but he assured me it would blend in, where I was going. It had taken him an hour and a half to get there, which meant I'd had a chance to eat and stock up on Starbucks stakeout specials—coffee blended strong and served in a small cup. That was essential if I was going to be up all night and still be comfortable. Not even CURVEs have bathrooms.

The built-in satellite navigation guided me as if I were heading to Midway Airport for the third time in three days. Then it changed its mind and sent me toward the Indiana Skyway instead. That sounded exciting, but it turned out to just be a large bridge that led to another freeway. The road itself was completely ordinary, but the view to the left was like a scene from some industrialized version of hell. I passed major railroad junctions. A nuclear power station. Chemical works, with miles of complex elevated pipe work spewing out dense clouds of evil-looking steam. Refineries, shooting jets of burning gas high into the darkening sky. There was no respite, anywhere. Any one of the places could trigger a major environmental catastrophe. Or provide the ingredients for one to be created somewhere else. It was a dirty-bomber's paradise. And somewhere in the middle of it I had to find a bunch of murderous kidnappers armed with biological weapons. I just hoped London's reluctance to involve the U.S. authorities wouldn't end up biting thousands of people in the backside.

I came to the junction the guy from the Vivaldi Suite had described after forty minutes, just as he'd told me to expect. The off-ramp dropped down sharply to the right, then swung around and doubled back under the highway. I followed it through to the other side and continued toward a line of warehouses. They were a quarter of a mile away, built of brick, and as I drew nearer I could see they were in bad shape. Most of their windows were broken and large patches of roof tiles were missing. Their perimeter fences were swathed with razor wire, stranding the half-dozen burned-out vehicles that had been left behind on the wrong side.

A patch of waste ground two hundred feet wide separated the derelict buildings from a line of newer ones that were still in use. Small manufacturing units I'd say, judging by the shape and the materials used to construct them. But I wasn't too interested in what they made. Just that people were there. People with cars I could park next to. Because the place I needed to watch was on the next street.

I wanted to get a sense of the place before stopping the

car, but couldn't risk more than one drive-by. Even if the man and woman who'd left the Commissariat together were there without reinforcements, they'd be insane not to keep a lookout. And there probably would be more of them to contend with, somewhere inside. Fortunately, though, the street was well lit. That made the building easy to observe. It was a hundred and twenty yards long. The roof was a single, continuous span, but below that the structure was divided into two sections. The left-hand part, two-thirds of the total width, was built of unfinished cinder block. There was a tall roll-up door at each end, big enough for medium-sized trucks to drive through. The right-hand section was made of brick. It had two stories, with evenly spaced, barred windows and a dark green personnel door in the center. The side walls at both ends were blank. The rear was completely obscured by a twenty-foot fence, topped with razor wire. There was no way to determine the number of inhabitants. But on a positive note—no sign of surveillance cameras, either.

I looped around past the disused warehouses, found my way back to the line of factories, and began looking for a suitable place to position the car. Several spaces were available on the street side of the parking lot, so I picked one at the far end, next to a pair of old, rusting flatbed trucks. It was pushing 10:00 P.M.—a little late for making deliveries—and I figured there was a good chance they'd be there for the rest of the night. That would be useful. A vehicle is always less conspicuous when it's not on its own. That just left me with the problem of sliding into the back without being spotted. Normally, you'd stop a couple of miles from your target, climb in through the tailgate, and have someone else drive you the rest of the way. I didn't have that luxury, so I had to switch to plan B: recline my seat as far as it would go, drop the backseat to leave a narrow triangle of space, and worm my way through into the rear compartment.

The amount of space in the observation area was limited, but if you were on your own, and you didn't wriggle around too much, it was tolerably comfortable. The floor was well padded, the side walls were cushioned, and the full-width view from the bottom of the tailgate took away any sense of confinement. And if I hadn't been alone—if I'd been with, say, Tanya—being confined could even have been a major benefit. But I knew that could never happen, now, so I pushed the thought aside and turned back to the job in hand.

The first area to focus on was the space surrounding the building. I wanted to be sure no one unfriendly was on the loose, in a position to spot me. Once I was satisfied I unclipped the binoculars from their mounting in the equipment bin and studied the front of the place in more detail. That revealed nothing new or significant, so I settled down into the main grind of the surveillance. Waiting for someone to move. In, or out. I needed a picture of how many people I was contending with. What kind of vehicles they used. What kind of weapons they carried. What kind of routine they followed on entry and exit. And what kind of loopholes they'd left for me to exploit.

Forty minutes passed without anything special to report, then my phone rang. It was Fothergill. He was still at his desk in the consulate.

"You're not going to like this," he said. "But London still aren't willing to send anyone to help."

"Why not?" I said. "You told me you could swing this."

"I thought I could. I thought it was a stitched-on certainty. But there's something fishy going on. Something someone's not telling me."

"Such as?"

"I don't know. It's a little awkward, actually. But I was wondering, exactly how many people have you upset over there?"

"You're blaming me?"

"Not blaming. No. Nothing like that, David. I'm just trying to make sense of this. They've never denied a request as watertight as this one, before."

"Then find another way to convince them."

"I've tried everything. And talked to everyone I can get hold of. I'm not a magician, you know. I'm sorry."

"I am, too. 'Cause that's going to make things a whole lot harder."

"No. Not harder. Impossible. Be realistic. It's time to rethink this. Get yourself back to Chicago. Get some sleep. Start again tomorrow."

"No. We'll be shorthanded, but that's no reason to walk away. We can work around it."

"David, you're pushing yourself too hard. You've had a hell of a day. Get back to your hotel. Rest. We can hook up in the morning. At the office. Get breakfast. Pull an alternative plan together then."

I took a moment to think.

"Have you picked up any word on McIntyre?" I said. "Any new ideas about where he might be?"

"No," he said.

"Or the gas they took?"

"Nothing yet."

"Then there's no alternative plan to make. I'll stay here. We'll carry on as agreed."

"That's crazy. You can't do this on your own."

I took another moment.

"We'll need another vehicle," I said. "One with Indiana plates. Could you get hold of something?"

"I should think so," he said. "If it's important. What kind?"

"Nothing too fancy. A regular sedan. Or a pickup. Anything like that would be fine."

"When?"

"First thing in the morning."

"OK. Leave it with me. Where do you want it delivered?"

"I don't. I want you to drive over here in it. I'll text you the GPS coordinates."

"Me? Why?"

"So you don't attract attention when you get here."

"That's not what I meant. Why do you want me there at all?"

"To take a spell watching this place. London won't send

anyone else, and I'll be tired by morning. I'll need some rest, ready for later on."

"Is it even worth watching it? Are you sure anyone's even there? Have you seen anyone?"

"No. Not yet. But that's going to change. By three P.M. tomorrow at the latest."

"Why?"

"Remember the guys you were following? They were heading this way. The only lead we have says they're here. And by four fifteen tomorrow, they need to be back at the Commissariat."

"Why?"

"To meet me. To buy the gas we told them I had."

"If we know where they're going, why not just snatch them up there? At the club? Why waste time making me travel to Gary, Indiana?"

"Because we don't want to pick them up."

"We don't?"

"No. Not yet. We just want them out of the way. So we can have a nosey round inside the building. Maybe lay our hands on our missing friend. Maybe his canister. Maybe both. Or at least find out more about what's going on."

"But hold on a minute. Wait. The rendezvous with you at the Commissariat isn't going to happen. The missing guys won't show."

"They will."

"They won't. Not once they hear about the Ritz-Carlton bloodbath."

"They will. Think about it. If they don't realize the events are connected, they'll show up with a sack full of cash. If they do join the dots, they'll break out a fresh carving knife and invite me into the women's bathroom. Either way, they'll be at the club tomorrow afternoon."

Fothergill didn't reply.

"Have you got a better idea?" I said.

He didn't respond.

"Something more than just hoping for divine inspiration over coffee and waffles?"

He remained silent.

"Seven o'clock sound about right?" I said.

"Make it eight," he said. "Talking about waffles, I'm not leaving before I eat. I spent enough years doing that."

"Eight it is, then. Bring coffee for me. And one other thing. Could you get your hands on a frequency grabber, as well?"

"Probably. I suppose. What for? Are we planning a hijack?"

"No. Getting into the building."

"Then why do we need a grabber? Wouldn't a key be more useful? Or a crowbar? Or maybe a brick to throw through a window? Wouldn't that be more your style?"

"Hey. Whatever gets the job done. And this place has roll-up doors. No handles on the outside. So, I'm guessing they have wireless openers. Spoof the signal, and in we go. No forced entry. No huge racket. No worried civvies swarming around, poking their noses in. Unless you want to stay outside and deal with them?"

"Members of the general public?" he said, after a

moment's pause. "No thanks. Count me out of that. I'll get the grabber. But it'll take me a while to finesse the quartermaster. Shall we make it eight thirty, instead?"

"Yeah, you take your time to finesse the QM," I said. "And there's me, thinking waffles take a while to cook."

I'd never been to Indiana before, but when Fothergill hung up the phone he left me in a state I was all too familiar with. One I've been in hundreds of times over the years. Suspended animation. The target building lay in front of me, almost close enough to touch, but there was nothing tangible to bridge the hours between now and morning. Nothing at all, aside from waiting and watching. Two of the most common activities in my line of work. If the circumstances were right, they weren't too great a trial. And things were pretty reasonable that night. I started with the same five questions I always ask myself. Am I in danger? Am I hungry? Thirsty? Too hot? Or too cold? The answer to all of them was no, so the only potential problem was boredom. And that should never be an issue, either. Because whatever kind of job you're on, you can always find plenty to think about.

Fothergill called to check in with me at just after eight, by which time we figured he was only about twenty minutes away. We stayed on the phone till he arrived, me confirming that no one had come or gone during the night, him confirming that he had the coffee and the frequency grabber. Other than that I just talked him through the directions, and endured the running commentary he kept up on all the unsavory aspects of the area. He was still reeling off ideas for reforming the droves of local vandals and graffiti artists when I saw him pull into the parking lot. He was driving a Ford Edge—a kind of small SUV they don't sell in England. It was silver, with a large dent in the driver's door. There were still plenty of spaces to pick from, so he backed into a slot on the far side of the truck to my left. I gave it another ten minutes so that no one would connect my departure with his arrival, then told him to get out, fiddle with something in his trunk, and keep an eye open for me while I wriggled my way back into the driver's seat.

We sketched out the day between us and agreed to split the time into blocks of four hours, with fifteen-minute overlaps. Fothergill didn't object to covering the next shift, which was lucky since I was already on the road, but I was well past the ruined warehouses before I realized I'd forgotten the most important thing. To collect my coffee from him. After that I couldn't shake the craving for caffeine, so I headed back to the highway. I remembered passing a diner on my way over last night. It was about fifteen minutes to the west so I retraced my steps until I found the correct turnoff. I'd missed breakfast so I ordered something more substantial than usual. A cappuccino. Extra large. With two extra shots to counteract the diluting effect of the milk.

I'd spent more than enough time cooped up recently so I stayed in the diner and drank the coffee standing at the counter. I glanced at a copy of a morning paper that someone had left there, then strolled back to the car. I looked around as I walked. The parking lot was well screened from the road. No one would be able to see I was there. There were exits in both directions. It wasn't too far from the industrial unit in case I got word from Fothergill that something had kicked off and he needed me back there in a hurry. And I could recline my seat, lie back, and be effectively invisible. All things considered, it was as good a place as any to grab forty winks.

Sleep came to me quickly, but it was snatched away again just as fast. The peace was shattered by compressed air blasting out of a truck's braking system, somewhere very close to my head. I woke with a start and checked my watch. It was dead on noon. I'd been asleep for two and a half hours. Not long by anyone's standards. I was tempted to shut my eyes again, but I knew there was no point. I only had a quarter of an hour before I'd need to wake up anyway, to get back in time to relieve Fothergill. I dozed uneasily for another five minutes, then forced myself to sit up and take stock. The thought of another cappuccino was very appealing. I was starting to get hungry, too. But in the end I decided against dodging back into the diner. The smarter option was just to get on the road right away. Arriving anywhere at a round half hour always seems contrived and suspicious to me.

I tried to get hold of Fothergill to let him know I'd be there early, but each time I called I was diverted to his voice mail. He was still on the phone when I pulled up opposite him, at twelve seventeen. The moment he saw me he dropped his other conversation and called me straight back. He spoke very slowly and made a real point of telling me just how little had happened, describing every mundane and irrelevant aspect in exaggerated detail. And while he didn't say it in words, his tone made it clear he thought we were wasting our time. I was starting to worry he was right. Then movement caught my eye. From across the street. The left-hand roll-up door was beginning to open.

"Quick," I said. "The grabber. Get the frequency."

"I'm on it," Fothergill said. "Wait a minute. There's no reading. Nothing's showing. We'll have to wait till it closes again."

The door slowly cranked its way up to the top of the frame. Nothing else happened for a moment, then a car rolled through the opening. A dark blue Cadillac. It would be too much to swallow for that to be a coincidence, but I checked the license plate anyway. Then there was no doubt. It was the one Fothergill had been following after it left the Commissariat, yesterday. Which was a relief. It meant we were on the right track, after all.

"I'm trying again," Fothergill said, as the door reversed its direction. "No. There's no signal. I'm not picking up a thing."

I got a better look at the Cadillac as it turned and passed in front of me. There were three people inside it. The guy who'd done all the talking at the club was driving. The woman who'd strip-searched me was sitting in the front, next to him. And a guy I'd never seen before was lounging lazily around in the back.

"They can't have been using a remote, after all," Fothergill said. "It must have been a regular switch.

Someone must have opened it from the inside. And closed it again."

I didn't reply.

"Problem is, what do we do now?" Fothergill said.

I stayed silent.

"Maybe it's time for a change of plan," Fothergill said. "I think we should head back to Chicago after all. There's still plenty of time."

"For what?" I said.

"Taking them at the Commissariat. Your rendezvous isn't until four fifteen."

"I told you. I don't want to take them, anywhere. Not yet, anyway. There'll be time for that, later."

"But if we could catch one of them, think of the leverage it would give us over London. They'd have to send a team, then. Quick results are good news, remember, and that's just what you need right now."

I didn't respond.

"David, we need to rethink," he said. "To adapt. To view this as an advantage, not a setback. 'Cause now, we know for sure where the key players are going to be. And when. Surprise would be on our side. And the environment there is favorable to us. It's a far more viable option than staying here and banging our heads against the wall."

"No," I said, after a moment's thought. "I'm going to find a way into the place. I need to see inside."

"But how?" he said. "You were right. Those roll-ups were the best option. Maybe if we at least wait, those guys will use a remote on their way back in. We could try grabbing the frequency again then."

"No. That would be too late. I need time to look around. Properly. Without them being there."

"I don't see how that's possible, David. We're out of options. Face it. This was a good idea, but it just hasn't panned out. We should head back to the city."

"Rubbish," I said, slipping the car back into gear. "There are always options. And I'm going to put one into play right now."

"Whoa, wait," he said. "What is it? What are you going to do?"

"Something you suggested yourself," I said. "Or a version of it, anyway."

The high-tech solution had failed, but I wasn't too concerned. I knew it wouldn't be hard to find something to replace it with. In the end, it took less than four minutes. One minute to drive to the warehouses. One second to open my door. Another second to scoop up a brick from the dozens that lay abandoned in the gutter. And two minutes to retrace my steps, call Fothergill, and tell him to keep his eyes peeled. I figured that if he was still there, he might as well be useful and watch my back.

I pulled the car up onto the sidewalk and parked nice and close in front of the green door. Then I tried the handle, just in case, but predictably the place was locked. I looked across at the factories. Fothergill was there, behind the wheel of the Ford, fiddling with his phone as usual. He saw me and nodded. No one else was watching. So I took out my Beretta with my right hand. Gripped the brick with my left. And swung it into the wooden surface. Hard. Two inches above the lock. End-on, to concentrate the force. The frame gave way, splitting all the way from top to bottom. The loose piece fell back into the corridor, bounced off the wall, and I dived clean through the gap before it had time to hit the floor.

The corridor ran the full width of the building. Four doors led off the stretch to the right. All were closed, and the passage ended with a blank, whitewashed brick wall. The stretch to the left was identical, except it ended with a double door. It was gray metal. A flight of stone steps stretched up straight ahead of me. A single light flickered at the top. I went up, two at a time. Turned left at the top. And stopped in front of a double doorway. I listened. There was no sound from inside, so I smashed my foot into the join between the two doors. I tossed the brick through the gap they left and dodged to the side. I heard a crash as it landed, but there was no other reaction. I waited another moment, then stepped into the room, gun raised. The space was large. Twenty feet by forty. And it was deserted. There was no furniture, but five sleeping bags were lying on the floor. Four were lined up together at the left-hand side of the room, parallel with the wall. The other was on its own on the right, facing the opposite way. Each had a black leather carryall sitting tidily at its foot. I unzipped the nearest one but it was just full of clothes—two pairs of jeans, a hoodie, and some underwear—so I closed it, picked up my brick, and moved on.

The other upstairs room was the same size. It was also vacant. There was no furniture here, either, but one item standing in the far corner told me what the place was used for. It was a chemical toilet. It looked ridiculous on its own in such a wide, empty space, but I don't suppose the guys from the Cadillac would mind too much. I'd seen plenty of temporary billets with much more spartan facilities over the years.

The derelict theme continued downstairs. I checked all eight rooms carefully, one at a time, and there was no sign of any of them having been used recently. Not by humans, anyway. Rodents and spiders were a different story. I avoided the worst of the webs and the droppings and finished my sweep at the far end of the left-hand corridor, next to the metal doors. Which told me that if there was anything to find, it had to be on the other side. I tested the handle. It was locked, so I lifted the brick and brought it down just hard enough to break the mechanism. Even with a minimum of force the sound still echoed alarmingly, so I crouched down low, grabbed the handle and eased the door open four inches. Thirty seconds passed without any unwelcome attention. I waited another thirty, then opened the door wider and darted through to the other side.

The space I entered stank of oil and burned carbon, and was much colder and brighter than I'd expected. The polluted air was being stirred up by giant fans and the whole place was flooded with harsh, artificial light. It was coming from a forest of heavy-duty lanterns. They were hanging on chains from metal beams near the high, corrugated ceiling. There were four rows of maybe twenty-five. All of them were switched on, and their efficiency was boosted by polished steel reflectors. Their main purpose would be to illuminate the dozens of industrial machines that were bolted in place all across the floor. I could see hydraulic presses. Radial drills. Bench grinders. All sorts of equipment I'd noticed in the machine shops on battleships, and plenty of other kinds I didn't recognize. The larger machines seemed to be concentrated at the far side, near a concrete loading dock. I moved across to take a closer look and spotted the entrance to a narrow office at the back of the raised area. I also saw the front fender of a vehicle, half concealed behind a turret lathe. It was another Cadillac, dark blue, just like the one I'd seen leave through the corresponding roll-up door. Wooden crates were lined up at the edge of the platform behind it. They were five-foot cubes, and there were five of them. At first I thought they were identical.

Then I saw one of them move.

TEN

Don't mock the afflicted, my parents always used to say.

That's kind advice. I've always tried my best to follow it. But there have been occasions when that's been pretty hard to do. I remember one of them very clearly. It was in my third week of training. A group of us had completed an exercise early, so we'd stopped at a café on the way back to base. We were sitting, drinking coffee, minding our own business, when a twenty-something businessman came bustling into the place. He had a shiny Armani suit, a mop of curly blond hair, and a walk that told you he had a more than healthy regard for himself. He picked a large round table in the nearest corner and plonked himself down with a newspaper. At first we assumed he was waiting for some colleagues, but after a few minutes it became clear he was there on his own.

I couldn't help watching him out of the corner of my eye, and soon saw he was fiddling with something underneath the table. It was a cell phone. A huge one, since this was back when even the most modern kind were the size of bricks. He poked at the buttons for a few moments, then went back to reading the paper. Until the peace was disturbed a minute or so later by a raucous electronic squeaking. The guy made a show of sighing, throwing down the paper, and whipping a radio pager out of a cradle on his belt. He studied its little screen, then produced the phone and embarked on a suspiciously one-sided conversation.

Ten minutes later, the whole cycle repeated itself.

The woman to my right nudged me with her elbow.

"He's doing that himself," she said. "He's calling his own pager, then pretending to talk to someone."

She was right. And faced with that degree of idiocy, it was hard not to be unkind about the guy. The jokes about him were still going strong a quarter of an hour later, when two policemen arrived. They walked straight up to him. Picked him up under the arms. And carried him outside, kicking, screaming, and showering electronic gadgets in his wake.

Back at base that evening we found out what had happened. Later in the program, pagers were due to be issued to everyone on our course. Officially they were to send urgent updates about changes to our briefs or exercises. In reality, though, they served two other purposes.

To give us practice in using gadgets discreetly, at a time when such things were a novelty. That's where the guy in the café fell down. A tout for the instructors in the town had mistaken him for one of us, and the police had been dispatched to make an example of him.

And to teach us that with access to up-to-date information, any given situation can be flipped on its head at a moment's notice.

For better. Or for worse.

The crate had been secured with a padlock, but that didn't concern me. I still had my brick. One sharp blow was all it took to remove the whole assembly. I kicked the pieces of wood and broken metal away, eased the side panel back a couple of inches, and peered through the gap. There was enough light for me to make out the outline of a person. A man. He looked about my age. And he was naked. A ball gag had been shoved in his mouth. His wrists were bound with rope and attached to a hook at the center of the crate's roof. His forearms were caked with dried blood. I couldn't see his ankles. He was kneeling awkwardly and seemed to be slumping over to one side. That would partly be due to the confined space, I guessed. And partly to relieve the pressure on the grimy bandage that covered the right-hand side of his abdomen.

I leaned inside and went to work again with the brick. It was hard to get the angle, but after a couple of minutes the hook was sufficiently bent for me to release the rope. The guy slumped farther into the corner, suddenly missing the support it had given him. He sprawled there for a moment, looking at me suspiciously. Then he pitched himself forward and with a little help managed to struggle to his feet.

"McIntyre," I said, "I'd like to say it was a pleasure. But that would be a lie."

The guy was in a seriously sorry state. Far worse than when I'd seen him at the apartment he'd been hiding in. He rocked slightly as he stood, unable to hold himself completely still. His naked body was streaked with more blood, and in the brighter light I could see bumps and bruises showing through the layer of grime that covered his skin. The guy obviously hadn't been treated well. Far from it. But even so, I couldn't summon much sympathy. In my book, you choose to sleep with the dogs, you wake up with the fleas. And you don't complain about it afterward.

"Hold out your hands," I said.

McIntyre shifted his weight to his other foot and braced himself against the crate. Then he leaned away from me and started to tug at the ball gag.

"Forget it," I said. "It won't come off. There's a little padlock at the back."

He continued to struggle.

"I'll find something to remove it with in a minute," I said. "Unless you want me to use the brick again?"

He stopped pulling, but his fingers remained hooked through the leather straps.

"The gag'll have to wait," I said. "But those ropes—they should be easy enough."

He lowered his arms, turned to face me, and for a moment I thought I could see an almost friendly look in his eyes. Then his focus snapped away to something behind my head. I spun around and saw what had caught his attention. It was two guys. They were charging through the office door, straight toward us. Both were holding guns. The lead guy raised his to shoulder height and fired twice, without stopping, which was just a waste of ammunition. The bullets rattled harmlessly off some machinery, way behind me. He never had any chance of hitting us but I pushed McIntyre back into the crate anyway, drew my Beretta, and jumped down off the dock. The second guy split away, trying to circle around to the left. I moved right, into the cover of a screw press, and looked out from the far side. I could see the first guy, still on the platform. He was closing in on McIntyre's position. Moving slowly. And leaving his legs exposed, which gave me a dilemma. It was unlikely I'd get a clearer shot, but I didn't want to kill him or leave him to bleed out. Not yet, anyway. I needed the chance to ask him about the missing gas. The guy stopped and stood still, almost begging for a bullet. I resisted. Then I heard a sound to my left. Something mechanized. It was the door, starting to roll itself up. I knew the game could have been changing completely right there, so that made the decision for me. I put a round in the guy's left leg, just below the knee. He went down, and I heard his gun clatter away across the concrete. Then I shifted myself around the base of the machine so I could catch a glimpse through the door. Nothing new was visible. No vehicles were coming in. No one was approaching on foot. Then I heard a car door slam. From inside the building. A car engine started. It was the Cadillac. Someone was leaving the place, not entering. I stepped out from my cover to get a better look. The car's rear tires started to squeal. They kicked up smoke as it surged forward. I couldn't see anyone in the driver's seat—he must have been lying sideways—but it had to be the second guy from the office. He was the only person I'd seen heading that way. He must have been planning to run, rather than ambush me. I put two rounds through the back window, but the car didn't slow down. I lowered my aim and went for the bodywork. I hit it four times, but still without effect. I didn't have the angle for the tires, so I jumped back up onto the dock. The first guy had crawled a couple of yards toward his gun. I kicked it away and put two more rounds through the roof of the Cadillac before it disappeared through the exit. That was as much as I could realistically do. There was no way I was going to catch up with a speeding car on my own, so I left the problem to Fothergill and turned to check on McIntyre.

I pulled back the side panel, looked inside, and found nothing but empty space. The crate was bare. McIntyre had gone. I turned to see if he'd somehow fallen off the platform when a bullet crashed through the woodwork, six inches in front of me. I hit the deck, unscathed, but severely bothered by something. The bullet had come from the wrong direction. There was no way the remaining guy could have fired it. Even if he could have retrieved his gun, he was in completely the wrong place. I wriggled back to check, just in case, and saw he had moved. But only marginally. He was still ten feet away from the Browning. So, someone else had to be loose in the main part of the machine shop. I crawled around the rear of the crate and slithered to the edge of the dock. Immediately my eyes picked up movement. A figure was darting between the machines. A man. He was coming in my direction. Quickly. Zigzagging across the open spaces. That wasn't a bad idea, in itself. But it would have worked out better for him if he hadn't left the same interval between each move. An even four seconds, every time. Like a target at a beginners' training course. So the next time he disappeared into some cover, I knelt up and raised my Beretta. I counted to four. The guy appeared, right on schedule. I lined up on his sternum and fired, twice. He crumpled and fell backward. It took a couple of seconds for the ripple of dust to settle around the body, but when it cleared I could finally make out his face.

And it was not what I'd expected to see.

The man I'd just shot was the second guy from the office. Which meant that someone else had escaped in the Cadillac. And I suddenly had a good idea who that would have been. I pulled out my phone and punched in Fothergill's number.

"Where are you?" I said, as soon as he answered.

"Don't know," he said. "Let's see. I've got burned out cars to my left. Desolate wasteland to my right. Is that any help?"

"What's in front of you?"

"The road."

"OK. I mean, who's in front of you? In the Cadillac."

He didn't reply.

"You did follow it?" I said. "Just now. When it came flying out of here?"

"I did," he said.

"And then you lost it, didn't you?"

He didn't reply.

"Didn't you?" I said.

"What do you want me to do?" he said. "This tub's no match for a Caddy. And whoever was behind the wheel was driving like a complete nutter. A psycho. No way could I keep up in this thing."

"Did you see who it was?"

"One of the ambush party? If you'd done what I'd said, you could have been sitting safe and sound in Chicago all along. Had him come to you. Saved us both a lot of time and trouble."

"No. He won't be going anywhere near Chicago. Trust me."

"Why not?"

"He's too well trained."

"How could you possibly know that?"

"Because it was McIntyre, in that car. He was naked. Tied up. Gagged. Wounded. And he still got away from you."

"It was Tony? Are you sure?"

"Certain."

"Damn, he's good. And he's thrown a pretty big spanner in the works, hasn't he? So. What now?"

"Just get yourself back down here. I've still got one guy left to talk to. Let's see what he can give us."

I ended the call and started work on the dead man's pockets. They were completely empty, so I got up and hauled myself onto the loading dock one more time. Right away I saw that the first guy had moved again. About ten feet, this time. But now he was lying stock-still, facedown, with his arms above his head. His injured leg was stretched out limply behind him. A shiny red streak marked the way back to the last place I'd seen him. It started out a couple of inches across, and grew noticeably deeper and wider as it approached the spot where he'd come to rest. Getting that far had cost him a lot of blood, and the rate of loss was clearly accelerating. I checked his pulse. It was there, but faint, and he'd lost consciousness. I pulled the belt off his jeans, wrapped it around his thigh, and pulled it in tight. It wasn't an elegant job. Probably too little, too late, but worth a try. I wasn't worried about his long-term well-being, after all. Only about keeping him alive for another few minutes.

This guy's pockets contained nothing, either, but I did notice one unusual thing when I was searching them. It was to do with his gun. The Browning was lying on the ground, away to the side, exactly where I'd kicked it earlier. But it didn't look like the guy had been trying to retrieve it. He'd crawled far enough to reach it, but hadn't gone in the right direction. The blood trail confirmed it. He'd dragged himself in a dead straight line from his starting point toward the office door. Back to where he'd started. Which suggested that something in there was more important to him than his weapon. I checked on his consciousness one more time, then went to find out what that could be.

The office was long and narrow. Maybe five feet by fifteen. There were three fluorescent tubes hanging from the ceiling. All were broken, so the space was only illuminated by the little light that could filter through the grimy internal window between it and the machine shop. There was enough to see that three high shelves ran the length of the room. They were metal, adjustable, and empty. A metal table was pressed against the concrete wall below them. That was the only piece of furniture in the place. Two wooden packing cases were sitting next to it, as if someone had been using them as chairs. Two more wooden boxes were lined up on its dented, scarred surface. And beneath it someone had shoved three clear garbage bags. Two were roughly crumpled up and empty, but the other was still around a quarter full with something multicolored. It looked like little S-shaped polystyrene peanuts.

The nearer wooden box was rectangular, around fifteen inches wide by twenty long. The lid was wedged in place, but not nailed down. I was curious to see what someone had been trying to pack away, so I wrestled it open with my fingertips and looked inside. And found a good candidate for what the unconscious guy had been crawling in there to fetch. An AK-74, with its skeleton stock still folded along the side. It was one of five that were peeping out from the polystyrene. Certainly a more effective weapon than the 9 mm he'd abandoned outside. If he'd got his hands on one in that confined space, dealing with him could have become a little tricky. Shooting him was turning out to have been an excellent decision.

The other box was the same height and width, but square. I figured that if the larger one contained assault rifles, this would hold ammunition. Or possibly grenades. Luckily it wasn't too hard to find out. The lid was lying at an angle across the top, completely loose. So I removed it, and saw I could hardly have been more wrong. There was only one item inside the box. A cylinder. It was three inches in diameter. Twelve inches tall. The body was divided into two unequal sections, with three locked spring clips holding them together. The top was domed, with two mounting points for attaching carrying straps. Standard army-issue webbing would fit them. The whole thing was painted matte green—a familiar military color—and it was plain except for two symbols down near the base. They were picked out in yellow. There was a skull and crossbones, meaning poison. And a saber crossed with a test tube. The emblem of Porton Down. The British Army's main chemical and biological laboratory. A place officially dedicated to defense research. But also where VX gas had happened to be invented. Among other things.

My phone started to ring while I was still standing, staring into the box. Fothergill's number appeared on the screen. I took a moment to answer. I'd been unsure about one thing before, but now it was crystal clear. He could promise whatever he liked about safety. But there was no way I'd be touching that flask.

"I'm nearly there," he said, when I finally picked up. "I'll be parked in a couple of minutes. Then I'll need you to wrap things up. Right away. We have to talk."

"OK," I said. "We can do that. But don't go back to the factory. Come over here instead. I've got something for you."

"What?"

"Richard, are you trying to spoil my surprise? I worked hard for this."

"Cut it out. This is no time for games. You still in the place opposite?"

"Yes."

"Where, exactly? How do I find you? I don't want to be wandering around some filthy garbage pit for hours."

"Don't worry about it. Just back in through the open door. Then hop up onto the loading dock. Watch out for the guy who's bleeding on it. Then come into the office. You'll see the entrance."

"Stay where you are, then. I'll be there in two."

It actually took Fothergill four minutes to reach me. He was moving slowly as he approached from the far side of the platform. His shoulders were hunched, and his face looked pale and spent. For the first time since I met him it looked like his years of service were finally taking their toll.

"Where is it, then?" he said. "This thing you want to show me?"

I nodded toward the box. He hesitated, then brushed past me and looked inside.

"Great," he said. "Better get it in the car. You'll have to do the carrying, though. Can't do it with one arm."

He turned back to me, and was halfway to the door when he stopped dead still.

"Wait a minute," he said, pointing at the other box with his good hand. "What about that one? What's in there?"

"Guns," I said. "A handful of old AKs."

"Oh. Damn. Guess we're SOL after all, then."

"Unless you were hoping for a little black market action, like your friend."

"That's not funny, David. Don't even joke about it."

"OK, then. Let's be serious. Tell me—what were you hoping for?"

Fothergill sighed.

"More gas," he said.

"How could there be more?" I said. "Those guys think they're on their way to buy more. From me. But that was a setup. I'm here. And now we've taken theirs. So think about it. They're the ones who are out of luck."

Fothergill didn't answer.

"McIntyre's our only problem, now," I said. "He's on the run again. But the job's done, as far as finding the gas is concerned."

"No," he said. "It isn't. I just took a call from London. While I was driving back here. McIntyre's canister? It was only half the consignment he brought over. He just held it back, to try to frame me. The other one, he'd already sold. To the same people. The ones you let drive away."

"Are they sure? About the quantity?"

He nodded

"So where is it?" I said. "The other canister?"

"If we'd taken those people like I wanted to, we might have a chance of finding out," he said.

I didn't rise to that.

"If it's not here, you can draw your own conclusion,"

he said. "This was their laying-up position, obviously. Where was their forward base?"

"Chicago."

"Right. At least we have to assume so, unless someone proves otherwise. And they're heading there now. Toward three million defenseless people. So McIntyre escaping is a nuisance, yes. But nothing more. His whereabouts are the least of our worries right now."

ELEVEN

Psychological profiling is used a lot in the navy.

Our bosses rely on it during selection. While you're on probation. And, of course, in your regular operational reviews. Some of the guys try to get a head start by really getting to grips with it, and learning all the latest theories and technical terms. Personally, I can see a use for it, but I don't go that far. I generally just divide people into two categories. Lean forward, who tend to be hands-on, seat-of-their-pants types who go out and make things happen. And laid back, who prefer to wait for all the information to emerge before they think, analyze, and respond.

Me—I'm a little of each.

But I guess I lean a little more one way than the other.

I pulled out the remaining bag of polystyrene peanuts and poured them carefully into the wooden box, like I was getting ready to send my grandmother's best china to a distant city on the back of a mule. When even the tiniest chippings were used up Fothergill moved in with the lid, brandishing it like a shield. He laid it across the opening, made sure it wasn't going to fall, and backed away. I held my breath and jammed it home with the heel of my hand. Then I picked the whole thing up, moved it to the back of his Ford, and secured it with a seat belt.

"You should get moving," I said.

"What about the guns?" he said. "Better not leave them lying around."

I stowed them in his trunk, then opened the driver's door and held it wide for him.

"I know," he said. "Don't worry. I'll be right behind you."

"I do worry," I said. "Driving around on your own with that stuff is a terrible idea. I should escort you."

"David, you need to show some faith. I've been around a lot longer than you. I can move a box from one place to another without your help. And at this point, there is no higher priority than getting a jump on those guys. Leaving them to run around the Midwest with another canister of gas is not an option."

I didn't answer.

"Just go," he said. "I'll close this place down. And deal with the mess you made. Someone has to figure out what to do with the guy you shot, for a start."

"Just leave him," I said. "Let nature take its course."

"That's pretty callous, David."

"Not really. Not compared to what they've got planned for their homeland."

"That's not our problem right now. We need to stay focused. I'm going to tidy up, dump the boxes at the office, and be outside the club before you know it. I'll have your back. You can depend on that. What you need to worry about is getting there. Fast. You know their MO now. The main group won't show up till after the advertised time. But they'll try to drop their joker in early. Get there before him, and you've got it cracked."

I'd covered less than three miles when Fothergill called again.

"What's up?" I said. "Have they caught you already?"

"What?" he said. "No. Don't be ridiculous. I've got good news. You can forget about the club. Head for the consulate. Meet me there. I'm going to show you why, after all these years, there's still only one Richard Fothergill."

"Why? What happened?"

"Meet me. I'll show you."

"No. Tell me."

He didn't respond.

"Has someone got a gun to your head?" I said. "If they have, just say the word consulate again. Anywhere in your next sentence. It's safe. They won't suspect. Then I'll come back and get you."

"There's no gun to my head," he said. "And I don't need you to come back. Will you just listen? The immediate danger's averted, thanks to me. You don't need to go to the club after all."

"Fothergill, I don't like riddles. Tell me why, or I'm going anyway."

"David, you're impossible. OK. Here it is. I've found the rest of the gas."

"You're serious?"

"I am. Which means those guys don't have it. There's no need to ambush them."

"Where was it?"

"In the office."

"Where? I moved the Kalashnikovs. There was nothing else left."

"There was. Two things. Right under our noses."

"The packing cases."

"Correct."

"Amazing. I thought they were makeshift seats."

"Me, too. At first."

"So what made you look inside them?"

"I have my moments. I've played this game a pretty long time, you know. You don't stay at the front of the pack as long as I've done without a damn good sixth sense. That's why I didn't want to leave when you did. I could feel something was about to break."

"What was it?"

"The garbage bags. Under the table. Remember them? Two were empty. I suddenly thought, why? Where were the peanuts?"

"Nice."

"I figured two bags, two boxes . . ."

"Bingo."

"Exactly. But I didn't think I'd hit the jackpot, right away. The first box was full of comms kit. Boring stuff. The canisters were in the second one. I pulled off the lid, and there they were. Thank you very much. Richard, you're a genius."

I didn't reply.

"Getting them in the car wasn't easy, I can tell you," he said. "Should have asked you to come back, really, but I didn't fancy hanging around the place."

I was still thinking.

"David?" he said. "You still there?"

"I am," I said. "But wait. Back up. Canisters? There was more than one?"

"What do you mean?"

"Go back to London's message. They said McIntyre's canister was half of the stolen consignment. Just now, when you got back from chasing him. Am I right?"

"Yes. So?"

"That means there should have been one more to find. A canister. Not two canisters."

"Oh. I hadn't thought of that. I guess you're right. London must have been sketchy about the consignment size. You know what they're like. The numbers thing hadn't struck me. I was just thinking about avoiding the ambush."

"That would be nice. But I can't avoid it."

"Of course you can. They don't have any gas left. I've got it here, in my car."

"We can't be sure about that. The intel about the consignment size is clearly unreliable. There could be more."

"I doubt it."

"Can you rule it out?"

"No. But I think it does downgrade the threat. And remember, didn't Young tell us these guys wanted the gas to use back home? You mentioned that just now. That's what reminded me."

"That was his theory, yes."

"And I'm thinking that makes a lot more sense than them using it in some sort of random civilian attack on U.S. soil. What good would that do them? Maybe we've been too quick off the mark on this one, David. A little carried away. Time for a reality check, maybe?"

I didn't reply.

"We need to refocus," he said. "Stopping the supply of more gas has to be the priority now. That means finding McIntyre. He'll be the first person they turn to. I know I told you to forget about him, but as of this minute he's back on top of the heap. And after all, there is a certain piece of paper from London with his name on it that we still have to deal with. What do you think?"

"I'm thinking, the ambush goes ahead," I said.

"No. There's no need. We've both seen those other guys. We can circulate their descriptions. There's plenty of time to pick them up later. Other people can do it, even. Finding McIntyre's what counts, now."

"Agreed. But the thing is, the ambush is key to both. It's a two-for-one deal. Buy one, get one free week."

"How so?"

"Where is McIntyre?"

"I don't know."

"Have any new leads come in?"

"No."

"So, who might know? Who knew how to contact him before?"

Fothergill was silent.

"The guys on their way to the bar," I said. "They're the only ones. Otherwise we'll just be driving around central America looking for a naked guy with a gag in his mouth."

"I'll speak to London," Fothergill said. "Get him on the watch lists at airports and border controls. Stop him leaving the country."

"That won't help."

"Wait. There's something else. In the comms gear I found. A laptop and two hard drives. The guys at the consulate can rebuild them. They're wizards at that kind of thing. They can decipher anything that was encoded. Restore anything that was deleted. Find anything that was hidden. We're bound to get something on him that way. I'll call ahead. Let them know to clear their desks."

"How long will that take?"

"I don't know. Not too long, I hope. And I could use the time to get back on London's case. Try and find a chink in their armor."

"It's worth a try, I guess. But it's a long shot. So here's what's going to happen. We'll back all three horses. You take IT and London. See what you can finesse out of them. Me—I'll stick with brute force and ignorance."

The Chrysler I was driving had been in the vicinity of the machine shop for over sixteen hours, which gave me a problem. I couldn't risk leaving it anywhere near the

Commissariat. The chances of it being recognized were too high. Instead I found a garage underneath a department store on the Magnificent Mile, parked where the car couldn't be seen from the entrance or the elevators, and went outside to look for a cab. I had the driver drop me two blocks from the club and I walked the rest of the way, circling the area carefully and keeping a sharp eye out for the Cadillac. There was no sign of it, so when I reached the corner of State and Rush I didn't waste any more time. I headed straight for the group of doormen at the entrance. I recognized them from my last visit. I don't know if they remembered me, though. None of the three would make eye contact as I approached, leaving me free to descend the stairs unmolested.

There wasn't a single customer in the bar, but that wasn't necessarily unusual for two thirty in the afternoon. The barman was leaning against the same spot on the wall, looking no more energetic than last time. The same DJ was crammed into her booth. But at least the music had progressed. She was up to the nineties, now. Although I wasn't convinced that was a good thing.

I moved over to the bar, and before I could order anything the guy brought me a Peroni and a grubby-looking glass.

"Thanks," I said.

"On the house," he said. "By way of an apology. For the misunderstanding, when I saw you in here before."

"Even better. But if you really want to make amends, answer me one question. Is there anyone else here?"

He didn't answer for a moment.

"I don't see anyone," he said, at last. "Do you?"

"You know, I still have the same phone," I said. "And I've been too busy to send that picture. So far. But that could change."

"There's no need for that. You should go ahead and delete it. Because what I'm saying is, there's no one else in here. No one in the bar. And not in the men's room."

"That's a much better answer. Thanks."

"For what? I didn't tell you anything."

"Of course you didn't. And to make sure you don't tell me anything else, perhaps you should get back to work, now. You don't want to be seen talking to me. I can't stay and chat, anyway. It's time I had a word with someone about the music."

The DJ was so absorbed with her iPod she didn't notice me until I was standing right in front of her booth.

"Oh," she said. "Hello. Sorry. Didn't see you. Got a request?"

"I do," I said. "But not the kind you're probably used to. I have a problem. It's my daughter. I'm trying to find her. She's missing, and usually turns up in a bar somewhere, drunk out of her mind. Have you seen her?"

"Here?"

"Yes. One of the doormen thought he'd seen her come in. She's nineteen, but looks a couple of years older. Five feet eight. Skinny. Blond. Blue jeans, white baby-doll top, black biker jacket. Tall black boots. Ring any bells?"

"No. Sorry."

"Could she be in the bathroom, maybe? She often hides out in one, when she gets a real load on."

"I don't know. I guess, maybe."

"OK, so here's the thing. I'm really worried about her, but I don't want to go charging into the women's room. There could be someone else in there. That would just be too weird. I'd probably get arrested or something. So I was wondering, is there any way you could go in and take a look for me? Tell me if any of the stalls are occupied?"

"I don't know. It's a little strange. And I'm supposed to be working."

"Please. I wouldn't ask if I wasn't desperate. You're the only woman here. There's no one else I can turn to."

"I'm just not sure . . ."

"Please. And don't worry about the work. There must be loads of music on that 'Pod. It's not going to need changing if you just step out of the booth for a couple of minutes."

"Well, OK then. One quick look."

"Oh, thank you. I really appreciate this. One other thing, though. When you go in, could you go up to the sinks and wash your hands or something? If she is there, she might get scared if she thinks someone's checking up on her. That would make it harder for me to calm her down, later."

"Sure. No problem. You know, would it be better if I actually used the bathroom? 'Cause to tell you the truth, I kind of need to go."

"That's a little too much information, but it would definitely be helpful. Thank you."

*

I waited next to her booth and fought the urge to rifle through her playlists and find something less annoying to listen to. She was gone for three and a half minutes, and as she hurried back toward me I could see she was excited about something.

"I think you're right," she said. "I think your daughter's in there. Someone was, definitely. They were locked in one of the stalls the whole time. And they didn't make a single sound. I peeped under the side, and I couldn't see their feet. They must have been holding them up, out of the way. So whoever it is, they're definitely hiding."

"Thank goodness," I said. "I was so worried. I can't thank you enough. But which stall was she in? The one at the end? That's where she usually goes."

"No. The end one was all closed up with some kind of tape. Must have been out of use. She was in the next one to it."

"That's great. OK. Well, I better go and fetch her now. I hope things don't turn too ugly. She can certainly be difficult when she's had a few."

"What's her name?"

"Pardon?"

"Your daughter's name? What is it?"

"Oh. Angela. Kind of ironic, don't you think?"

"I guess. But I was thinking. Do you want me to come back in with you? Maybe talk to her? She might respond better to another girl."

"That's a lot to ask. Are you sure?"

"Absolutely. Come on. Let's go. We're up to '97 already,

and I need to be back before the new millennium starts. I've got a bunch of embarrassing stuff on it after that."

"OK, thanks. I appreciate it. But let's do this. You go in first. I'll follow, stepping when you do so she doesn't hear me coming and freak out. Then maybe you could just wash your hands and head back out? Leave me to take care of the messy part? She'd never forgive me if I let someone new see what kind of state she was in."

"Sure. I understand. I don't want her to feel bad. I just hope she's all right."

"Oh, she will be. It takes a while, sometimes, but we always get there in the end. Actually, it can take a really long time to get her back on her feet. Up to a couple of hours, worst case. So if I'm in there for ages, I don't want you to worry. That's just the way it goes with Angie. It's the price of being a parent, these days."

The DJ was as zealous at the basin as anyone I'd ever seen. She washed her hands twice, used a paper towel as well as the air dryer, and finally turned back to give me a smile before the door to the bar closed behind her. I stayed completely still throughout her whole performance. Thirty seconds passed in silence after she left, then I heard a rustling sound. It was coming from the closed cubicle. A pair of feet hit the floor. They sounded heavy, but somehow also made a crunching noise. I looked under the door and saw a pair of black trainers. They were large enough to be a man's. Transparent plastic covers were stretched over them. The ankles were elasticated, like the kind crime-scene technicians wear when they want to avoid contaminating evidence.

Or getting soaked with blood.

I drew my Beretta and launched myself forward, smashing the ball of my foot into the door to the stall. The lock shattered and it flew open, connecting with some part of the guy who was lurking inside. He swore, but I could tell the flimsy wood was too light to have done him any real damage. Four latex-covered fingers appeared around the doorjamb, so I lashed out again, just as hard, before he had the chance to push it away. It was still touching him when my foot made contact, which was just what I wanted. It ensured that this time, none of the force was wasted.

I stepped into the stall and closed the door behind me. A man was lying on his side, stranded between the side wall and the toilet bowl, struggling to get back on his feet. He'd certainly come well prepared. As well as the shoe covers and surgeon's gloves, he was wearing a set of baggy gray coveralls and a dentist's-style mask over his mouth and nose. But what he was holding was even more telling than his outfit. Still clasped in the fingers of his right hand, despite his fall, was a knife. It was six inches long with a watermarked cobalt-steel blade.

"Is that Japanese?" I said.

The guy didn't speak, but I saw his eyes narrow with surprise and the skin of his forehead wrinkle into narrow folds.

"The knife you're holding," I said. "It looks Japanese.

That's not good. I prefer Sheffield steel, myself. But then, I am a little biased."

He didn't respond.

"Have you ever used a Fairbairn-Sykes commando knife?" I said. "I went to the factory, once. And saw how they make them."

This time his eyes grew wider, but he still didn't speak.

"You should try one," I said. "They're a lot better than kitchen utensils. Less likely to snag on someone's rib. If you want a job done properly, you need the right tools. Remember that. Now. Take the mask off."

He removed it gingerly with his left hand, and confirmed what I'd suspected from the moment I first heard him move. It was the guy I'd seen leaving the machine shop in the back of the Cadillac, nearly two and a half hours ago.

"Have you been in this business long?" I said.

He didn't answer.

"How's it working out for you?" I said. "Are you enjoying it? Does it give you much job satisfaction?"

His eyes were starting to glaze over.

"No?" I said. "Can you tell me the money's good, at least? 'Cause I've met your co-workers, and they're nothing to write home about."

By now he was looking thoroughly confused.

"Let's try this, instead," I said. "Do you know who I am?"

He shook his head.

"Well, we need to put that right," I said. "My name's David Trevellyan. I'm your victim. You're supposed to be killing me, right here, in less than two hours."

That took a moment to sink in. Then his whole body recoiled, pressing hard against the cubicle wall to get away from me.

"So, we can do one of two things," I said. "Bring the schedule forward, and you can kill me now. Try to, that is. Or you can put the knife down, and we'll think of another way to handle this."

The knife hit the floor and for a moment it hummed like a tuning fork, but the expression on the guy's face didn't relax one bit.

"Good," I said. "Now, there's one more thing I need to find out."

The guy capitulating like that gave me a tough choice to make. He was no use to me. He was clearly new to whatever business his employers were in, and if he didn't even recognize my face or know my name, there wasn't a snowball's chance he'd be privy to McIntyre's contact information. Obtaining that was my only valid objective, not furthering my case for the Nobel Peace Prize. Keeping him alive was a liability. I knew that. If we were part of a well-resourced, official operation, things might be different. You could maybe make a case for holding on to him. He was never going to be primary source material—that was immediately obvious—but some conscientious interrogator with time on his hands might have been able to dredge up some useful background information from somewhere inside him. But with circumstances as they were, however, the requirements of the mission were clear. It was my job to shut him down. Permanently. Except that I was reluctant to do that. He wasn't like the guys at the machine shop or the Ritz-Carlton or the apartment. He was quivering. Up close, he didn't seem much more than a kid. Not much of an adversary. More of a rabbit in the headlights. So I decided to delegate. To let him make the decision for me. And to do that I kept him at the limit of my peripheral vision, half turned away, and started to open the stall door.

"I have to just step outside for a moment," I said. "You stay there. Don't move."

He moved. I was still midstep when I heard his coveralls start to rustle. I saw him sit up and lean forward. He was stretching. Going for the knife. He reached the handle. His intent was clear. He was still trying to pose a threat. So I changed direction and planted my left foot firmly on the flat side of the blade, pinning it to the floor and trapping his fingers. Then I drove the edge of my right foot into the bridge of his nose. His head snapped back and smashed into the hard tiles on the back wall. He started to slide. He was out cold. But he didn't fall all the way, because I leaned in and caught him.

A couple of seconds later I did lay him down. Only by then, there was no chance of him regaining consciousness. Ever again.

TWELVE

I come from a very healthy family.

We live till ripe old ages, and hardly spend any time in bed, sick. In fact, during my whole childhood, I can only remember my mother taking to her bed on one occasion. It was just after we'd moved into our new house in London, and I guess looking back the stress of relocating from Birmingham had taken its toll. My father filled the void as well as he could, but after three days he sent an SOS to some obscure relatives in Ireland and headed back to the safety of his office.

Two old ladies answered his distress call, and they had an almost immediate effect. Within hours of them arriving, my mother was out of bed, cooking, washing up, and making sure the guests were comfortable. And within two days, she was in the hospital. The Irish ladies were well meaning, but hopeless. She felt she had no option but to look after them, even though it was supposed to be the other way around. And the effort required was simply too great.

I heard the grown-ups referring to the whole episode as the Curse of Good Intentions.

I didn't really understand what that meant, at the time. But later in life, it became only too clear.

Sixty minutes is a long while to spend on your own in a women's bathroom. Especially in one like the Commissariat's, where there isn't even a window to look out of. Instead, I sat on the counter between two basins and tried to make the time count for something. I wanted to put myself in McIntyre's shoes. To picture what he might be doing or where he might be going, in case the afternoon's meeting didn't yield any new information. I'd infiltrated groups who were trying to buy arms—and secrets, and even people—but I'd never sold anything like that on my own initiative before. There were too many factors I had no experience of, and too many gaps in our intelligence. I guessed the main one was not knowing how big the consignment he'd stolen had actually been. If he'd sold all his stock already, maybe he'd just fade into the background until his wounds had healed. If not, greed might lead him to show his face one more time. These thoughts just kept chasing themselves around my head, never leading anywhere conclusive, so I still hadn't made much progress when I saw that my watch was showing three forty-five. Only half an hour to the rendezvous. I decided it was time to take my seat in the bar.

Charades had never been my forte as a kid, but I did my best to mime "putting makeup on" to the girl in the DJ booth as I came out of the bathroom. I didn't want to speak to her again, and that seemed like the best way to avoid it. I was in luck. She just smiled and turned back to her iPod, leaving me free to walk across to the table I'd used yesterday. I'd been there less than a minute when the barman arrived at my side. He was carrying a new bottle of Peroni, as well as the empty one I'd been drinking earlier.

"You must have been sitting here quite a while," he said, setting the bottles down together. "Assuming you don't drink too fast."

"I never left the table," I said. "And I'm very responsible when it comes to alcohol."

The guy who'd done all the talking and the girl who'd searched me arrived fifteen minutes late, just as they had done yesterday. They paused at the foot of the stairs, surveyed the room, then approached the table and sat down on either side of me without saying a word.

"I guess your knowledge of the city hasn't improved any," I said. "It's a good thing I'm a patient man."

"Once again, my most sincere apologies," the guy said. "I would offer to buy you a drink as compensation, but I see you've already been well tended to. Perhaps we should move directly to the matter in hand?"

"As long as you've brought the money, I have no objection."

"I have it. Outside, in the car. And the item you are furnishing us with?"

"It's nearby, too. Somewhere safe. Given what it is, I thought that was better than bringing it into a public place."

"Then shall we proceed?"

"In due course. Pardon my cynicism, but I'd like to see the color of your money, first."

The guy reached into his jeans pocket, pulled out his cell phone, called up a picture, and held it out for me to see. The screen showed an aluminium briefcase loaded with cash, but the image was too small to make out the denominations. I wondered where he'd taken the photo. Nowhere close, I'd be happy to bet. And I'd wager double the contents that there was no sign of the case in his car.

"That looks good," I said. "But I hope you won't be offended if I count it, before we complete our transaction."

"A very prudent attitude," he said. "I would do exactly the same thing. Now, in return, some indication that we are not wasting our time?"

I showed him the picture that Fothergill had given me of a typical gas canister three days ago, when he'd first briefed me on this whole mess. It was almost identical to the one I'd found at the machine shop. You couldn't see any emblems or markings, and the spring clips were slightly different, but it was clearly from the same family. The guy studied the image intently for a moment, nodded, then folded the paper and placed it carefully on the table between the beer bottles.

"Excellent," he said. "Then there's no need to delay any further. Just one final precaution, as is our custom. I think you know what I'm referring to. Perhaps one of the restrooms would be appropriate, for privacy?"

The woman stood up and reached back greedily, taking my right arm. I grabbed the picture, then let her help me to my feet and lead me away from the table. She was moving faster than yesterday, and her body was much more tense.

Either she hadn't killed many people, or she enjoyed it too much. I suspected the latter, which wasn't a bad thing. It would make her easier to neutralize. I wasn't sure about the guy, though. He seemed a much calmer character. I kept expecting to feel him take his place on my left, but when I looked around I saw he hadn't moved from his seat. He must have thought that two of his people could take me, with the benefit of surprise. The fool. I couldn't wait to see his face when I came back from the bathroom. And then hear what excuses he could come up with.

I waited till we were halfway across the bar, then looked over at the DJ. I wanted to make sure the appearance of this new woman wasn't making her too suspicious. I needn't have worried, though. She was completely occupied with her iPod again, which made me wonder which song she'd choose next. Without realizing it, she was effectively picking the sound track to this stranger's death. I couldn't help wondering what would be appropriate. And whether any music would be playing when my time came. If so, I hoped someone with better taste would be selecting it. I was still thinking about that when I heard a different kind of noise altogether. Something extremely familiar, but totally unexpected. Like someone swatting flies on a table with a rolled-up magazine. Twice, in rapid succession. It was coming from the foot of the stairs. I spun around and saw a man standing there. It was Fothergill. He had a pistol in his hand. A twist of smoke was still leaking from the suppressor attached to its barrel. The gun was pointing at the table I'd just left. I turned to look.

The man I'd been talking to had been hit. He was still in his seat, but his head had been thrown back against the wall and two ragged holes were torn in his chest. One had dissected the *I* of the word "Chicago," and the other had hit the center of the *O*, like the writing on his hoodie had served as a target.

"David," Fothergill said, whipping the gun around in my direction. "Get down."

The muzzle flashed before I had time to react, and the woman at my side screamed and pitched headfirst into the door to the bathroom. She lay there for a moment, gently twitching, until Fothergill had moved in close enough to put two more rounds through the back of her skull. Then he went back to the table, poked the guy cautiously with his toe, and finally leaned over to check for a pulse.

"What kind of insane world do you live in?" I said, as soon as we both had our feet on the sidewalk. "How does killing those two even come close to being a good idea?"

Fothergill didn't answer.

"What on earth were you thinking in there?" I said.

"You could show a little gratitude, perhaps," he said. "I just saved your life."

"You nearly got me killed, is what you did. And what about the witnesses? The barman and the DJ. What's going to happen to them?"

"They'll be taken care of. The club owner will see to that. He's an old friend. And he owes me."

"Taken care of, how, exactly?"

"You're not getting squeamish, now, are you David? Don't worry. They'll just be paid off."

"What makes you think that'll stick? Either one of them could take the cash and go to the police, anyway. Or both of them could."

"No. Carlos runs a tight ship. It doesn't work that way in his place."

"How naive can you be? It works that way in every place."

"Time will tell. You'll see."

"Maybe. But why did you do it, in the first place? Two hits, in public, for no reason?"

"They were going to ambush you."

"No shit. If only someone had told me."

"No. Really. They weren't just planning a knife fight in the bathroom, like with Young. They were going to snatch you. Take you somewhere else. Probably torture you. Then dump the pieces in the lake, I wouldn't be surprised."

"How do you know?"

"I saw their vehicle. When I arrived. The blue Cadillac. They pulled it around the back of the restaurant, next door. It's only a few seconds to the club from there, if you cut through the alley. Easy to carry someone's unconscious body."

"So?"

"I saw inside the trunk. They were checking it over. It was lined with thick, black, rubbery sheeting. Some kind of heavy-duty PVC, I guess. And it was full of other weird stuff. They had gags. A straitjacket. Rope. Chain. Padlocks. All sorts of nasty things."

"Maybe the two of them were just bondage freaks."

"David, be serious. This was heavy-duty stuff. And it had your name all over it."

"Maybe. They could have been planning to lift me, I guess. It's always possible. But there's a difference between planning and succeeding."

"You could be right. But I had a decision to make, and I just didn't feel like I could take that chance. This is your life we're talking about. I wasn't about to gamble with it."

"There was no gamble involved. Everything was under control."

"Really?" he said, lifting his injured arm and pointing to the spot where the bullet had struck. "Look what happened last time I made that assumption."

"OK, I appreciate the sentiment," I said. "But the thing is, Richard, that wasn't your call."

"Really? That's how you feel? I can't believe you're upset about this. Killing children, remember? No reason to keep those other guys alive? Or is it a case of one rule for you, and one for everyone else?"

I didn't reply.

"I thought so," he said.

"When they parked the car, was anyone with it?" I said. "I mean, anyone other than the two people you shot?"

Fothergill took a moment to think.

"No," he said. "Just them. The man and the woman. Why?"

"'Cause they were no ordinary pair," I said. "I don't care about her, but the guy was clearly running their show. We needed to take him alive. To talk to him. He was our last link to McIntyre. Without him, we have no idea where to look."

"It was a question of priority. Taking him wasn't worth losing you. Not in my opinion, anyway. And I'm sure not in London's, either. You might be a royal pain in the ass, but you're an expensive pain, too. I wasn't about to lose you on my watch."

"There was no question of losing me. The situation was completely under control. Until you got there. Now we're back to square one."

"So you say. I saw it differently. And we still have all that computer stuff, remember. That I found at the machine shop. Which you missed, when you were having that little gun battle of your own. It's all at the consulate, already. The gurus are working on it. They'll find something. They always do."

"Let's hope so. Do they have a timescale?"

"Not yet. It's a question of 'How long's a piece of string?' They're no slouches, though. Shall we make our way back and see if they've made any headway?"

"We might as well. Since there are no warm bodies left to interrogate."

"Come on, then. And let's stop bickering. We're like spoiled kids. One quick question, though, first. You said you didn't care about that girl?"

"That's right."

"So how come, after I'd shot her, you went back and took something out of her jeans pocket?"

I shrugged.

"Some kind of memento, perhaps?" he said. "That speaks of a slightly less disinterested attitude than you've been letting on. I hope there are no conflicts of interest emerging here?"

"No," I said. "None."

"Then why did you want something of hers?"

"I didn't."

"So what did you take?"

"Something of mine."

"What?"

"My shorts."

Fothergill's eyebrows arched, and his mouth began to open.

"Don't even ask," I said.

He was alluding to a road I knew I'd never be going down again.

THIRTEEN

All change is for the worse.

That was a phrase I heard a lot when I was growing up. I guess the advances of the sixties didn't sit too comfortably with my parents. I sometimes thought they'd be happier if time had stood still at the start of the thirties. As in, the eighteen-thirties. They didn't see the potential for changing your life, to take advantage of circumstances. For changing your routine, to benefit from new facilities. Or for changing your plans, to make the most of whatever the gods of fate saw fit to throw in your path.

We reached the consulate without incident, but once we got there three interesting things happened, one after the other. When the guard on duty at the garage saw Fothergill approaching, he came straight out of his booth and offered to park the car for him. Then the doorman from the foyer walked across with us and hit the button for the fourteenth floor, without waiting to be asked. And the receptionist left her desk and unlocked the door that led directly to

Fothergill's corridor, saving us from dawdling our way through the sniffer machines.

I watched each one carefully. They behaved in exactly the same way, and their expressions and body language told me exactly the same thing. They weren't acting out of sympathy for Fothergill's injury. They weren't in a rush to get him out of their hair, even though it was pushing five and they probably wanted to go home. They were doing these things because they all seemed to genuinely like him, and were happy to see him back in the fold, safe and sound.

It was a strange phenomenon to observe, especially since it involved someone who wore the same uniform as me. Someone who'd cut his teeth in the field, like me. Who'd also lived a large portion of his life on the outside, looking in. Fothergill had somehow turned all that on its head. He'd been absorbed by the crowd and was now on the inside, looking out. At me. I wondered how that would feel. To be part of something that wasn't temporary. Something with some stability—transfers and repostings permitting. I hadn't known Fothergill as an agent, but it was clear that now he'd put down roots. He was welcome here. He was flourishing. And for the first time, I began to wonder if my future could ever hold anything like that. I'd never really thought about it consciously before. My long-term planning had never gone beyond a vague image of my number coming up, leaving me sprawling in an alleyway or a hotel room. And everything after that going dark.

Fothergill dropped into the chair behind his desk and started to swing lazily from side to side, reinforcing the image of comfort and familiarity. I wouldn't have been surprised if he'd produced a couple of cigars for us to smoke, like we were at some kind of exclusive club. Instead, though, he pulled out his phone and called down to the IT guys for a progress report.

"Anything?" I said.

"Not yet," he said. "But they're good. And they're pulling out all the stops. They'll come through with something. I'm pretty confident."

"I hope you're right. I can't see what you're hoping to get out of this, though. Who would leave vital contact details lying around on some laptop? These guys weren't amateurs."

"All the data was encrypted. And they'd need some sort of backup, in case of injuries or fatalities. That's how teams work. Not everyone runs around on their own, with everything stored in their head."

"I'm not saying there'll be nothing useful, when you get it all deciphered. But encrypted or not, they wouldn't have just left McIntyre's cell number in their address book for anyone to find. And even if they did, what are the chances of him still using the same phone? He'd have dumped it the moment he got out of the building, after he shot you."

"You'd be surprised what we find. People are careless. And it's all about lateral thinking. Finding oblique ways to achieve the same goal. Like nicking Al Capone for tax evasion. All they cared about was getting him behind bars, not how or why."

"Excellent point. Maybe McIntyre won't have paid his cell phone bill. Then we could dress up as debt collectors and catch him that way."

"See? You're getting it. In the meantime, you sound tired. Do you need a caffeine fix?"

Fothergill reverted to small talk until after his assistant had delivered the coffee. Then he called IT again.

"Still nothing," he said.

"And there won't be anything if you keep harassing them," I said. "Give them the time they need to do their jobs."

"You're right. I can ride people too hard, sometimes. I just keep thinking back to those people in the bar. I can't see that stopping them will really be a long-term problem. Can you? I mean, what would they have told us?"

I shrugged.

"Probably nothing," he said. "Or whatever they thought we wanted to hear. Either way, we'd be no further along. Dispassionate, factual evidence is what we need. Taken directly from their computers. Properly analyzed. That's what's going to break this. As long as we get it quickly enough."

Fothergill drained the final drops of his coffee, then sat for a moment and stared into the empty cup.

"Need a refill?" he said. "Or something to eat? I could call back down."

I declined. I wouldn't have objected to another drink, actually, but I was used to fetching things when I needed them. Not sitting back and waiting for them to be delivered.

Like the situation with McIntyre. My preference would be to get out of the office and start shaking things loose for myself. I was itching to move, but I knew that in the circumstances, waiting for a solid lead was the right thing to do. And I had to confess, part of me was fascinated with Fothergill. Watching him work was a revelation. He wasn't in the field anymore, but he could still get things done. Unlike most desk jockeys, who are completely useless. And he'd shown at the Commissariat that he could still get his hands dirty when he thought he needed to. It's just that he worked in a different way, now. He'd pulled himself into the center of the web. Nearly everything was achieved through other people. As it was with me, really. Only in a way, his approach was more honest. At least the people who were involved knew what was happening to them. They knew what they were part of, and stayed on board voluntarily. That was a galaxy away from the lies and deceit that are the basic building blocks of my world.

I listened to Fothergill call his assistant and order a sandwich, and realized there was still plenty to think about. There was bound to be more to his situation than met the eye. But I'd never previously been able to see any kind of life beyond what I knew in the field. Now I was feeling something new. For the first time, I felt like I was maybe looking at a future version of myself.

"I think I'll pass on a drink, too," Fothergill said. "Just stick with the snack. Then I need to check that McIntyre's description went out to everywhere that needs it. The U.S. is big enough, but having to chase him all over the world would be worse. If we can keep him from leaving the country, we might still have a chance."

"How did he get into the country?" I said.

"We don't know. He didn't leave any trace."

"So how do you expect to spot him sneaking back out?"

"No one was looking, before. Everyone is, now."

"He could use the same route in reverse, and no one would know. Or try something else, completely different. He'll have all kinds of tricks up his sleeve. You can count on it."

"Maybe. But don't forget—something's changed. We're expecting him. He won't have such an easy run this time."

"Expecting him, how? He won't use his real name, for a start. He'll have a choice of IDs. And all of them will be indistinguishable from government issue. There's no net tight enough to catch him. Not without a huge slice of luck."

"We're also distributing his photo. An up-to-date one, before you object. From the CCTV in this building, taken a few days ago."

"There's no point. No one's going to recognize him from a picture. You'll just have to accept it. If he wants to leave, he's as good as gone."

"We'd better hope he decides to stay, then."

"That won't help, either. If he goes to ground there's no way we're going to unearth him. Not without enough feet on the street. London need to get over whatever's been bugging them. Maybe I should fly over there and have a word, myself."

Fothergill was shaping up to reply when there was a

knock on the door. A woman I'd never seen before came in, placed a sandwich in a brown cardboard wrapper carefully on his desk, and left again without ever making eye contact with either of us.

"David, this negativity is getting tiresome," Fothergill said as he unwrapped his food. "Sure you won't join me? I could split it."

I shook my head.

"Look, I know there are problems," he said. "I'm doing my best to work around them. But right now we need helpful suggestions. Not criticism. So if you've got anything useful to add, let's hear it."

"OK," I said. "If we're going to catch him, we're going to have to make him come to us. Trick him into breaking cover. We need to come up with a ruse."

"Good. Interesting idea. Lure him out. I like it. How?"

"I don't know yet."

Fothergill grunted. Then he picked up half of his sandwich and moved to gaze out of the window, standing in the same spot he'd been in when I first saw him. I went over and stood next to him. The cars were sitting stationary on the bridges, but below them the city lights were starting to dance in the darkening water of the river. I watched them for a moment as the sun slowly sank, and decided that if I ever did end up in an office, it would need to have plenty of windows. And a view no less stunning than this one.

"You know, I need to talk to those techies again," Fothergill said, after he'd finished chewing on the last morsel of bread.

"You don't," I said. "Leave them alone. You'll only make them go slower."

"No. You don't understand. If we're going to trick McIntyre, like you suggest, we'll need a hook. There could be something we can use on that laptop. Something weird, that the techies wouldn't expect we'd need. I never told them to look for anything off-the-wall. So, I need to change their brief. Right now. Before they miss everything."

"I guess that wouldn't hurt. But be careful how you phrase it. No one works slower than a disgruntled engineer."

"You're right. Only, don't worry. I'm the master of careful phrasing. But you know what? I won't do it on the phone. That's too impersonal. I'll head down there and do it face-to-face. It's much easier to fake sincerity, that way."

Normally when I'm left alone in someone's office I take that as a cue to nose around the place. Old habits die hard. But in Fothergill's case, he had everything set up so minimally that there wasn't much to get my teeth into. There was nothing on the glass desk. Only newspapers on the coffee table. And if there was a safe anywhere, it was so well concealed I certainly couldn't find it.

Ten minutes later I was back at the window, watching the traffic making no progress around the city center. It made me think of the cabdriver who'd picked me up at Midway when I first arrived, three days ago. He'd told me there were two seasons in Chicago—winter, and road construction. I was beginning to understand what he meant.

Fourteen floors below me I saw two cabs from rival

companies—a red one and a yellow one—vying for position at an intersection. The sound-deadening glass they use in all consulate buildings made it impossible to tell if they were honking at each other, and I might have been too high up to hear anyway, even if I'd opened the window. I bet myself that they were, and was wondering how I could find out when a noise did reach my ears. A sound like an old church bell. It was coming from my pocket. I realized it was my phone. Or rather, the one I'd inherited from Young. A new text had arrived.

u here yet?

I was intrigued. I didn't know where Young was supposed to be but figured there was only one way to find out.

Where's here? I texted back. *What am I? A mind reader?*

chicago, arsehole, someone replied a minute later. Another Brit, judging by the insult.

I'm in a truck. Problems en route! Had to hitch the last part of the way. Nearly there, though. ETA twenty minutes. Where are you?

problems—tell me about it! but be careful! all safe houses blown. consulate not safe either. specially fothergill. avoid at all costs.

Got that. Will avoid. Where are you? What's happening?

eta chicago 30 minutes. meeting our friends 2moro night. should be last time, then free & clear. need you to watch my back, if youre finally there.

Will do. No problem. Where & when do you want to rendezvous?

6.45 bench next to navy pier ferris wheel photo booth.

Today or tomorrow?

you today. friends tomorrow!

Got that. Confirmed. Out.

Fothergill returned five minutes after the final text had arrived. His face had changed, and I thought he was looking a little haggard again. Perhaps the technicians hadn't been as easy to manipulate as he'd hoped.

"That went well," he said. "I put them in the picture. They got it easily enough. But finding what we need will widen the search parameters, apparently. That means it could take longer to turn anything up."

"That may not be a problem," I said. "'Cause we just caught a break. In fact, it landed right in our laps."

"Really? What did?"

"McIntyre just resurfaced. Via text, would you believe. Asking Young to meet him. In Chicago. In seventy-five minutes."

"Seriously? How do you know?"

"Because I have Young's phone."

"Oh my goodness, you do. I never replaced your last one."

"No, you didn't. Very remiss. I was going to report you, only I thought, come on, the guy's getting old, he's banged up his arm . . ."

"You know, David, I could get used to working with you. You're all right. Whatever those other people say. So where does Tony want to meet?"

"Somewhere called Navy Pier."

"Hmm. Good choice. Very public."

"What is it? Literally a pier?"

"Yes. It sticks out into Lake Michigan. But it's bigger than what we're used to in England. Big enough to land planes on."

"Yeah. Of course it is."

"No, seriously. The U.S. Navy used it for training in World War II. New pilots had to practice there before being deployed. In fact, did you see a plane hanging from the ceiling at Midway, the other day?"

"I did. Some kind of Dauntless?"

"Right. That came courtesy of a guy who needed a little more practice. They dragged it out of the water after the war was over."

"McIntyre mentioned a Ferris wheel?"

"Yeah. The place is all built on, now. There's a big complex full of restaurants—and a cinema. Then a space with a few fairground things and the wheel. It's not as tall as the London Eye, but you can still see it for miles. Then there's another building with a garage and a theater."

"So it's not too hard to find this place?"

"Not at all. You can't miss it. And it's lit up like a Christmas tree. You go left out of the building. Right on Illinois. Down the steps. Past the cinema. Then keep on going past the big cloverleaf-shaped building near the water."

"That doesn't sound like a problem."

"It shouldn't be one. And it's only a few minutes' walk, which means . . ."

"Someone's going to be meeting McIntyre tonight. Only it won't be Young. It'll be me."

"It'll be both of us. Oh, no—wait. Seventy-five minutes? That makes the rendezvous, what—a quarter to seven?"

"Yes."

"Damn. There's no way I can make it. I won't be back."

"Where from? You're going somewhere?"

"Yes. I have to. Didn't I tell you? The establishment officer's been on to me. She's not happy about keeping the gas containers here overnight. In fact, she downright refused. She's got herself all frothed up, worrying about the contents."

"She might have a point, you know. They probably are too dangerous for the office. But what does she want you to do with them?"

"There's a place out near the carpool that can handle them. A hazardous materials depot. I have to take them out there. They probably won't know what to do either—this stuff is pretty new, apparently—but at least they can lock the containers down properly. Keep everything controlled and stable."

"Maybe they can. But they should come and fetch them. You can't transport them. Bringing them back from Gary was bad enough, but there wasn't an alternative. Now there is. Don't take them on your own. Not through the city. It's not safe."

"Don't worry. I won't be on my own. The depot's sending one of their guys to ride shotgun. He'll have special equipment to transport the flasks. And he's a fully trained-up biochem expert. So it'll be fine. I'll be in good hands."

"I don't know. That doesn't sound so bad, I suppose. But where was this guy before? Tell me he's just been flown in from somewhere, or I'm not going to be happy."

"Sorry, David. No. He hasn't been flown in. He's been at the center all along."

"How come?"

"He's based there. He's the best guy in his field in North America, apparently. New York is always trying to poach him, but he's too much of a Cubs fan. Which some folks around here would tell you is evidence enough to question any claims of intelligence. But that's another story."

"So Cubs fan or not, where was he this afternoon? We needed him in Gary."

"That would have been handy. I did ask, but the place is very specialized. You wouldn't believe the rules of engagement. They only come out to play when someone has a confirmed contact. And it has to be something on their Dangerous list. Until today, we just had a rumor. Now we have the gas. And its working name. Spektra. And that changes everything."

"Bureaucrats. You've got to love them. And their rules. But still. Given your recent history, it's probably a good thing your path won't cross with McIntyre's. That would be as dangerous a formula as the gas, I expect. Especially in public."

"Maybe you're right," he said, lifting his bandaged arm. "And with this albatross, he would hardly be able to miss me."

"It does stand out, a little," I said, thinking about the impression the sling had first made on me.

"It does. But back to business. I'm puzzled. How's this all going to work? Tony knew Young. And he's seen you before. He's going to know that you're not the right guy."

"If he sees me. I'm going to head down there now. There'll be time. He hasn't arrived in town yet. Then I'll lay up near the rendezvous point and snatch him when he comes by for his initial recce."

"That's a tricky procedure. You'll have to hope the place isn't too crowded. But it might work."

"It might. And if not, I'll come up with something else. But here's another thing to think about. When McIntyre texted, he said he was meeting friends again tomorrow night."

"Friends? Who are they?"

"Must be the people from Gary. So either he doesn't know they're dead, in which case he's going to get two nasty surprises, later. Or there are more of them than we thought. Which means more loose ends to tie up."

Fothergill sighed.

"Like we don't have enough flies in the ointment," he said. "What do you think we should do? Go ahead with the hard arrest as soon as you get hold of McIntyre? Or cut him a little slack, and hope he leads us to more miscreants?"

"Well, I don't know," I said. "Option B is tempting. I could always use more contact with miscreants."

"David, I'm being serious."

"OK. This is what I think. McIntyre is so damn slippery

that if we can get him in the crosshairs, we should pull the trigger there and then. Bring that chapter to a close. And worry about these other guys—who may not even show up—when and if."

"I agree. That sounds like the way forward. Plus, if you could get hold of McIntyre's phone, they might even get in touch to see where he is. If we're very lucky."

"I think we're due a little luck."

"You're right. We are. But listen, here's an idea. Talking about McIntyre's phone, why don't you give me the number he texted you from? I'll get onto the network guys. Then we can at least get a GPS trace on him, in case he gets lost in the crowd tonight. Or, heaven forbid, slips the net again altogether."

FOURTEEN

Toward the end of our training program the instructors really cranked up the pace.

Instead of setting one exercise and giving us the chance to complete it before moving on to another, they took to handing out three or sometimes four different tasks at the same time. Everyone was feeling the added pressure, but no one was prepared to buckle beneath it. We'd come too far for that. So we just worked longer and longer hours, juggling ever-increasing volumes of written work, physical training, practical assessments, and library research. Pretty soon a full night's sleep had become nothing more than a distant memory.

We tried our hardest, but after a few weeks our scores had begun to suffer. Our marks had declined, but not to a disastrous extent. Or so we thought. Until one Friday afternoon when, after a particularly brutal week, we were summoned to the main conference room. It was warm in there, and more than a few eyes were beginning to close as we waited for the chief instructor to arrive. He came in after twenty anxious minutes, carrying a stack of paper. I was near the front, so I could see it was the work we'd been set the night before. The instructions had been shouted at us as we staggered into the locker rooms after a six-mile run. Write two thousand words about Wales. Must be completed by 10:00 P.M.

The one thing on our minds at that time was getting to bed, so no one queried what was required of us. We just each found a space in the gym and started scribbling down anything we knew about the place. Geography. History. Politics. Sport. Anything to burn through the specified number of words. Then one of the guys gathered the papers up, took them to the office, and no one thought any more about it.

"Hands up who's read *Moby-Dick*," the chief instructor said.

A couple of people complied.

"Hands up anyone who started it, but didn't make it to the end," he said.

About three-quarters of the group raised a hand this time.

"Well, you lot have certainly got no excuse," he said. "For getting no marks. Zero. Nada. Nil points. To be clear, you've all failed. All of you. Now go back to your rooms and write four thousand words this time. About whales."

The moral of the story was clear. Doing the right work was even more important than doing the work right.

And once you're in the field, you find the same thing applies to place.

*

Fothergill was right. McIntyre had chosen an excellent place to set up the meeting. But not for the textbook reason. You'd normally pick somewhere like a pier when you knew you were under surveillance, but that whoever was watching you was still gathering evidence. Your identity would already be known, so you wouldn't mind being seen or photographed. You'd meet at the very far end, so you had the maximum warning if anyone tried to approach or apprehend you. And the physical inaccessibility, married to the ambient noise from the wind and water, would make it nearly impossible for anyone to eavesdrop. Even if they had access to the best electronic enhancements.

Navy Pier didn't work that way. It was just too big.

There were two official entrances for pedestrians to use. One was to the right, outside, leading to where the leisure boats and cruise ships were tied up. The other was in the center, which brought you inside the main building. It looked like you could make your way through either of the restaurants at the front of the complex if you needed to, as well. A driveway for vehicles led away to the left, allowing access to the garage. An abundance of windows and polished surfaces made it easy to check for tails. There were obliging crowds everywhere to lose yourself in. And a virtually unlimited number of places to observe the rendezvous point from without any chance of being spotted in the process. I had to confess—the location stacked the odds hugely in McIntyre's favor. He'd pulled out another rabbit, just like with the abandoned apartment. I wondered whether Young's network was still helping him. And whether there was any mileage in tracking them down, if I found myself needing a real plan B.

I reached the pier complex at a minute after six, which further restricted my options. It meant there wasn't time to set up any of the usual tricks. Even the simplest were out of the question. Like one of my favorites, which involves a second person. It works because generally speaking, your target will be on the lookout for an individual. So if you show up as half of a couple, you can stand or sit in plain sight—arm in arm, or even cuddling and kissing—without attracting attention. Another trained operative is obviously preferable, but I've had to rope in civilians on more than one occasion. The kind that bill themselves as members of an even older profession than mine, and charge for their time by the hour. But in this case, I had no idea where to look for one. And no chance to find out. So instead, I resorted to something you learn on your first field exercise. Something that's surprisingly effective, but so basic that with luck McIntyre would never believe anyone would try it for real.

All you need is a newspaper. And something to make a hole.

None of the shops in the main building could help me, but a guy from a souvenir kiosk pointed me toward a trio of vending machines to the side of the taxi rank. I bought a copy of that day's *Tribune,* and headed for the area surrounding the Ferris wheel. The photo booth was to the left, against the parking garage's outer wall. A line of benches ran back from it, at ninety degrees. There were seven. All were vacant, despite the hordes of people that were still swarming throughout the place. I sat at the edge of the second one and unfolded my paper, making it as large as possible. The keys to the Chrysler were still in my pocket so I took them out and selected the sharpest. I used the tip to make a tiny hole two-thirds of the way up the paper's spine. Then I sat back, raised the *Tribune* like a shield, and settled down to wait.

I never paid much attention to physics at school, but I'd learned one thing about light waves since then. If I put my eye near enough to the hole, I could see out. Yet anyone looking back at me would be hard-pressed to notice the pinprick, let alone anything on my side of the paper. There were only two things to be careful about. Holding the paper in a convincing position, like I was actually reading something. And keeping it still.

The photo sellers were kept busy that night. A constant stream of people flowed past their booth—there was no other way to go once you left the Ferris wheel—and the group from every third or fourth gondola stopped and gathered around to gawp at their pictures. They formed quite a crowd. Maybe half of them handed over some money. But six forty-five came and went without anybody sitting on the bench. Or approaching it. Or even looking at it. I scanned every face in the vicinity. There were hundreds. It was impossible to say that McIntyre's wasn't one of them. But if he was there, I couldn't pick him out.

I decided to only wait until seven fifteen before abandoning the plan. I took a final, careful look around the area.

Then I folded the paper, found the shortest route across to the garage building, and called Fothergill. I wanted to know if he'd got anywhere with the cell phone company. I knew it was a risk. McIntyre had shown he was patient. If something had made him suspicious, he'd have been prepared to watch the bench for hours. But on the other hand, the GPS signal from his phone would give us an idea of where he was. If it turned out he was miles away from the place, the sooner I found out, the better.

There was no answer from Fothergill's desk phone, so I tried his cell. I figured he might not be back from the depot yet, or he might be tied up en route with the technicians. He didn't answer that one, either. I moved to a window to keep an eye out, just in case, and gave him five minutes. I tried again. And got the same result. No answer on either number. So then I wondered about the IT guys at the consulate. Perhaps Fothergill was down there again, harassing them. I didn't have their department's number so I tried the switchboard, hoping they could put me through. But when the operator picked up, she recognized my voice. She sounded tense. I was put on hold, and after thirty seconds the receptionist from the fourteenth floor came on the line. She took a minute to run me through some pedantic security routines—a kind of telephone version of the sniffer machine—and then told me why I couldn't reach Fothergill. He wasn't in the office. And he wasn't in a place where they allow cell phones.

He was in the hospital.

The car he'd been driving to the depot had been involved

in an accident. A serious one. The other occupant had been killed. Paramedics had collected Fothergill and taken him to the emergency room at Northwestern. It was nearby, on Huron. There was no word yet on his condition.

The receptionist had no idea whether Fothergill had made any headway with the cell phone company before he'd left. There was no one else there who could find out. But by then, at least the first part of the answer was irrelevant. I knew for a fact that McIntyre had been nowhere near the pier that night. He'd obviously been too busy elsewhere.

I've always hated hospitals. They may look different in other countries, but the smell is always the same. And so is the atmosphere. The moment you set foot in one, the sense of sickness and decay floods over you, seeping into your pores and dragging you down into a pit of despair. At least that's how it feels to me. And judging by Fothergill's face when I finally found his room at Northwestern, he saw it pretty much the same. Which was a good thing. People who enjoy getting medical treatment worry me deeply.

A doctor and two nurses were gathered around Fothergill when I arrived, so I retreated to the corridor until they'd left. Then I went back in for a proper look at him. He was wearing pajamas—crumpled green ones—which was a little disconcerting after his usual beautiful suits. The fancy sling was gone, replaced by a standard white one, and his right hand and forearm were bandaged, too. But other than that, barring a few scratches on his face, he didn't seem too badly banged up.

"Grapes?" I said.

"Whisky?" he said.

"Haven't got either. Sorry. So. What happened to you?"

"Had a fight with an iron girder. Holding up the top deck of Lake Shore Drive, where it crosses the mouth of the river. A couple of hundred yards from where you were, ironically."

"Good spot for it?"

"Perfect."

"Hit and run?"

"Officially."

"And do we know who did the hitting and running?"

"Take a guess."

"McIntyre."

"Right in one."

"I'm not surprised. But are you sure? Did you actually see him? These things can be so sudden."

"It wasn't sudden at all. He actually stopped, after running us into the pillar. Came up to the car. Opened the door. Saw Milton was dead. Pointed his gun at me. I thought he was going to slot me there and then, David. I really did."

"Milton was the techie they sent?"

"Yes. Seemed like a good guy, too."

"And he bought it in the crash?"

"He did. Poor bastard. It was the air bag's fault."

"Your car has air bags?"

"He brought the car from the depot. That's how they have them, apparently."

"I got the impression you were driving."

"I was. Milton asked me to. Said he hates doing it, especially in the city."

"So what went wrong with the air bag? I guess you weren't wearing seat belts?"

"No. The techies are properly trained. It's just their cars that are weird. And nothing went wrong with it, exactly. It's kind of hard to explain. Milton was holding this thing. On his lap. And I don't really know what happened. I guess he went forward, with the momentum. The air bag burst out and hit him. And somehow, this object ended up getting driven straight into his chest. Like a knife, almost."

"What was it made of? Metal?"

"Yes. It was some kind of tool. Long and thin. A bit like a wrench, with a special end. For fastening the lid onto the container."

"What container?"

"For the gas. The safety thing."

"What, like a key? You had to keep it separate?"

"No. Just a regular tool. They always go together, as far as I know."

"So why did Milton still have it? Oh. Wait."

Fothergill looked away.

"Tell me you weren't on the way to the depot when this happened?" I said.

He fixed his stare on the wall, and didn't speak.

"Tell me the gas wasn't in the car?" I said.

"Well," he said, after a moment. "Put it this way. It isn't there now."

Neither of us spoke for a good two minutes. Then Fothergill shook his head and finally broke the silence.

"So," he said. "Here's where we stand. Tony's back on the loose. So is the gas. And it sounds like the buyers could still be on the scene, based on what Tony texted you."

"Not just 'the gas.' Three times as much gas as there was when we started."

"No. There's the same amount. We just didn't know about all of it. But either way, this is not good. There's some serious broken glass for us to sweep up here, my friend."

"There's more than broken glass. Things are spiraling out of control, is what's happening. This is about much more than a hard arrest, now. Or saving face with the Americans. It's time for you to call London. Light a fire under them. We need more feet on the street if we're going to contain this mess."

Fothergill didn't answer.

"What's the matter?" I said. "Don't you think they'll listen?"

He glanced at me, then looked away again.

"Is this about covering your arse?" I said. "Are you trying to hide the fact that McIntyre put one over on you again? Because if you are, you can forget it. Trust me. The truth's coming out, anyway. A man's dead, remember."

"It is my arse that's on the line," he said, slowly turning back to face me. "But that's not the problem. I didn't break any procedures. There's nothing I can't talk my way out of. I've been backed into worse corners, dozens of times."

"So why the reluctance? We need to escalate this, and escalate it fast."

"There's something else," he said, after a moment. "Something you need to know."

"So go ahead," I said. "What is it? Level with me."

"I didn't handle things too well, back there. When I saw Tony coming up to the car, I froze. He looked at both of us. Then he went to Milton's side and opened his door. He had a gun, and he was setting up for a double tap when he realized Milton had already gone. So, he pointed the gun at me. Told me to pop the trunk. And, guess what? I did."

"So?"

"I was sitting next to a guy who Tony had effectively just killed. I was armed. And did I get a shot off? Try to stop him? Do anything at all to even the score for Milton? No. No. And No."

"Where was your weapon?"

"Holstered."

"Where was McIntyre's?"

"In his hand."

"So if you'd tried to draw, you'd be dead now. How would that have helped?"

"I feel like I should have tried to do something, at least."

"You'd just driven into a metal girder. That's traumatic in itself. And you're already injured. You already had a gunshot wound, in your arm."

"To tell the truth, that was part of the problem. I saw him pointing a gun at me, and all I could think of was what happened last time. That was the first time I'd ever been shot, in all these years, and it really messed me up."

"That's understandable. It happens to a lot of people. And anyway, what about your other hand? That looks hurt, too."

He lifted his right hand and looked at it, as if noticing the bandages for the first time.

"Yes. It got burned, somehow. The doc thinks it was from the air bag. I must have reached out, instinctively, when I saw Milton flying forward. He was a large lad. Guess I was trying to stop him. Pretty stupid, huh?"

"Not stupid at all. You did what you could. And you got hurt trying to save a guy you hardly know. That's admirable, Richard. Now stop beating yourself up. It's time to focus."

"Thanks for the kind words, David. I appreciate it. But the truth is I didn't do enough. Not for me. I can't walk away from this yet."

"No one's asking you to walk away. We just need some help to reach the finish line."

"That's not how things work, and you know it. If we send the balloon up, London will parachute in a whole new team. They'll replace both of us."

"We don't know that."

"We do. It's how things work. Like my friend Callum, in Edinburgh. Did I tell you about him?"

"No. I don't think so."

"Well, Callum's ex-navy. And he was in bed one night, fast asleep, with his wife. Then a noise woke him up. It was coming from outside. He looked through the window, and saw four guys burgling his garage. So he called the police, right away. And do you know what they said?"

"No."

"I can't remember their exact words. But it was along the lines of 'Tough luck, pal.' They couldn't have been less interested. So do you know what Callum did?"

"Went outside and shot the burglars?"

"Nearly right. He called the police back a few minutes later and pretended that's what he'd done. And guess what? Four squad cars and an armed response unit were on his lawn inside four minutes."

"That's a lovely story, Richard. But it doesn't mean we'd be replaced."

"Of course it does. It just goes to show. People like the brass in London can put their hands on whatever resources they want, whenever they want. The preferences of people like us don't count. Which may be OK with you—you never wanted this assignment in the first place. But it's a major problem for me."

"Why? You can't bring Milton back. Finding the gas and stopping McIntyre is what counts. Your job is to make that happen as quickly and efficiently as possible."

"David, please. There's something you need to know about me. I'm old school. That doesn't just mean I wear good suits and drink vintage champagne. It means I'm not an 'end justifies the means' type guy. It means I care about how the job is done, not just getting the right result. I care about the people I work with. And never, not once, have I turned my back on an obligation. I've never left a man behind, and I've never left a score unsettled. And I'm not prepared to start now."

I had nothing to say about that.

"So," he said. "I'm asking you. For Milton's sake. For my sake. Give me twenty-four hours?"

I didn't respond.

"Please," he said. "They're only keeping me in overnight. We could meet at the office, first thing. Get our heads together. See if we can't find a way to make this right."

FIFTEEN

If there's one thing the navy relies upon, it's the ability to make plans.

I've been subject to literally thousands of them over the years. They make them in response to every conceivable situation. Some have worked well, so I've adapted them to other situations. Others have been shambolic, so I've abandoned them halfway through. You get to the point where you can tell from the first few lines whether they're going to be any good. Sometimes you can even recognize who wrote them, from the style and layout and general approach. But there's one thing I've noticed that applies to all plans, regardless of purpose or quality.

The danger or difficulty is always inversely proportional to the degree to which the author will be personally involved.

I'm no fan of mornings, but even so, Fothergill's idea of early didn't match mine. I'd been in his easy chair for a good half hour before he finally showed his face. He was freshly shaved, his silver hair was glistening from the shower, and he was wearing an immaculate charcoal gray suit I hadn't seen him in before. There was no sling to match this one, though. Just the standard-issue hospital one the medics had given him last night.

"Oh, David, there you are," he said, when he'd stepped into the room and closed the door. "Sorry to keep you. The doctors were very sticky about letting me go. Seems they were worried about this burn on my hand. I talked them around in the end, but they wouldn't back down till I'd let them change the bandages, at least. And then I had to pop home on my way over, to grab some fresh togs."

"Did you grab any coffee, while you were there?" I said.

"No. Sorry. I wanted to get over here as quickly as possible, so we could get started."

"OK, then. Let's start. Thoughts?"

"Well, time is limited. So I think we should go for two birds, one stone. Tony, and the gas."

"Good in theory. Any ideas for making that happen?"

"Yes. Start with Tony. Last night. He was pretty motivated to get his hands on the gas, wasn't he? Acting like a pirate in the middle of a city street? Taking Milton's life?"

"He was. But that seems to be his mode. He comes across as a fairly wholehearted kind of guy."

"True. But my point is this: Why was getting the gas back so important? To want it so badly, he must really need it. For something specific. Something urgent."

"OK. Seems reasonable."

"So, tie that in with what he said about meeting his

'friends' again. By which I'm assuming he meant those guys from Myene."

"You think he'd risk being involved with them again? After the state they had him in at the machine shop?"

"I do."

"Why?"

Fothergill moved over to his favorite window and started to gaze out.

"I can't tell you, exactly," he said. "But it's the only explanation that makes any kind of sense. Maybe it's about the money."

"You think he's that greedy?" I said.

"It could be greed. Or something less straightforward, like a kind of revenge. Forcing them to buy back their own stuff."

"That seems like a pretty convoluted kind of revenge. I don't buy it."

"Something else altogether, then. Like he thinks they won't stop chasing him till he's made good on what he owes them. But the point is this: It gives us a key advantage. It tells us where he's going to be, and when."

"What do you mean?"

"He'll be meeting his buyers. Tonight."

"Well, obviously. But where will he be meeting them? What time?"

Fothergill moved closer to me.

"I don't know the specifics," he said. "Not yet. But I know how to find out."

"How?" I said.

"The IT guys. They've been in all night, working on it."

"Working on what?"

"Those hard drives. They're bound to dig something out of them. I bet they'll have something for us pretty soon. Maybe this morning, even."

"Was it just hard drives you gave them? Or crystal balls, too? 'Cause I don't see how they're going to find details of events that weren't even dreamed of when you found all that stuff."

"Sorry, David. I skipped ahead. I meant to say, what I'm looking for from the IT guys is some way of getting hold of the buyers. That's all we need."

"How will that help?"

"This is what we do. We know they want as much gas as possible. That's why they were prepared to buy from you, yesterday. So, we hook you up again."

"So I meet them. String them along a little. What then?"

"Well, assuming you don't kill any of them, you worm your way in. Gain their trust. Make your way along the chain till you come across Tony. Then you finish things."

"All before tonight? Did they slip you some steroids, at that hospital?"

"I know. There's a lot there. But let's break it down. The first dependency is IT. If they can't find some way to get in contact, we won't have much chance."

"Given the time pressure, make that no chance."

"I guess you're right. But that's out of our hands, so let's not worry about it. Let's assume, for now anyway, that the eggheads come through. The next problem will be getting a meeting set up. We need it to be today. What do you think? Doable?"

"Maybe. Depends on where."

"Let's assume a hundred-mile radius of Chicago."

"OK. Then we could probably persuade them."

"I would think so, too. Maybe by unsettling them? Suggesting that McIntyre might not be able to deliver?"

"We could do that. Make them afraid to have all their eggs in his basket. Or offer a much lower price. Or promise to provide a regular, guaranteed future supply."

"Good. I like it. One of those should work. So we're looking pretty good. Why don't I head downstairs for a minute and prod the IT guys. It's all hanging on them, right now."

"Hold on. What about the infiltration part? How's that going to work?"

"It'll be easy. A few people from their crew had seen you, but they're all dead now, remember. So you should have no problems with being recognized."

"I'm not concerned about recognition. I'm worried about getting under their skin before tonight. Going from total stranger to inner sanctum in a couple of hours is a lot to ask."

"It would be—if it wasn't for one thing."

"What?"

"I have an idea. I've got that part all figured out."

"Hallelujah. What are you thinking?"

"Something like this. We let these guys choose whatever location they feel comfortable with. You show up, as agreed.

You make like you're itching to get down to business. Then, a couple of other guys appear. Maybe they're drunk. Maybe they're just idiots. But either way, they try to pick a fight. They pull guns, knives, whatever. Things are about to get really nasty and—boom. You step in, risking life and limb for your new friends."

"That's not an idea. That's straight from cliché central."

"There are no marks for originality, David. Only effectiveness. And this works. I've seen it half a dozen times."

"I guess it might not be a complete disaster, if it was staged just right. Where would these rent-a-goons come from?"

"Leave that to me. I have contacts. People who'd be happy to help."

"I don't care if they're happy. I care if they're good. 'Cause I don't want some Keystone Kop fiasco."

"Don't worry. They're excellent. I've used them before, a dozen times. No one will ever know they're staging it."

"So assuming you can get them in, and I pull it off. I then have to convince the buyers to let me tag along when they hook up with Tony."

"Right. But you could do that in your sleep, David. It's more or less what you suggested before, with the Commissariat. Only more elegant. Food and drink for a guy like you, surely?"

"It's next to impossible, is what it is."

"Let's be realistic. It's not going to be easy. I know that. But it's not out of the question, either. And here's the thing—have you got a better idea?"

I didn't answer.

"OK, then," he said. "Right now this is the only plan that has legs. Shall I head downstairs? Turn the screw on our technical friends? See if we can get ourselves out of the starting gate?"

"I suppose you better," I said. "I'm not thrilled with the idea. But we've got to do something. We need to get the gas back under wraps. And I want this business with McIntyre over and done with. I want to get back to some work that doesn't leave a bad taste in my mouth."

Fothergill offered to send some coffee up for me, but I declined. There was no way of knowing how long he'd be gone. I guessed the IT guys wouldn't make him all that welcome, but he also said there were loose ends to tie up from yesterday's accident. That sounded pretty vague, but the chances still were that he was going to be a while. And with the prospect of meeting another set of buyers, dealing with the fake fight and possibly having to finish things with McIntyre, the last things I needed were random strangers and office small talk. I felt like I needed some time to myself. I needed somewhere peaceful to prepare. So I took one more look around his office, found nothing of interest, and made my way back to the hotel.

I picked up some coffee of my own so I'd have something to drink as I walked. I went for cappuccino again, since I'd missed breakfast. It took five minutes to reach the counter, and the line of customers at Starbucks kept growing steadily as I waited near the wall for the barista to weave her magic. There was nothing to do but stand back and watch the people coming in. It seemed like there was an endless stream of them, and that sparked another image in my head. I thought about the people who were so desperate to buy this gas. I'd neutralized two of them at the abandoned apartment. Three at the Ritz-Carlton. Two more at the machine shop in Gary. One at the Commissariat. Fothergill had accounted for another pair. And yet more kept on appearing. I couldn't help wondering what would be next. Would the whole population of their little country end up coming after me before we were done?

This thought was still floating around in my head when I arrived at the hotel. It wasn't unusual to go up against people without knowing much about them. Sometimes it was even an advantage, despite what Sun Tzu might have said, because you weren't bogged down with preconceptions. But this time, the longer things went on, the more it felt like I was missing something. And with nothing else to fill my time, it was turning into an obsession.

I took off my boots, lay down on the bed, and tried to focus on something else. Really hard. For ten minutes. And failed. The part that was eating me up was the geography. I knew the people who wanted the gas were from Equatorial Myene, but I had no idea where that was. I'd never even heard of the place until Young mentioned it the other day. That made me wonder about what else I didn't know. Their history. Their culture. Their traditions and institutions. Whether they were seriously considering using illegal military weapons against their own population. And how a serving naval intelligence officer could come to be supplying them.

I reached for my phone and called Fothergill's number. I wanted him to see what background information was available. If Chicago was like most other places I'd been to, the consulate archive would have plenty of detailed files on more or less everywhere in the world. I lay on the bed and listened impatiently to the slow, drawn-out American ringtone. It went on for thirty seconds. Then the call tripped through to voice mail. I left him a message, but didn't give up there. I called the switchboard and asked to be put through to the analysis team, directly. That seemed like a good idea, but it didn't get me any further. The call diverted to Human Resources. The analysts were all out to lunch. Already. It wasn't even eleven o'clock yet. At first I was annoyed. But then a smile spread across my face. Analyzing data couldn't be that hard. And with hours like that, maybe I'd just found another possible future home for myself.

Fothergill had a lot on his plate that morning, so I didn't expect he'd be returning my call anytime soon. It was possible that at least one of the analysts might venture back to his desk before the day was much older, but I wasn't inclined to wait and see. The IT guys were allegedly pulling up trees in their quest to uncover some contact information. If they were successful I'd have to move pretty fast. And my itch needed to be scratched before that happened, which left me with only one option. Peace and quiet would have to take a backseat. I'd have to find out for myself. Even if it meant doing things the old-fashioned way.

I'd seen a branch of Borders at the far end of Michigan Avenue so I grabbed my coat, left the hotel, and started to walk in that direction. I needed an atlas. Then I'd at least be able to find Equatorial Myene on a map. And if I was lucky, pick up some basic data about the place. I had a memory of the Philip's School Editions from my youth being full of charts and graphs and statistics that looked impressive, even if they were absolutely irrelevant to my life at that time. Beyond that, I'd have to find an encyclopedia. I was wondering whether bookshops still sold that kind of thing or whether it had all gone online when an alternative idea presented itself. I remembered passing an Apple store on my first day in Chicago. That was also on Michigan, in the same general direction as Borders. And Apple stores are stuffed full of computers, which they leave conveniently connected to the Internet. Computers that anyone can stroll in and use.

I crossed to the other side of the street, and the alternative source for finding information led to another thought. There was another place I could make inquiries. The consulate in New York. Fothergill had been pretty disparaging about them, but before I'd left four days ago I'd built up a pretty good rapport with the staff there. And with Lucinda in particular. She'd been Tanya's assistant, and the way she'd watched my back in the days that followed the official end of my assignment had been invaluable. She'd called me on my way to the airport to thank me for what I'd done, and to give me her private cell number in case I ever needed anything. I got the impression she really meant it. And whether she did or not, I'd committed the number to memory. Just in case.

I texted Lucinda with my name, and Tanya's initials and serial number in case she was spooked by the unknown number I was using. I waited a moment, hoping she'd read it and understand what I meant. Then I cursed the handset for not letting me dial the number without keying it in all over again on another screen. I'd have to be more careful about the kind of phone I stole in the future.

Lucinda answered on the eighth ring.

"Yes?" she said.

"You don't have to keep the accent out of your voice," I said. "It's me, David."

"David? Really? Excellent. How are you? How's the Windy City?"

"So far, so good. What I've seen, I like. How's things with you?"

"Quiet, since you've been gone. I've been doing some work I can actually tell my bosses about, for a change. And I was beginning to worry about you. I've been watching the news every night. There hasn't been a single report of riots or civil commotion in all the time you've been there."

"That's because you're not here. You were a bad influence."

"David, that's not fair. You're the one who made all the mess."

"Not all of it. And I've reformed, now. I've been keeping a low profile."

"That I can't believe. But talking of profile, have you

come across a guy called Richard Fothergill? I heard he's in Chicago these days."

"I've heard the name."

"You'd know if you'd met him. He's an older guy. A real character. And a really sharp dresser, I remember."

"Where do you know him from?"

"Training. He was one of my instructors. The best thing was he used to wear a bow tie every time his class passed an assessment."

"Bizarre."

"In a way. But a much more popular incentive than what some of the guys liked to use. I felt quite lucky to be in his group."

"If you were in his group, I'd say he was the lucky one."

"David, you're too kind. Either that, or you want something."

"You think I'm only calling 'cause I want a favor? I'm hurt. And shocked. Such cynicism in one so young . . ."

"Come on. Out with it. What are you after?"

"Well, now that you mention it, there is something. If you're sure you don't mind?"

"After what you did for Tanya, you name it. Whatever you need."

"Thanks, Lucinda. I really appreciate it. But it shouldn't be too hard. I'm just looking for a little background information, if you've got five minutes. It's a little delicate, though, so best kept to yourself."

"No problem. I can research whatever I like. No one's going to ask any questions."

"They might, with this one. There's a decent chance that what I'm working on won't have a happy ending. So I wouldn't leave anything that could point back to you, just in case."

"OK. I'll be discreet. Just tell me what you need, and when."

"All right. Two things. First, as much background as you can get on a country I'm interested in. The Republic of Equatorial Myene."

"Never heard of the place. But I'll get what I can. What else?"

"Something more scientific. And it might be harder to find. I need the lowdown on a chemical agent. It's some kind of prototype. Officially it doesn't exist, but you know what that means. Its code name is Spektra."

"I've never heard of that, either. Give me a little while to get to grips with it, and I'll call you right back."

"Thanks, Lucinda. And I don't mean to hassle you, but as soon as you can would be good."

I kept on going down Michigan, weaving my way through the knots of shoppers and businesspeople who were constantly meandering along the sidewalk. It seemed like none of them had any purpose in being outside, from the aimless way they were moving. And it seemed like every kind and age of person was there, doing their best to get in my way. Except for kids. I couldn't see many of them. Not counting the ones in strollers, anyway. I guessed the older ones must be in school. Or if they were playing truant, they must have found somewhere more interesting to hang out. I was still wondering what kind of place that would be, and thinking back to the haunts I used to disappear into, when I reached the entrance to the Apple store. But I didn't go in right away. Because I realized my phone was ringing again, already.

"Ready for the first installment?" Lucinda said, when I got around to answering.

"That was quick," I said.

"It was easy. All you needed to do was google the name of the country. Or look it up in an atlas."

"Why use books or computers when I could ask you?"

"Cheeky bastard. I don't get paid to—oh, wait. I don't get paid for this at all. I'm on my lunch break."

"I'm sorry, Lucinda. And seriously, I was on my way to do those exact things when I called you. I just don't know how much time I have."

"The consulate in Chicago doesn't have computers?"

"It does. But there are reasons why I don't want to use them."

"OK. Sorry, David. So, are you ready?"

"I am. Fire away."

"Grab your pencil. Here we go. The Republic of Equatorial Myene. Well, what can I say about the place. It's a small, landlocked country in West Africa. Population, five hundred thousand. Allegedly democratic. Relatively stable. As in, they haven't had a coup since 1979. That's when the nephew of the existing president decided he could do a better job than his uncle."

"Have they got elections coming up soon? Or are there any more nephews waiting in the wings?"

"Elections, apparently. They're due within a year, unless the government suspends them again. And there are always nephews."

"Do you know anything out about the opposition? Do they have much of a chance?"

"Ha. I wouldn't hold out much hope, if that's where your sympathies lie."

"No?"

"Put it this way: do you know what the population was in 1979, when the current guy took office?"

"How many?"

"Closer to seven hundred and fifty thousand. Which means it's fallen by a third in thirty years. And there've been no famines to account for it. No natural disasters. No mass emigration. The people have just disappeared."

I took a moment to think about the implications of the statistics. I didn't like where that was leading, but it did seem to tally with the picture that Young had painted.

"And there's more, if that's what you're interested in," she said. "This isn't on Wikipedia, obviously, but I checked our own internal files, too. It seems the rate of decline has increased recently. Say in the last four years or so."

"How steeply?"

"I can't put an exact figure on it. We've only got what the aid agencies tell us, informally, and that's not always consistent. But the best guess would be an initial fall of maybe six to eight thousand a year. That held fairly steady for the first twenty-six years of the regime. Since then it's gone through the roof. The current rate's possibly as high as fifteen thousand. And if you think of that as a percentage, it's even worse, 'cause the base population is shrinking all the time."

"That's a lot of people to misplace. Why's it accelerating so much?"

"I don't know for sure. But the file says there's one candidate that's head and shoulders above the rest."

"Who is it?"

"Not who. What. Something called dysprosium."

"What's that?"

"It's some kind of mineral. Very rare. Or rather, you get it from a mineral. One called xenotime. It's only been available from one other place, so far. China. So naturally everybody wants to get their hands on it."

"What's it used for?"

"Manufacturing. It's a component in nuclear reactor control rods. But the real action is hybrid car batteries. You can't make them without it. But whatever, loads of corporations are busting their guts for it. The rival car makers. The gas companies. Engine component developers. And the upshot is that money is literally gushing into the place."

"So if the place is getting richer, why are the people suffering so much more?"

"Because none of the money is reaching them. The ruling elite—maybe two or three hundred—are siphoning it all off. Nothing filters down to the bottom of the heap. And that's fueling the discontent. Leading more and more people to find their voices."

"Leading to more and more being killed."

"Exactly. Things are escalating, by all accounts. It was bad enough when only power was on the line. Now it's power and money. And not just ordinary money, either. Out-of-this-world riches. Which is a powerful motivator."

"It is. And that's really helpful. You've joined a lot of dots, there, Lucinda. Any news on the other thing? The gas?"

"Not yet. No sign, so far. If there is anything, it must be buried pretty deep."

"It will be. That's the nature of the thing. Are you OK to keep looking?"

"I can give it a bit longer. No one pays too much attention to what I'm doing, anymore. That might change when Tanya's replacement gets here, though."

Lucinda's words set me back for moment. The idea of massacring thousands of civilians was hard enough to understand. But replacing Tanya? Impossible. For me, anyway.

"Call me when you find something?" I said, pushing those thoughts away.

"Of course," she said. "No point in doing the work, otherwise."

"Good point. I'll keep my phone switched on . . ."

Under normal circumstances I'd have turned and walked straight into the store, found a vacant computer, and looked for some softer material to flesh out the information Lucinda had given me. Photos. Video. News reports. Diary entries. Blogs. Anything to add a human element to the facts and statistics she'd just dug up. But it was precisely the human element that stopped me, this time. In my world, you get used to a degree of constant, ongoing tension. When you're working a regular case, there's no way to avoid it. Every conversation, every interaction, every time you walk into a room or pick up the phone you're risking exposure. And if that happens, the chances are you've reached the end of your particular road. But at least it's a road you've chosen. You've been trained to spot the pitfalls along the way. And there are people, albeit at arm's length, ready to try to help you if the sky does fall in. It can be stressful enough, at times. So I could only imagine what life was like for the ordinary villagers in Equatorial Myene. They hadn't signed up for any such thing. But due to no better reason than someone else's greed, they had to live every minute of every day in fear of a knock at their door. With the constant, gnawing knowledge that they could be taken away at the drop of a hat. Or that their friends could be. Or their families. People were vanishing faster all the time. The bastards who were responsible seemed to be gearing up for even more killing, with this Spektra gas. And it was McIntyre who'd put it in their hands.

All of a sudden I wasn't feeling so bad about the hard arrest being ordered. Or that I was the one who'd get to carry it out.

*

I did go into the store, in the end. I saw a crowd of people checking their e-mail and tweeting and updating their Facebook pages, but there was still no shortage of available computers. I set up on one at the end of the left-hand table, near the door, but with the screen facing the wall rather than into the room. The Internet connection was fast, the first set of keywords I used hit their marks, and I had no trouble finding useful material. There were plenty of good Web sites. They yielded lots of intriguing detail. But none of it made me feel any better about what was happening. I spent a good half hour intensively browsing, thinking less and less favorable thoughts about McIntyre and his buddies from Equatorial Myene, and was just about ready to leave when Lucinda called back.

"You were right," she said. "There was something about the gas. As in, one thing."

"Only one?" I said.

"Only one that I could find. I used every tool we have, and searched every source we know about. And that's all I could turn up."

"OK. Well, one's better than none. What can you tell me?"

"That I won't be sleeping well tonight. Probably not all week. I hope you're not anywhere near this stuff, David. It's not very nice."

"I didn't think it would be. How bad are we talking?"

"Pretty bad."

"Can you describe it? I need to know what I'm dealing with here."

"Oh, you're going to absolutely know in a minute. The resource I found includes a video clip. Have you got an e-mail address? A private one, I mean. One that the service knows nothing about."

"I do—hclpqz63819@yahoo.co.uk."

"Wow. Nobody's going to stumble across that one by mistake. OK. I'm going to send the link to you. You won't recognize my address, either, and you won't be able to reply. It's a throwaway."

"No problem. I'll go back inside and log on."

"Wait. Inside where?"

"The Apple store. I'm right outside. I was just using one of their machines."

"David, no. You haven't been listening. You cannot—cannot—view this anywhere that a civilian could catch even a glimpse. Absolutely not."

"OK. I'll head back to the consulate. Like you said, they have computers."

"No. You can't do that, either. You shouldn't be going anywhere near this Web site. It's on a classified server we're not even supposed to know about. Service computers are way too easy to trace. The cyberfuzz would be all over you before you got halfway through."

"Where can I view it from, then?"

"Didn't you bring a laptop of your own?"

"No. I don't own one."

"Oh. Really? Then I don't know what to say."

"How about, maybe it's time I put that right? I'll go inside and buy one. Then take it to my hotel."

"OK. That would work. As long as you don't have anyone stashed away, in there."

I didn't reply.

"Oh," she said. "I'm sorry. I didn't mean that. It was really insensitive of me."

I took another moment.

"Going and buying a laptop is a great idea, by the way," she said. "And I like the direct approach. Another reason why it's always a pleasure."

"The pleasure was all mine," I said. "And thanks for your help, Lucinda. If it wasn't for a couple of little details, I'd commend you to your boss."

"Like, what I just said? I feel horrible about that."

"Like, if he knew what you were helping me with, you'd get fired. Probably arrested. Possibly deported."

"Oh. Yes. Any one of those would suck."

"So how does lunch sound, instead, next time our paths cross?"

"It sounds like the proverbial tomorrow. You don't have to make any empty promises. I was happy to be of assistance."

"You're a princess."

"Thanks. I am. And actually, if there's any way lunch could ever work out, that would be lovely. If I've recovered from watching that damn video by then."

SIXTEEN

I read an article recently about job-related stress. Funnily enough, though, my job wasn't covered.

I looked at all the factors that were listed and tried to relate them to the times I'd been sent to offices and factories and call centers and other, more mainstream places to work. I found I could relate to quite a few of the issues, from what I'd seen in other people. But what surprised me most was that despite the lack of knives and bullets and explosive devices, there were several areas that corresponded pretty closely with how I felt. In particular, the impact of seeing a tangible result of your labors.

Jobs where I investigated and found there to be no verifiable threat were by definition good for the service, but boring for me.

Where I found a threat and neutralized it, that was bad for the service and satisfying for me.

And where there was a threat that remained unresolved, that was the worst of both worlds.

*

It doesn't show up in my service record anywhere, but a while ago I was given a job in Ulaanbaatar. It's in Mongolia. I was there for a week, and the place I stayed in couldn't really call itself a hotel. The most it could honestly claim to be was a hostel. It cost six dollars a night. And it had free wireless Internet. So you can imagine how irritated I was when I got back to my expensive room that afternoon in the center of Chicago. Unpacked my shiny new aluminium-bodied MacBook Pro. Fired up the browser. Typed in my Web mail details. And got redirected to a screen that demanded twenty-five dollars for a day's Wi Fi access.

When I'd parted with the cash, I found I'd received three new e-mails that day. One for cheap Viagra. One for cheap copies of expensive watches. And one with no subject. It was from someone called koala32. I guessed that would be Lucinda. I opened it. A URL had been pasted in, but nothing had been written. I crossed my fingers and followed the link. The Web page it led to took a long time to open. And when something did appear on the screen, it wasn't very helpful:

Error 404: page not found.

I closed the browser and tried again. The screen was just as slow to react. I sat and watched as nothing happened, until eventually it returned the same error message. This wasn't the result I wanted. Fothergill's people could break something loose at any moment. It's as if computers know when you're short of time, and deliberately move at a snail's pace to show you who's boss. I didn't have time to mess around so I picked up my phone. I was going to call Lucinda and ask her to check the details she'd sent when I remembered something I'd seen once in a similar situation. A trick someone had used at a logistics firm I'd been sent to infiltrate in the Czech Republic. I moved the cursor to the top left of the screen. Clicked. And dragged it down to the bottom right. The blank space turned blue. And within it, in the center, three words appeared:

File 1
File 2
CCTV

The error message must have been a fake. Just text on the page, not a real status report generated by the system. The server must have opened the page slowly on purpose to simulate a routing problem. And the file names were displayed in a white font on a white background, making them seem invisible. I was impressed. But I didn't waste any time admiring anyone's ingenuity. I just clicked on File 1.

The link opened a text file, but there weren't any words involved. It was only being used as a vehicle to display photographs. There were two. They were both large, high-resolution color shots. The subjects were similar. Both showed the inside of large rooms. The first was some kind of auditorium, like a theater or cinema. It was full of curving rows of fixed red velvet seats. The photographer must have been standing near the stage or screen, looking back at the audience. There were maybe a hundred and fifty people in the shot, out of a capacity of probably two thousand. But they weren't evenly distributed throughout the space. At least eighty percent of them were concentrated in four main groups, at both sides, near the walls. The remainder were spread out among the other seats, but with fewer and fewer remaining toward the center. The people were lying back, slumped listlessly in their places. I guess there was a chance they were asleep. In theory, at least. But my money said they were all dead.

The background in the second picture was far less luxurious. The floor was plain, scuffed wood. The walls were a dirty, blotchy version of white. The chairs were the interlinked, removable kind. They were arranged in straighter rows, and looked hard and uncomfortable. But they held a similar share of bodies. Again, I'd say well over a hundred. The people were sprawled out in the same way, as if they'd all suddenly fallen asleep. But this time, they were spaced out pretty evenly throughout the room. I couldn't see any distinct groupings anywhere, front to back or side to side. So either the occupants had been distributed differently from the outset, or whatever had gone to work on them had done a more thorough job.

File 2 turned out to be a spreadsheet, but again it wasn't being used in the normal way. There were two worksheets—labeled IV and V—and neither contained any numbers. Someone had drawn black outlines around large blocks of cells, and then colored them in to form a kind of pattern or diagram. Some were filled in with red. Some with green. And the rest, yellow. The only marking on either sheet was a lowercase *x* in a few of the cells. There were four on each side of the first sheet, and three on each side of the second.

The red cells were predominantly bunched up in groups near the edges of the first worksheet. The pattern looked familiar. I thought about it, and realized it reminded me of how the bodies had been arranged in the first picture. I opened the text file again to check, and saw there was a definite correlation. It was as if someone had used the spreadsheet to re-create a kind of bird's-eye view of the room. Red clearly represented the seats where people had died. I guessed green meant that the people in those ones had survived. Yellow was less obvious. Maybe the people had died later. Or perhaps those seats had been vacant. I was still mulling over the options when another thought struck me. There were hardly any green cells at all in the second sheet. If I was right, that meant nearly the entire population of the second room had been killed. Which left just one element to identify. The *x*'s. And when I went back to the photo, it was obvious what they were, too. Air vents. Large ones, set into the walls. I was looking at a record of the carnage caused by something airborne. It had to be Spektra. The gas that McIntyre was selling to the Myenese.

I clicked on the final link, and for a moment I thought nothing was going to happen. Then a separate window opened. A video viewer appeared and automatically began playing. I hit the FULL SCREEN button and realized I was looking at the inside of a large inflatable structure, like a blow-up marquee. Or part of one, at least. I could see a long expanse of bulging horizontal panels, like giant cigars. They were bright, shiny white. The part of the wall in the shot was at least fifty feet wide, but the frame wasn't big enough to see either end. There was no sign of any doors, either. Just windows. There were five, evenly spread out. They were flat, but so thick they were barely transparent. I could just about make out rough cinder-block walls on the far side, interspersed with heavy iron girders. If I was pushed, I'd say it looked like the tent had been built on the inside of an abandoned factory or warehouse.

A row of chairs ran parallel to the wall, facing away from the windows. I counted twenty. They were arranged in one single, unbroken line. The seats and backs were covered with rough, khaki canvas that was stretched over simple tubular frames. The chair legs disappeared into a continuous concrete plinth, twelve inches high and three feet deep. I guessed that was to anchor the chairs firmly in place. No one would be able to knock them down, now, or tip them over. Assuming that anyone sitting in them was able to move. Higher up the sides I could see where straps had been attached. There were three on each chair. One at shoulder height. One at waist level. And one that would wrap around the thighs. They were made of black webbing, and had silver buckles at the ends like the seat belts on passenger planes. Once they were fastened up tight, with your arms pinned to your sides, there'd be no getting them off. Not on your own.

The line of chairs was bookended by a pair of square wooden frames. They were held up with scaffolding and filled with narrow parallel louvers, which were angled toward the ground. An electric fan stood behind each one. They were large, industrial models like they use on movie sets, mounted on battered mobile stands. And in between each fan and frame, I could see a tripod. Each tripod had a metal cylinder clamped to it. The size and shape of the cylinders was familiar. They were just like the one I'd found in the machine shop in Gary. The color was the same, too. Matte green. But at the top, things looked different. The normal clamped-down lids had been replaced with black spheres, about four inches across. They were peppered with tiny holes. And a thin radio aerial snaked out from the top of each one.

The kind of aerial you use to trigger remote explosive devices.

I was studying the base of the closest cylinder, checking for telltale yellow markings, when the screen went blank. Nothing happened for five seconds. Then a caption appeared:

Live subject exposure test #2
Variant A
Spektra IV (no BMU8)

A bar at the bottom showed the date, which was almost eighteen months ago. There was a clock, which was showing just after 6:00 A.M. And there was another figure for elapsed time. This seemed to be frozen on one second, but as I watched it jumped forward to ten minutes and then kept running. The black screen bled away, and the interior of the tent became visible again. Everything looked the same, except that now the line of chairs was no longer unoccupied. A person was sitting in each one. There were men. Women. Boys. Girls. Toddlers. Geriatrics. Some looked strong and healthy. Others were frail and feeble. At least one of the women was pregnant. All the people were different in some way, like some kind of carefully constructed social cross-section. But they also had one thing in common. They were all strapped down.

There was no sound to go with the picture, which I was extremely glad about. You could see people's mouths opening and shutting as they yelled and screamed. Some fought and struggled against the straps, heaving and pulling and wrenching with all their might. Others sat quietly, almost serenely, waiting for their fate. I scanned along the line and saw a pool of liquid appear under one woman's chair, near the center. It grew steadily then flowed off the concrete platform and splashed onto the ground, twelve inches below. But no one around her cared. In fact, no one even noticed. Everyone's attention was taken by a sudden movement at both sides of the room. The giant fans had sprung into life. Their curved blades started slowly, then spun faster and faster until you could only just make out a gray blur behind the protective wire mesh covers. And it may not have been visible to the people in the room, but thanks to the camera I could see another thing that had changed. Something at the top of the cylinders. As soon as the fans had reached full speed, a tiny red LED light on each one flashed three times. And after the final time, they remained illuminated.

Most of the eyes in the room remained locked on the fans, but a few people started to glance at their neighbors. Fear and helplessness were etched clearly into their faces. A couple of them started to struggle again. Then the person third from the left—a boy, maybe fourteen or fifteen years old—was suddenly thrown back in his seat. His legs straightened out like staves and his neck bent so far back that his head seemed to disappear. All I could see was the underside of his chin. He hung there for a moment, rigid and still. Then his body began to shake. He was twitching so fast and so hard you'd think he had hundreds of volts running through him. The movements were so violent you wouldn't have been surprised if one of his legs, or even his head, had been torn clean off his body. The fit lasted maybe thirty seconds without any sign of letting up, then stopped as suddenly as it had started. It was as if someone had thrown a switch and the kid was freed to slump back down, torso sagging, legs slack, head lolling to the side.

It was impossible to know this for sure, but I imagined the inside of the tent was completely silent. The nineteen survivors were all fixated on the dead boy. The people nearest him were trying to look away. And failing. The ones at the far end were craning their necks and stretching for a better view. All their faces were pale and shocked. No one was unmoved by what had just played out. Things seemed tense, but a few notches down from hysterical. They stayed that way for maybe a minute. Then the woman at the end on the right jerked back in her seat. The same thing happened to the next two people in line—a man, and a girl who looked less than ten years old. They started thrashing at virtually the same moment, and before they collapsed another nine people had succumbed to the same fate. The computer screen was a mass of uncontrollable movement. It was such a frenzy my eyes could hardly make out what was happening. But within a minute, the outcome was clear. Thirteen people were dead.

Everybody had died except for the three to the left of the central point, and the four to the right. And while I knew they were alive—I could see their rib cages move as they breathed—I couldn't say they were unaffected. As the people nearer the edges were in the midst of their final agonies, I'd noticed the ones in the middle were starting to sag. Their legs had grown limp, their eyes had closed, and their chins had rolled down onto their chests. I expected that someone would come to release them, or treat them, or at least find out what state they were in. But nothing happened. The scene was static for another two minutes. Then I noticed the LEDs on the cylinders were no longer glowing red. The fans slowly wound back down until their blades were stationary again. And just as the last one stopped spinning, the screen faded softly to black. It was inert for ten seconds, this time. Then another caption appeared. It looked for all the world like the next installment in a series:

Live subject exposure test #4

Variant A

Spektra V (inc BMU8)

The information bar at the bottom showed that a day had passed since the video sequence I'd just watched. The clock said we were back to six o'clock in the morning. The elapsed time had reset to one second. I kept an eye on it, and once again it sprang forward to the ten-minute mark. The black background dissolved. And I saw that another group had been brought into the tent. The mix of age and gender and condition was similar to the first sample. The range of reactions was equally broad. And the people were strapped to the chairs in exactly the same way.

The fans began to turn. The LEDs on top of the cylinders flashed red, then stayed lit up. And the people began to drop. They jolted back, convulsed, and collapsed like they were in some kind of macabre ballet. I watched them suffer through the same cycle of agony as the victims from the first group. Only this time, there was a difference. Every single person died. It took less than four minutes, and there wasn't a single man, woman, or child in that tent with a breath left in their body. Not one out of the twenty there'd been to start with.

I closed the computer and waited for my stomach to untie itself. I knew there'd been no way to stop any of what I'd seen. In fact, there wasn't really anything to have stopped. It was only a recording. The actual events had occurred eighteen months ago. They'd unfolded in some unknown location. It may not have been on the same continent as me, let alone a place I could have reached in time. And I had no idea who was responsible for it.

All of that was true. But none of it was any consolation. So I reached for my phone and called Lucinda.

"Have you watched it?" she said.

I didn't answer.

"I thought so," she said. "Pretty sick-making stuff, wasn't it?"

"Where did it come from?" I said.

"The Spektra gas? You know where. You saw the emblem on the cylinder. And you know I can't name the place over the phone. Just in case."

"No. I mean the video. Who made it? Who did those—what did they call them—exposure tests?"

"I don't know."

"How did they get the gas? Was it sanctioned?"

"I don't know."

"Is this some kind of arm's-length bullshit? Did the government want the data without getting its hands dirty?"

"David, I just don't know. But I can't believe they'd do that."

"No. They just happened to be hiding a secret video of someone else doing it. That's bound to be a coincidence."

Lucinda didn't answer.

"So either the government colluded with the experiments, or they lost the asset," I said. "Either way, it stinks."

"To high heaven," said Lucinda. "Put like that."

"So what else do we know? Where was the video made? Can we identify the location?"

"I don't think so. There's no audio, so we can't do a language or dialect analysis. And I doubt you can gather enough detail through the windows for a database match. Or even a manual comparison."

"What else can we do? What about the background files from the Web site? Is there anything in those we can work with?"

"No. Everything's been stripped out. They're content only. But I have found out a couple of other things since we spoke."

"You're an angel. Tell me."

"OK. Well, first, did you notice that the video said the difference between the two clips was something called BMU8? The first time the gas had it, the second time it didn't?"

"It was the other way around. That seemed to be the difference between Spektra IV and V. Whether it had this BM stuff."

"Oh. Right. The other way around. But do you know what BMU8 is?"

"No. Never heard of it."

"Nor had I. So I checked. Turns out it's something quite simple. A stimulant. It aids breathing."

"So why's it added to the Spektra gas?"

"I've just been reading about it. Turns out it's a technique they borrowed from the knockout gases that SWAT teams use. When they first tried them, it nearly always went wrong. If they pumped in enough gas to take down any hostage takers, for example, who were usually young and fit, it would kill any hostages who were old or ill or vulnerable. So, they added the stimulant to cut down on collateral damage."

"But with a poison gas, you want as many fatalities as possible, surely?"

"You do. But with poisons, you've got the opposite problem. If a person doesn't breathe in enough gas to kill them straight away, they might just go unconscious or end up restricting their airway or something. That reduces the volume of poison they ingest, and increases their chance of being resuscitated. Adding the stimulant increases the chance of instant death, and makes a higher yield achievable from a lower initial concentration."

"So you're saying it makes the gas more lethal?"

"Yes. Paradoxical, isn't it?"

I didn't have an answer to that.

"Oh, wait," Lucinda said. "Actually, no. I'm not saying it's more lethal. Something's either lethal, or it's not. You can't have degrees of lethal, obviously. What I'm saying is, it's more practical. It can be deployed more easily. Either by inexpert personnel, or against targets with more diverse levels of fitness."

"Such as civilians?" I said. "By them, and against them?"

"Exactly. Which brings me to my next point. That country you asked about. The Republic of Equatorial Myene. I put the word out on the grapevine for information. And something interesting has come back already. Word is, a coup is on the cards."

"It's in Africa, Lucinda. Of course a coup's on the cards. There've been two hundred since 1960, alone. Attempts, anyway. It's a standard political tool, in some places I've been to."

"I understand that. But this is a serious one, apparently. I'm hearing that the rebels have some major-league backing. Money. Weapons. Mercenaries, ready to help them fight."

"Are you sure? Most coup attempts turn out to be all talk and no trousers."

"I'm hearing that it is, David. And it would explain the government being so keen on acquiring Spektra gas. Imagine whole villages being wiped out by one guy in a jeep. It would take a single cylinder. That would be quite an incentive to stay loyal to the regime."

"One cylinder? Wouldn't most of the gas just blow away?"

"No. Not if they have the right kind. On the videos, did you see the captions saying 'Variant A'? That signifies the indoor version. It's a fraction of the concentration. And the external type will be loaded with additives to make it more dense. Keep it close to the ground."

I didn't reply.

"I know what I'm talking about, David," she said. "I was in the Balkans before New York, and we were all trained on this stuff."

"Don't worry," I said. "I believe you. I was just thinking, coup attempt or not, we need to keep the Myenese and the gas apart. On separate sides of the ocean, preferably. And on that, there's something else I need to check. Call me if anything else breaks?"

"I will. But I might have to increase my price to two lunches."

*

The more I thought about the video, the less I liked the idea of the Myenese getting their hands on the cylinders of Spektra gas. Or of McIntyre continuing to be on the loose. The only link we had to either was the consulate's IT guys, but I couldn't put in a direct call to them. Hassling them would only slow things down. But at the same time, I was impatient for news. That just left me with Fothergill. I guessed he was busy, since he hadn't returned my call from earlier. I was a little annoyed about that. I was still mulling it over, and wondering if he was worth another try, when his number appeared on my phone.

"Richard," I said. "I was just thinking about you. Any sign of a rabbit?"

"Perhaps," he said. "A bunny, maybe. A chink of light at the mouth of the burrow, at least. The Tefal-heads have found something. We think we know how Tony was communicating with his contacts."

"Have you got a number? Let me have it. I'll try to get hold of them right away."

"No. It's more sophisticated than that. It seems they were swapping messages via an Internet dating service."

"Online dating? Are you sure he wasn't just lonely?"

"Positive. This came from the other guys' computer, remember. It was hard to spot. The messages were coded, but they'd kept enough of them for our boys to break their system."

"Are they sure? Can we use it?"

"They think so. We've just planted our first seed. We're waiting for a response, now."

"I'll keep my fingers crossed, then."

"I'm keeping everything crossed. And I'll keep you posted. I just wanted you to know where we were up to. Things could break in a hurry, so keep your boots on and stay by the phone. I'll be in touch."

SEVENTEEN

Scratch the surface of a corporation, and you might be surprised what lies beneath.

Even organizations that appear similar on the outside can have dramatically different cultures. That makes infiltrating them all the more interesting. But also more difficult. The last thing you want to do is stand out, and it's the little behavioral quirks that can so easily trip you up. Birds of a feather flock together, so you have to gauge very quickly how competitive your new colleagues are likely to be. Or how secretive. How helpful. Or in one place I went—a semiconductor manufacturer—how nice.

It's not quite true to say that everyone at that company was nice, actually. The majority was. But one person definitely was not. One of the secretaries. She wasn't to me, anyway. She went out of her way to make my life miserable. So when it was revealed that she had some horrible disease, I had mixed feelings. I wouldn't have wished it on her. If there was anything I could have done to make her better, I would have. But I wasn't about to shed any tears, either. So I had to be careful about that. It could have driven a wedge between me and the others in the office. And I found that annoying.

A horrible person who's sick is still a horrible person.

Just like an evil person who's no longer inconvenient is still evil.

Having a computer that wasn't bursting with navy spyware was a novelty for me. It had the potential to be a real luxury, especially with all this time to kill. I could use it to watch movies. Play games. Contact people I'd fallen out of touch with. Do all the things on the Internet that civilians take for granted. There were endless possibilities, but the memory of watching the Spektra gas tests had killed my appetite for all of them. Stone dead. I was tempted to just close the machine down and wait for the phone to ring, but I forced myself to check another couple of Web sites instead. I looked for more information about the Myenese, but nothing new or significant came to light. Then I moved on to dysprosium. The miracle mineral. It may have been rare, and it may have generated untold wealth, but it didn't make for interesting reading. It didn't fill me with enthusiasm. And that meant I was only half way through the first article I'd found when Fothergill called me back.

"Good news," he said. "Time to move. Got a pen and paper?"

"I don't need one," I said. "Go ahead."

"OK. They took the bait. The meeting is on. Two o'clock at a hotel called the Drake. It's a little farther up Michigan than the Ritz-Carlton, where we were the other day. They have several bars, but you need to find one called the Coq d'Or. It'll appear closed when you get there, but the left-hand door will be unlocked. You should have no trouble getting in. You won't even have to break anything."

"McIntyre's contacts will meet me there?"

"They will."

"Good. How many will there be?"

"I don't know. They didn't say. And I couldn't really push them. It would look too hokey."

"Agreed. And it's not a problem. Just a nice-to-know."

"I understand. The IT guys are still digging, so if they come up with anything that could throw any light, I'll get straight back to you."

"Thanks. So that just leaves our unwelcome guests. Where are we up to with them?"

"All done. They're lined up and waiting. I just need to call them with the green light as soon as we're finished. I'm really happy, actually. I managed to get the best two under-the-counter operators in Chicago. They're going to do an excellent job. I know it."

"They better. There's a lot hanging on this. What's the setup?"

"Nothing fancy. I believe in keeping it simple with deals like this. Both guys will be wearing White Sox gear. They'll stagger into the bar, pretending to be drunk and belligerent. Then they'll act like they recognize the Myenese as opposing fans from some recent game and come over all nasty. And that's where you step in."

"Do you think that will work? Do they have baseball hooliganism here? This isn't England, you know."

"I'm sure they do. Sports are sports. And anyway, who cares? The Myenese aren't going to know the difference. And they only have to buy it for about ten seconds before you ride in and save the day."

I still wasn't convinced.

"It'll work," he said. "Trust me. And besides, have you got a better idea?"

I didn't reply.

"OK. I'll text you when I've spoken to them. In the meantime, any questions, call me."

The conversation with Fothergill had blunted my interest in research, so I closed the computer and put on my coat. The rendezvous point was within walking distance if I left in enough time. The need to set off wasn't urgent yet, but it never hurts to get to a place first. Especially when the people you're meeting have a habit of carrying knives and guns.

Fothergill's text arrived when I was halfway across the hotel lobby. It confirmed we were all set for two o'clock. That was all I needed to know, so I didn't expect to hear from him again until after the setup had either succeeded or failed. But in the event, he did call me. Just as I was passing the Wrigley Building.

"Got any sandwiches up there?" I said.

"Why would I have sandwiches?" he said. "Up where? What are you talking about?"

"I'm right outside the office. I thought you'd maybe seen me out of the window and were going to invite me upstairs for a snack. Save me having to stop and buy something on the way to this Drake place."

"Oh. I see. No. No food. And I'm not in my office. I'm with the IT boys. We've got some news. It's hot off the press. We haven't even had the chance to think through what it means, yet. But I thought you should hear about it straightaway. Before you reach the Drake."

"OK. That sounds serious. What's up?"

"Well, remember how we figured that Tony was communicating through a dating service?"

"Right. That's how you set up the meeting I'm heading for right now."

"Exactly. So, we found that out via historical information on the Myenese guys' computer. Now what we've done is work back the other way. We've managed to track down Tony's live dating account. And we've found it's become active again."

"I guess it would have. How else would he have set up his own rendezvous with them, later? The one I'm supposed to crash?"

"That's logical. But it's only part of the story."

"So can we find out when McIntyre's meeting them? And where? 'Cause then we could cut out this whole charade at the Drake. Avoid the chance it all blows up in our face. Sidestep that, and go straight for the throat."

"I don't think so. And this is where things get a little strange. What we've found out is, Tony's been using a new set of addresses. And his messages seem to be using a completely new version of the code."

"So he's suspicious? He's picked up that his meeting tonight's been blown?"

"No. I don't think that's it at all. The code changed before we even started looking. We think it means that he's in touch with someone new. He's ditched the Myenese, and he's selling to someone else."

"OK. That could be. Remember how he texted me something about meeting friends? On the pretense of hooking back up with Young? When he was setting up to ambush you? We took that to mean the Myenese. That must have been a red herring."

"Right. And it nearly worked. But the question is, what next? How do you think we should play this? Your meeting with the Myenese is probably irrelevant in the circumstances."

"It may be. Figuring out when and where McIntyre's seeing these new buyers has to be top of the list, now. And that's down to the code they're using. How do the IT guys feel about it? Have they got enough to work with?"

"They think so. It might take a little while to break it, though. They're on it as we speak."

"Have they got any idea how long?"

"All they can go on is the last one, that led to us contacting the Myenese. Based on that experience, they reckon four hours, minimum."

"Four hours. Is there any way they could go any faster?"

"No. I'm here with them, and I can tell you they're pulling out all the stops."

"That's fine. I have every faith. I just wanted to know how much time I have to play with."

"I'll let you know as soon as we have anything. You'll be at your hotel?"

"I might be back by then. Depends how it goes."

"How what goes? Where?"

"This thing at the Drake."

"But that's irrelevant now. Tony's not selling to the Myenese. He's not seeing them later. You don't need to infiltrate, anymore."

"He may not be selling to them. But doesn't make them irrelevant."

"For today, it does."

"Child killers are never irrelevant. They may not be getting any gas today, but it won't stop them looking elsewhere. Or trying to use it when they do get their hands on some."

"So what are you going to do, when you see them?"

"Persuade them to change their plans. Think of it as my public service for the day."

"How will you do that?"

"Some things, you're better off not asking about. And it might be an idea to cancel your White Sox guys, as well. We may not want people seeing what happens. Or talking about it, afterward."

The farther north I walked on Michigan Avenue, the stronger the wind became until by the time I turned into Walton Place the flags on the angled poles above the

Drake's entrance canopy were blowing out sideways like solid boards. Three uniformed doormen stood in a huddle near the valet stand, clearly hoping I was going to walk past the hotel and not bother them. The youngest of the group finally peeled away and approached me when it became obvious that a trip to the far end of the street was not a part of my immediate plans. He held the door for me, and looked longingly toward the warmth of the foyer as I went inside.

The reception area was a festival of red and gold and crystal and flowers. It made me wish I'd brought my sunglasses as I made my way up a short flight of stairs and looked around, taking my bearings. I saw seven people in line at the check-in desk, away to the right. Twelve people waiting for the elevators, straight ahead. Double doors leading to one of the bars to the left. And next to them, I spotted a sign for the Coq d'Or. It was pointing to the entrance to another corridor, tucked away in the corner, dark, and uninviting.

Progress at the check-in counter seemed very sedate, so I joined the end of the line and focused on the opposite corner of the foyer. It took twelve minutes to get within two places of being served, and in that time no one entered or left the far corridor. When the person in front of me stepped forward I peeled away and headed for the elevators. That bought me another five minutes of observation. Still I saw no one, so I decided it was finally time for a closer look.

There were no lights in the narrow corridor so I took

two steps—just far enough to be out of sight of anyone watching from the foyer—and pressed back against the wall until my eyes had adjusted to the meager glow from the emergency signs. When I could see again I moved forward and found myself at the top of a flight of stairs. I made my way down and followed the next corridor around to the left, which I figured brought me back underneath the main foyer area.

The corridor continued into the distance, eventually disappearing into the gloom, but I had no reason to follow it any farther. The wall to my left gave way to a row of double doors. There were eight. They were made of wood at the bottom, and frosted glass at the top. A gilded, fowl-shaped motif stretched the entire length, and interlaced within its long exaggerated feathers I could make out the words COQ D'OR—CHICAGO'S FINEST.

I moved to the side, took out my Beretta, crouched down, and tried the first door. Fothergill was right. It opened easily. I swung it back around forty-five degrees and paused. There was no response from the other side. I waited another minute. The inside of the room was even darker than the corridor, which put me at a disadvantage. I listened carefully, straining for the sound of breathing or movement or the rustle of clothing. There was only silence, so I dived through the gap and rolled away to the right.

"Hello?" I said.

There was no response.

"Anyone there?" I said.

No response.

"Get your coat," I said. "You've scored. Whoever said online dating doesn't work?"

There was still no answer, so I took out my phone. I placed it on the ground as far to my left as I could reach, pressed a key so that the screen lit up, and snatched my hand away again as quickly as I could move it. The little square was surprisingly bright in the surrounding darkness, but it drew no reaction. The light faded to nothing after thirty seconds, but I didn't move for another five minutes. I remained still, crouching in the dark, listening intently. Again, I came up empty. As far as I could make out, I was alone in the room. So, cautiously, I picked up the phone, reactivated the screen to serve as a flashlight, and began to explore.

A brass panel with twelve old-fashioned switches was mounted on the wall to the right of the open door. At random, I picked the one in the center of the bottom row. I flicked it up. The room filled with light. It came from behind my left shoulder. And lasted less than one second. That brief moment was all the time I had to absorb an impression of the interior of the room. I remember seeing a bar, running the whole length of the back wall. A mass of round tables—maybe forty of them—pushed together at the far end. A sea of chairs in the space to their left. An expanse of empty, floral-pattern carpet spreading out around me. And in the center of it, two bodies. They were male. Both were wearing White Sox jackets. They were lying a few feet apart, arms and legs twisted at unnatural angles. And each had a bullet hole in the side of his head.

When the light snapped back out the room seemed even darker than it had been before. My night vision was completely shot. But I did hear something this time. The sound of the door slamming shut. And I could smell something, too. A heavy, oily odor laced with a hint of bitter almonds. It was a scent I knew well. Fulminic acid. Its fumes were poisonous, but I wasn't too worried about that. Because most often when people use it, they have another purpose in mind. Forming part of a detonator.

I stepped to the side and tugged at the handle. It wouldn't budge. Whoever had just closed the door must have fastened it, as well. Behind me I heard a low crump and the room began to glow a deep, volcanic red. I stepped back and flicked up the other light switches. A whole row at a time. None of them worked. Acrid smoke was starting to reach my nostrils, so I moved left again and tried the other doors, one after the other. They were all locked, but with the top halves being glass I guessed that wouldn't be too much of a problem. I struck out at an angle and kept moving till my shin crashed into something wooden. It was a chair. I grabbed it, felt for its neighbor, and retraced my steps. I lined up on the first door I reached. Swung the chair. Felt it make contact. Let go as it crashed through into the corridor in a flurry of jagged shards. Then I picked up the second chair. Used it to clear the remaining glass from the window frame. Prepared to climb out to safety. And flung myself back down to the floor as a bullet ripped into the frame near my head.

I could hear the flames crackling behind me, near where

I'd seen the bar. They could only get worse with the extra oxygen that would be sucked in, now that I'd broken the window. That left me with some pretty stark choices. I could burn to death, if I stayed in the room. Get shot, if I tried to leave. Or possibly suffocate, if the oily fumes continued to grow thicker.

None of those options really grabbed me so I decided that since Fothergill's buddies had shown up anyway, it would be nice for one of them to lend me a hand. I crawled across toward the spot where I remembered them lying and stopped when I came in contact with a body part. It turned out to be a leg. I worked my way up until I reached the face. Then I found the guy was no use because he'd been shot in the right-hand side of the head. I left him in peace and kept on going till I stumbled across his buddy. He'd taken his slug in the left side, so I dragged his body back to the safety of the wall. Then I propped him up and wrestled him out of his baseball jacket. I'd forgotten just how hard dressing corpses can be, so combined with the smoke and rising heat I was breathing pretty hard by the time I'd replaced it with my own.

The person who'd shot at me had been somewhere to my right, so I dragged the body I'd dressed to the far side of the left-hand door. I went back for the remaining chair and used it to break the window. Another bullet hit the woodwork. I dropped the chair and waited for thirty seconds. Then I hauled the body upright and maneuvered it close to the door. I tipped it forward so that its right hand flopped forward, as if trying to grab hold of the frame, ready to climb through. Another shot rang out. A bullet smashed into the body's chest. I simulated jerking it back under the impact, but kept him on his feet. Two more rounds hit him, both in the chest, and I decided enough was enough. His last stand had been a glorious one, after all, so I let him slip to the floor for the final time. There was silence from the corridor. A minute passed. The smoke was growing noticeably thicker. My eyes were beginning to water and it was becoming hard not to choke. And then I heard the sound I'd been waiting for. Footsteps. Running away. I risked another thirty seconds in the room. Then I went back to the first window I'd cleared and vaulted through to the other side.

EIGHTEEN

There are many reasons for a person to take action.

Some are positive. They lead to doing things because you actively believe in them. Such as joining the army in 1939, like my father had done. Or in 1914, as his father had done before him.

Others are negative. They lead to things you wouldn't normally do, simply to avoid alternatives that strike you as worse. Like not wanting to spend time in a hotel room with nothing but certain red-raw memories to keep you company.

An old boss of mine once warned me against the second kind.

But it's a lesson I still haven't learned very well.

The first assistant I saw at the Gap store on Michigan Avenue wrinkled her nose when I walked in. Then she dumped the stack of shirts she'd been folding on the nearest table and retreated to the back of the store. Normally I'd have been insulted by that kind of reaction, but on this occasion I couldn't really blame her. My clothes and hair stank of smoke. A film of gray soot coated my skin. My jeans were ripped from the broken glass in the door at the Coq d'Or and specks of blood from the White Sox guy had ended up on my shirt. All things considered, I looked and smelled pretty damn unpleasant.

I picked out suitable replacements for my ruined garments, including a new jacket to replace the one I'd loaned to the dead body, and made my way back to my hotel. I went straight up to my room, locked the door behind me, and headed for the bathroom. Taking a long shower is something I usually enjoy, but in this case it wasn't an option. It was a necessity. I stayed under the cascade of warm, cleansing water for nearly twenty minutes, not moving. Then I pulled on my new outfit and retrieved my phone from the pocket of the discarded jeans. A message on the screen told me that Fothergill had been after me. He'd tried twelve times since I'd been in the bathroom. I guess he must have been anxious to reach me. It was tempting to leave him dangling after he'd ignored my message, earlier, but I had ulterior motives. I was hoping he'd have some interesting news, so I called him right back.

He picked up on the first ring.

"Seems like you're having communication issues with your people," I said.

"David?" he said. "Are you OK? What happened?"

"I'm fine. I can't say the same for your guys, though. Looks like you'll be needing new rent-a-goons from now on."

"What do you mean?"

"Maybe you can find ones that can follow instructions. And understand simple concepts, like being stood down."

"They showed up? At the Drake?"

"They did."

"I don't understand. I told them not to go. Well, I got a message to them, telling them not to."

"Well, I guess it never got through."

"So what happened? I'm hearing that shots were fired. Something about a fire breaking out. I can see smoke from my office window, right now. And fire trucks. The whole north end of Michigan is closed off. People are being evacuated."

"Someone torched the place."

"While you were there?"

"Oh, yes."

"Really? Who?"

"You tell me."

"It was a deliberate torching? Are you sure?"

"It was a pro job. No doubt about it. They used incendiaries, triggered by a light switch. Not explosives. They wanted the place to burn, not blow up."

"It was a trap?"

"From the start."

"But you got out."

"Evidently."

"And the guys I sent? Or tried not to send. Lady Luck wasn't smiling on them, quite so much?"

"She wasn't smiling on them at all."

"So what was it that did for them? The fire? The fumes?"

"Neither. They were shot in the head."

"By the Myenese?"

"I presume so. I don't know for sure, though. Your guys were dead when I got there."

"When you got there? Were you late?"

"Me? No. I'm never late."

"So they were early?"

"They were both. Early, and late. At the same time. Sounds like a riddle."

"David, this isn't the time. Didn't the Myenese say anything? Shed any light on what they did? Or why?"

"No. I never saw them, let alone spoke to them. They just locked me in the bar with the dead guys and tried to incinerate me. And then shot at me. They were persistent. I'll give them that."

"So nothing happened to derail things. It wasn't like you were leading them down the garden path when my guys jumped out and knocked everything out of kilter?"

"No. It was a setup from minute one."

"Which points to one person."

"McIntyre."

"Exactly."

"Which is why I was calling. I want some news. Good news, preferably."

Fothergill didn't respond.

"Any progress on McIntyre's new contacts?" I said. "Any word from the IT guys?"

"Maybe," he said. "In fact, yes. We think so. They've narrowed the dating site traffic down to a defined range of

IP addresses. And with a bit more work, we should be able to pinpoint a specific user."

"Excellent. How long will that take?"

"David, after what you've been through, don't you think that's a question for tomorrow?"

"No. I'm asking now."

"Don't be so hard on yourself. No one would bat an eyelid if you took a few hours to reset."

"How long will they take?"

He didn't answer.

"Do I need to come down there and ask them myself?" I said.

"No," he said. "I'll find out. But don't worry. They don't think it'll take too much longer."

"Good. I want to know where to find McIntyre's new friends. And in the meantime, I want you to set up another meeting with the Myenese."

"Really? Are you sure?"

"Would I ask, otherwise?"

"The thing is, I think we should focus now, David. Those people are out of the picture. It's time to let them go."

"No. We need to keep after them."

"Why? This is no time for revenge."

"It's always time for revenge. Especially since they ruined my favorite jacket. But that's not the point. Think about it. McIntyre tipped the Myenese off about this afternoon being a bust. Which means they've been in contact, in the last few hours. So they might be able to get in touch again."

"Oh. I hadn't thought of that."

"So, we need them back on the hook. That way, if the new buyers don't lead us anywhere, we may still have a back door into McIntyre."

"It'll give us a plan B. Excellent. Or where are we up to now? Probably about plan Z, I should think. But whatever it is, I'll talk to the IT guys. See if they can get something coded . . . Oh, can you hold on a second?"

The line went silent.

"OK," Fothergill said, after two minutes. "I'm back. And we're in business. We know who Tony's been messaging with. It's an architect. Or someone in an architect's office, anyway. A firm called Pascoe, Kershaw, and Reith."

"That's good," I said. "Where are they?"

"Guess."

"Where?"

"About three hundred yards from where I'm standing."

I was beginning to learn that Fothergill was sometimes prone to exaggeration, especially where directions were involved. Pascoe, Kershaw, and Reith's building was something over half a mile from the consulate, not three hundred yards. That didn't matter enormously in the great scheme of things, but it did cause me a little inconvenience that afternoon. Because before approaching it, I decided to hit Starbucks one more time. And not just 'cause I was ready for another cappuccino. The main reason was that if you buy four drinks to take out, they give you a cardboard holder to carry them in. And if you approach an elevator hanging on to one of those with both hands, looking like you're on the verge of spilling a couple of pints of hot liquid all over your neighbors, something magical happens. People's natural inclination to ask who the hell you are and why you're poking around their building instantly disappears. And is replaced with a simple, courteous question. Which floor do you want?

Fothergill's lack of accuracy meant I had to lug the drinks twice as far as I'd expected, but when I arrived at the correct address they did the trick just as beautifully as usual. The architects had the top floor of an anonymous building on Washington and State, not far from the old Marshall Field's department store. I loitered outside for a moment, observing the steady stream of office workers, before a young woman in a plum-colored suit paused to open the door for me. I followed her inside, glanced up at the list of tenants displayed over the concierge's desk, and made my way across to join a gaggle of telemarketers who were waiting to head back up to their suite.

No one else asked for the same floor as me, but when the elevator doors opened I realized that wasn't just a happy coincidence. It was because the architects' firm had closed for the day. The lights were off, and the place looked locked down and deserted. Which wasn't necessarily a problem. It just meant that getting inside would be a different kind of challenge.

I stepped out of the elevator car and into the reception area. A single chair was tucked neatly away behind a pale wooden counter, next to a computer screen and a phone.

A blue leather couch was pushed back against the wall to the right, beneath two large black-and-white prints of the Chicago skyline. A pair of frosted glass doors filled the space to the left, with the partners' names etched vertically in bold, modern letters. There wasn't much else to see. Except for a digital keypad that was fixed to the frame. And a CCTV camera above my head, keeping watch over everything.

A drop of coffee slopped onto the floor as I flipped the lid off the backup cappuccino I'd bought. It was lucky I wasn't planning on drinking it. All I needed was the foam. I scooped some out with my fingers, stretched up, and daubed it all over the camera's lens. It wasn't an ideal substance—not sticky enough—but I figured it would keep any images sufficiently indistinct as long as I didn't hang around too long. I'd known people improvise with all kinds of foodstuffs before. Mayonnaise. Peanut butter. Hummus. And while steamed milk may have been a little more unorthodox, necessity is, after all, the mother of invention.

My next priority was the alarm, and that was just as easy to find. The control box was mounted on the far side of the counter, under the main shelf, at knee level for anyone who was sitting down. It had a keypad, an LCD display that confirmed it was armed, and a key switch to reset the system. I quickly searched the receptionist's drawers, just in case. That wasn't as long a shot as it sounds—human laziness and stupidity dictate that you can find either the override key or a note of the code in probably three tries out of ten—but it wasn't to be this time. Instead I took a six-inch ruler, a well-sharpened pencil, and returned to the control box. I'd noticed that the manufacturer's logo was attached to a circle of metal about the size of a dime at the top left of the case, and that had given me an idea. I eased the pointed corner of the ruler under the edge of the little disc and pressed down hard. It pinged off, snapping the ruler in the process, and rolled away under the counter. But I wasn't concerned about the damage or the loss. Because at the center of the circle I'd just exposed was exactly what I'd been hoping to see. A tiny hole. I inserted the tip of the pencil into it and pushed. The box beeped. All the LCD characters flashed in unison. Then a message appeared:

ENTER RESET CODE?

I was relying on the fact that while practically all users changed their PINs to something secure after installation, not many of them knew how to reset their systems. That's because you only find out if you lose your keys, forget your code, and call the manufacturer's helpline. So I took a deep breath, crossed my fingers, and keyed in the most common factory default:

0 0 0 0

The system beeped twice. The LCD characters flashed. And a new message scrolled across the screen:

DISARMED

The cappuccino foam on the camera lens seemed to be holding up pretty well, but I smeared a little more on for luck before moving on to the final hurdle. The keypad next to the door. I took a closer look and saw it was divided into three sections. A narrow rectangle at the top, which housed a red and a green LED. An empty central section, the approximate size of a credit card. And the numbered buttons at the bottom—0 through 9, plus * and #.

I guessed the central panel would be a proximity card reader. That would probably be the way most employees would gain access, because it's quicker and easier than having to enter a code. The keypad would be used by people who'd forgotten their cards, guests—unless they were given temporary passes—and contractors, and to allow the system to be disabled in case of emergency. Which I guess was a fair description of the situation I found myself in right then.

The emergency services can't be expected to memorize the codes for all the alarms in all the offices in all the buildings they protect, so the systems come with what's known as a fire number. In a sane world, there'd be just one of these. In fact, there are close to twenty. I knew six of them from past cases I'd been involved with, and I was pretty sure Fothergill could get me the others if I needed them. I started with the ones I could remember. The little red light glowed in response to the first three I keyed in. But when I entered the fourth, it turned to green. Life was good. I was clear to enter.

The moment the door swung open I could see why the architects had chosen that particular office. The place was incredibly bright. Even at that time, the late afternoon sun was flooding in through a huge rectangular light well in the ceiling. Four draftsmen's desks were arranged beneath it, to take full advantage of the natural light. Six tall document cupboards, large enough to hold full-sized plans, were lined up along the left-hand wall. Regular desks and filing cabinets filled the space to the right, with one at the end reserved for a giant printer and photocopier. The area straight ahead was divided into three glass-fronted offices. There was a fair selection of the usual office paraphernalia lying around—phone chargers, pens and paper, coasters with advertising slogans on them—and lots more specialized items like containers full of rolled-up plans and piles of half-finished plastic foam building models. But there was one kind of thing that was conspicuously absent. The thing I'd specifically come to find. Their computers.

Except for one.

I stepped back into the foyer, jogged the mouse that was lying on the countertop, and the receptionist's screen sprang back to life. The desktop picture showed a bloated ginger cat curled up on a floral sofa. That wasn't a promising sign. I did my best to ignore it, and clicked on the Internet Explorer icon instead. The cursor gave way to an hour glass, and I had to wait for what seemed like an hour until a little box appeared in the center of the cat's stomach.

> You are not connected to the Internet. Would you like to launch the Network Connection Wizard?

I clicked on "No," pulled out my phone, and called Fothergill.

"I need another address," I said.

"Why?" he said. "Couldn't you get in?"

"Of course I could. I'm inside now. But their computers aren't here. They must use laptops, and have taken them home."

"The people aren't there?"

"No. The place is empty."

"Damn. I hadn't expected that. OK. Let's think. What else can we do?"

"Is there any way to trace the computer McIntyre's contact was using? Can you talk to the IT guys? See if they can trace it, if it's gone online from another location?"

"I'll talk to them. I don't know if that kind of trace is possible, though."

"I don't either. But this place is a wash, otherwise. And it might be too late if I have to come back tomorrow, when they're back at work."

"Tomorrow could well be too late."

"What about their home addresses? Could you track any of them down? Starting with the partners. I could pay a couple of them a visit. See if I can't loosen some tongues."

"That's a good thought. I'll get the boffins on it, right away. But depending on where they live, it might not be quick. There might be a lot of running around involved, and these guys might not even be home. So before we go down that road, are you sure there's nothing at your end we could use? Already in the office?"

"Maybe. I'll nose around, see if I can find the personnel files."

"No. I wasn't thinking about addresses. I was thinking about these guys' jobs. If they're trying to buy this gas, there's a chance it's related to something they're working on."

"It could be. Or it's just as likely that whatever pie they've got their fingers in is completely separate."

"It could go either way. But we know that someone who works there is the linchpin. The only one left who can connect us with Tony and the gas. So while you're there, it makes sense to take a thorough look, doesn't it?"

"I want to find that computer. And the guy who was using it."

"I understand. But here's how I see it. The guy's computer is what led us to that office, but it doesn't follow that the information we need is on it, too. The key could be right there, on a desk, in a drawer, on the wall, who knows?"

"Maybe they signed a confession and left it in a sealed envelope?"

"I'm serious, David. This used to be my specialty. Residual Analysis. You can always tell what someone's up to by what they leave behind."

"If they leave anything behind."

"You're right. Sometimes they leave nothing. Sometimes you figure it out by what's missing. But either way, the clues are always there. You just need to know how to find them, and how to put them together. And the starting point is always careful observation. So come on. Let's try. Is it a large place?"

"No."

"OK. Why don't you walk me through it. Start with the shared areas. For some reason people are always more careful in their personal spaces. We're looking for something current, not lost in the mists of time. And something big, if they need multiple canisters of this gas to poison it with."

I did what he asked, and as I made my way from desk to desk I found the firm was keeping itself pretty busy. It was involved with all kinds of diverse projects. High-end housing developments. New build, as well as conversions. Boutique-style shop renovations. And interior design, for a couple of fancy restaurants and cafés. With some of the buildings, they were handling the design from scratch. With others, they were supervising the work the contractors were doing. And in one case, they'd been hired to validate the structural calculations another practice from out of state had come up with.

The hardest part of assessing the threat came from the inherent versatility of the gas. Houses are small. They hold five or six people at most. You'd think an apartment building would make a better target. Or an office. But houses are rarely built on their own. Especially in the suburbs. Factor in wind patterns and climatic conditions, and one residence could be used as a springboard to infect hundreds of others. Or maybe thousands. Which meant that several of their projects could be suspicious. Or none of them. A number of schemes had the potential, but nothing really stood out. And most of them were still in the "possible" pile when we reached the final item. It was the only thing I hadn't been able to identify right away. One of the plastic foam models. It didn't look familiar, and at the same time it didn't look finished. Fothergill seemed suspicious. It was like his internal antennae had picked up on something, and he just wouldn't let it drop.

"Describe it to me again," he said. "I'm just not getting it."

"It looks like the cross-section of a room," I said. "It's rectangular. There's nothing inside. One of the long walls is missing. The two shorter walls have floor-to-ceiling windows. But the other long wall is where it gets strange. Three boxes are sticking right out of it."

"Boxes? Like cardboard boxes?"

"Right. Like the kind you get at arenas and stadiums. Only smaller. They look like they can move, in and out. And they're transparent."

"Transparent? Like they're made of glass?"

"These are plastic. I have no idea what the real ones are made of. But glass wouldn't be impossible, I guess. If it was properly strengthened."

"And the place, itself. Is it definitely just a room? Or could it be a whole floor?"

"Not a whole floor, I'd guess, since one of the walls is missing. Maybe a third of a floor. Perhaps a quarter."

"You know what I mean."

"Then, yes. It probably represents a whole floor."

"Is there any way to tell how high up a floor it is?"

"No."

"Is there anything attached to the top? Like aerials?

Ventilation equipment? Anything to suggest it could be a roof?"

"No."

"That's a shame. It would make things clearer. But David, I think I've got it. I think I know what we're talking about."

"I'm excited. Did you ever think about the stage? You could be one of those illusionists who resurface every Christmas. I saw one for real, once, at a ball. He was called the Regurgitator. I bet you can't guess what his act involved."

"David, will you listen? Do you want to know what the model's of, or not?"

"OK. Go ahead. Surprise me. But I bet it can't beat what the Regurgitator did with a goldfish and a cigarette."

"I think it's the Sears Tower."

"Oh well. I was right again. Never mind."

"What do you mean, you were right?"

"About the Regurgitator. He was far more entertaining. I thought so, anyway. The goldfish would probably have been in your camp, though."

Fothergill didn't reply.

"And you should have seen his outfit," I said. "Yellow spandex. Very tight. You're a bit of a fashionista. You'd have loved it."

He didn't respond. I thought perhaps he was sulking a little bit.

"And if you want to be pedantic, it's the Willis Tower, now, apparently," I said.

"No one in Chicago will ever call it that," he said.

"If you're even right about it being the Sears Tower, of course."

"I am. It has to be that. The glass boxes are the clue. They were added to the observation level a little while back. They're pretty cool, actually."

"And they're broken, I heard. Or the mechanism is, at least. The magazine in my hotel said the whole of that level was closed again while they were being fixed."

"That's right. I'd forgotten. I wonder—David, stay on the line a moment, will you please?"

I heard some rapid typing from Fothergill's end; then everything was quiet for a moment.

"Listen to this," he said, when he returned. "Guess which structural engineer is involved in the repair project?"

"Can I go for best of three?" I said. "OK. I'm going right out on a limb, here. Is it Pascoe?"

"No."

"Kershaw?"

"No."

"OK. Reith?"

"Yes. It's Reith. And guess what? There's more. He's not charging a dime for the work."

"What a public-spirited kind of guy. Sounds like the city could use more people like him."

Fothergill sighed.

"You don't understand," he said. "I think we're onto something here. Think about it. Everything fits."

"What fits?" I said. "I don't see it."

"You've got the tallest building in the United States. It's

taller than the World Trade Center was. Goodness knows how many people work in it. And there are all the tourists. Talk about a juicy target. Now here's a guy, trying to buy poison gas, with engineering knowledge, bending over backward to get access to the inner workings of the place."

"You seriously think there's a genuine terrorist threat against the Sears Tower?"

"It's possible."

"Then why are we even messing around? You should kick it to Homeland Security, right away."

"I don't know about that. If we're wrong, we could cause a panic. People could be killed. And we would expose everything to do with McIntyre and the missing Spektra gas, which is just what London doesn't want to happen."

"I think you're jumping the gun. We don't know it was Reith who was chumming up to McIntyre. Any one of their staff could have been using that dating service. Or someone entirely unrelated could have been piggybacking off their wireless, even."

"You're reaching, David. It's just too big a coincidence."

"Maybe. But I'm not convinced. And I still want those guys' home addresses."

"Yes, we'll get them for you. But in the meantime, do any of their other projects honestly seem like a hotter target?"

"No. But we don't know the target has anything to do with their work."

"True. But think about it. Right now, this minute, have we got anything better to go on?"

I didn't answer.

"I think you should head over there and take a look," he said. "Will you go?"

I didn't reply.

"I'll meet you there, if you like," he said. "We'll check the place together."

"I'd like you to check their home addresses," I said. "That's how we'll move this forward. Not by replacing one wild-goose chase with another."

"I'll get the analysts on it. Straightaway. All of them. But while they're doing that, what else are you going to do? Sit around in your hotel? See a movie? Go shopping? Get a pedicure?"

I didn't want to wait, at all. I didn't see why finding three addresses had to be so time-consuming. None of Fothergill's suggestions had even crossed my mind. I was just going to tell him to turn the heat up under the IT guys when my eyes fell on a flyer pinned to a notice board near the photocopier. It was advertising *Richard III* at one of the local theaters. That was Tanya's favorite play. We'd seen it together, years ago, in Madrid. I could almost feel her head on my shoulder, and the tension building in her body as we waited for the curtain to go up. And I knew that memory would only grow on me, if I allowed any time to hang on my hands.

"How are you helping anyone, just spinning your wheels?" he said. "Maybe it is an old-timer's hunch. Maybe we're stretching logic a little, here. But if a building full of people get killed because of this, how are you going to feel?

Knowing that's all on you? Or if Tony escapes permanently this time?"

"I'll have a look at the place," I said. "But I'll take my phone. And I'll expect a call the second you get an address. Preferably Reith's."

"Perfect. You have my word. I'll sit on it, all the way. You'll hear the second I do."

"I better."

"You will. And there's something else I can do to help. Could you find your way to the Quincy El stop?"

"If I needed to. Why?"

"It's only a stone's throw from the Sears Tower. Wait there, and I'll get the plans of the building biked over to you. If someone's planning to gas everyone inside, they'll need access to the ventilation system. And this way, you'll know where to look for them. If you think that's a good idea."

"It's definitely a good idea. As long they're up to date. If we're going to take potshots at a place, it's better not to do it completely in the dark."

"OK, then. Why not head over there now? I'll try not to keep you waiting for the messenger. It's good you're going, David. I'll sleep a lot better, knowing we've left no stone unturned."

NINETEEN

When I was in school, I had a teacher who liked to crack people's heads together.

That certainly grabbed their attention, but I can't honestly say it helped them to learn anything. In the navy, we had an instructor who used a different approach. He used to crash different quotations together to make his points. Or his own versions of quotations, anyway. For example, when it came to teamwork he liked to tell us—

Lads, remember this. No man is an island.

Followed by—

Be not afraid of helpfulness. Some men are born helpful. Some achieve helpfulness. And some have helpfulness thrust upon them.

I did remember what he said. I agreed with it. And I came across all three types of people, over the years.

I found the first group is always the easiest to work with. But the last group is a whole lot more fun.

*

The Sears Tower completely dominates West Quincy Street between the El stop and its east facade. It's unmissable, but its black frame, dark glass, and irregular profile make it seem moody rather than magnificent. It may be taller than the World Trade Center used to be, but to look at, I'd never have guessed. It just doesn't have the same brutal, uncompromising presence of the Twin Towers. Or the elegance of the Empire State Building. The exuberance of the Chrysler. Or even the symmetry of the Hancock Center, a few blocks away. But as I stood and stared up at the tips of its antennas, a hundred-plus stories above me, I couldn't help feeling a sense of awe. It was still the tallest building in the United States. It had been the tallest in the world for over twenty years. And that was without any shenanigans over the way it was measured, which in itself demands respect. It would be a shame for something bad to happen to it. I was pretty sure Fothergill was just seeing ghosts in the shadows, but making completely sure no longer felt like such a waste of time.

The plans that Fothergill had supplied gave me exactly the level of detail I needed. They showed three obvious places for gaining access to the ventilation system. The main plant room in the lower basement, and subsidiary control points on the thirty-fourth and sixty-eighth floors. Checking those would be quick and easy. The dilemma would come if I didn't find anything at any of them. Because it looked like you could get into the risers at nine separate locations on each floor. Which was a thousand or so places. And there was only one of me. Those weren't the greatest of odds.

The main pedestrian entrance to the Sears Tower is on Jackson Boulevard, but I ignored that and headed for the loading dock at the opposite side of the building, on Adams Street. The truck door was rolled all the way down, and the personnel door was closed. Both were locked. Access for vehicles was controlled by an intercom mounted on a tall, skinny pillar. I checked, and saw it included only a call button and a video camera. Ignoring the voice in my head that said I should have fetched more cappuccino, I examined the touch pad on the nearby door frame. It was for proximity cards only. There was no keypad, so no chance of using a fire number. Which left three choices. Try my luck with the receptionist, around at the front. Wait for a vehicle to arrive, and use it for cover. Or talk my way past anyone I could get to open this door.

The door was made of hollow metal, and it made a decent amount of sound when I banged it with the flat of my hand. I did that repeatedly, but no one came. I'd just about decided it was time for a new approach when I heard a voice behind me. I turned around slowly and calmly, like I was entitled to be there, and saw two men approaching. One was in his twenties, and was wearing a security guard's uniform. He was walking backward, keeping an eye on the other guy who could have been anywhere from fifty to eighty. His filthy clothes and unkempt, straggly hair made it impossible to be sure. He was following the younger man, and grasping at his jacket as he struggled to keep up.

"Come on, Pops," the guard said. "Nearly there. Come on. Keep moving."

He was leading the tramp along the drive toward the vehicle entrance. Then, when he was only about halfway down, he veered off to the side. He seemed to be heading into a corner formed by two brick walls, next to where the three of the building's Dumpsters were kept. I guessed he had something hidden there, but I couldn't see what. Maybe food, I thought, saved from one of the restaurants. Or clothes, that careless visitors had left behind.

"Come on, you worthless piece of crap," the guard said.

The old guy kept on moving, and the expression on his face didn't change. He still looked like an excited kid in a toy shop, not quite daring to believe he was going to be given a long-dreamed-of treat.

"Move, you sack of shit," the guard said. "Did I tell you to stop, you useless asshole?"

All of a sudden a completely different theory entered my head. I looked up the side of the building. I counted six security cameras. They were all pointing in different directions, covering the area outside the loading bay. But if you looked closely, you could see there was one blind spot. One place where nothing you did would be recorded. It was the spot near the Dumpsters. The spot that the guard had almost reached.

"I'm going to show you what happens to scumbag assholes who prefer not to work," he said, grabbing the tramp by his lapels and spinning him around. "You hobos make me want to puke."

"Excuse me," I said, stepping out of the shadows. "Are you related to this gentleman in some way?"

"What?" he said. "Who are you?"

"I'm his assertiveness counselor. I keep an eye open, and anytime I see him in an adversarial situation, I help to explore alternative strategies for bringing about a more positive outcome. From his perspective, anyway. So unless you're his long-lost nephew or some other family member, you're going to need to take your hands off him."

"Me? Related to him? Screw you, man."

"Sometimes I offer advice. Sometimes I give practical demonstrations. Today I'm thinking that advice just isn't going to be enough."

"I'll give you advice, man, if you don't mind your business."

"Speaking of business, I'm also his financial adviser. I help out whenever money needs to be transferred. Take this current situation as an example. The cash that's in your pocket? It needs to move into his."

"The hell are you talking about?"

"I'm talking about you apologizing to this unfortunate gentleman, and giving him all your money."

"Why would I want to do that?"

"Because if you don't, I'm going to break your legs, then take it anyway."

"Oh yeah? Go for it, man."

"One other question, first. Do you work here, in this building?"

"Yeah. Why?"

"Do you have a card to open that door?"

The guy didn't speak, but his face gave me the answer I wanted.

"OK, then," I said. "The terms have changed. The Early Bird Discount is no longer valid. Now it's a case of money and apology to him, ID card to me."

He didn't respond.

"Normally I'd give you three to comply, but as I don't have time to teach you to count, I'm just going to have to—"

I punched him in the face. Hard. The back of his head hit the brick wall, his legs turned to jelly, and he went down in an undignified, uncoordinated heap. I reached down and took the proximity card from his shirt pocket, then rolled him over and fished out his wallet. His Social Security card was the only thing I needed, so I handed the rest to the tramp. He was standing in front of me, rooted to the spot, looking mildly bemused.

"Are you OK?" I said.

He nodded balefully.

"Take what you need," I said. "It's yours now. Just don't get caught with his credit cards, OK? Or you'll end up in jail."

He nodded again. Then he turned and wandered away, shoving the wallet deep into his layers of underwear.

It would have made sense to snap the guard's neck, but since he was a civilian I decided on a more lenient option. I could see three pens sticking out of the shirt pocket on the other side of his chest, so I helped myself to the center one and started to write on the back of his hand:

I have your SS number. 737-65-4344. I know where you live. Report your ID missing, and you'll be hearing from me again.

TWENTY

During our training, not all the exercises turned out to be a success.

For some people, that was hard to take. But it wasn't always their fault. It wasn't necessarily down to not trying hard enough, or not having the necessary skills, or even not having the rub of the green on a given day. It was down to some of the tasks we were given being literally impossible. They were designed that way. Not out of cruelty. Not to torment anyone who had a perfectionist streak running through them. But because in the field, not everything you try will come out right. So you need to know how to deal with that. And learn how to boil things down afterward, to make sure you gain from the experience.

Sometimes, though, things went wrong because people did make mistakes. And in our line of work, the most common one has to do with calling for backup. Specifically, when to do it. Because there are two ways to get it wrong.

You can do it too early.

Or you can leave it too late.

*

Throughout my time in the navy I've observed a kind of law that governs the process of looking for things. It states that whatever you need to find, you never come across it in the first place you try. It seems like there's a kind of invisible force at work, making sure you put in an arbitrarily determined amount of effort before being allowed to walk away with your prize. And though it might sound crazy, this principle certainly held true when I was sneaking around in the Sears Tower, searching for the Spektra gas.

In the absence of any rational way to choose between the most likely locations, I flipped a mental coin and decided to start at the bottom of the building and work my way up. And even though the lower basement was the closest of the three destinations to the entrance I'd used, it still took a good ten minutes to reach it. The floor plan helped me avoid any wrong turns—as well as the security stations—but it didn't do justice to the size and scale of the corridors and stairwells. Close your eyes and you could easily believe you were on a treadmill, it took so long to get from one end of the building to the other.

The facilities in the lower basement were fantastically well organized. The plan referred to a plant room, but plant suite would have been a more accurate description. There was one room for the wet services, and another for the dry. Everything was clearly labeled. All the service and maintenance logs were present and complete. I checked everything thoroughly, and found no sign of anything untoward attached to the ventilation system. And no record of anyone having worked on it recently, either.

It was the same story in the second place I tried, on the thirty-fourth floor. The rooms were smaller and there was less documentation, but I saw nothing to make me suspicious. And while I'm no expert on heating or air-conditioning, I've seen plenty of sabotage attempts over the years. Consulate staffers all around the world are well trained. They're told to raise the alarm whenever they're unsure about any part of their infrastructure, and then we're called in to investigate. I've been sent to look into strange additions to water systems. Electric cabling. Data networks. E-mail servers. Even kitchen appliances, in one strange case. And because the overall attitude is better safe than sorry, a lot of the things I've seen are perfectly innocent. Which has helped me develop a pretty good sense of when things have been tampered with, and when they haven't. And how people disguise the things they'd rather you didn't see.

By the time I reached the sixty-eighth floor, I was getting a real feeling for life in the building. It reminded me of several of the organizations I'd been sent to infiltrate over the last decade. The offices looked perfectly ordinary, with all the trappings of people's daily lives left strewn around for anyone to see. There were birthday cards on six different desks on four separate floors. Cardigans hanging on the back of chairs. Chipped mugs left to drain in sinks. Small soft toys displayed in cubicles like mascots. All kinds of little details that brought home the reality of the corporate routine. It was starting to feel so familiar that when I reached the service position, despite what that would mean in terms of searching the risers, I was actively hoping I wouldn't find anything.

And once again, I was disappointed.

Space was tight in the utility area, but right away I could see that something was wrong over on the left-hand side. Someone had managed to divert one of the core ventilation pipes so that it ran in a D-shape just in front of the wall. A line of connecting valves had been added along the lower horizontal section. There were four. Two were empty. Two weren't, and when I saw what had been attached, my stomach knotted and my hand reached immediately for my phone. It was a pair of matte green cylinders. Spektra gas. There was no doubt. And on the floor, next to an old, scratched wrench, was another one waiting to be installed.

Fothergill had just correctly predicted the most audacious terrorist threat since 9/11. He'd convinced me to break into the Sears Tower to find proof of it. And I was happy to take my hat off to him. But when I called his number to tell him he was right, I got his voice mail. I hung up, and decided to give him another minute. If he still didn't respond, I'd be left with no choice. This was too important to gamble with, or worry about saving face. We needed all hands to the pumps. So as much as he'd be upset, I'd have to call the police. And then London.

My next attempt at reaching Fothergill produced the same result, and I'd got as far as dialing the 9 of 911 when I heard movement. It was nearby. Someone was in the corridor. No. It sounded like two people. They were approaching fast. I dodged back against the wall to the side of the door and held my breath. The footsteps paused for a moment, right outside the little room. I heard voices. There were definitely two people. Both were men. They had heavy South African accents, and were discussing recent football matches in the Dutch league, of all things. One guy reached the punch line of his story, the other laughed, and the door swung open. Both guys came in, and when the door closed again they were less than four feet away from me. Close enough for me to smell their aftershave. I saw they were dressed identically. They had crisp blue coveralls, with *W* logos on their chests. Shiny black safety boots on their feet. And on chains strung around their necks, building security passes. Just like the one I was using.

Thoughts of calling anyone had to go on hold.

"Gentlemen," I said, slipping the phone in my pocket and leveling my Beretta at the nearer guy's chest. "I hope you have an eye for a bargain. Because you're in luck. Today's two-for-one day."

Neither of the guys reacted.

"Let me be more specific," I said. "You're going to be disconnecting two gas canisters, instead of installing one."

Neither guy moved.

"Or, we could try an alternative version," I said. "Two of you get shot in the head by one of me. Two bullets each. Your choice."

The guys glanced at each other, shrugged, and raised their hands to chest level. Then they looked at me straight in the face, calmly and sensibly, and evaluated the situation. I knew they were considering jumping me. They had the confident, controlled manner of people who were used to taking care of themselves. The confined conditions were in their favor, as well as their numerical advantage. And if they were professionals, they'd know the odds were that one of them would end up taking the gun.

But they'd also know the odds were that the other would end up taking a bullet.

Discretion won the day.

Until the third guy arrived. He was older. Most likely in his fifties. He was dressed in an expensive-looking black ribbed sweater and loose beige cord pants. And he had a gun. It was already in his hand when I saw him, standing in the doorway. But instead of pointing it at me, he aimed it at the loose cylinder on the ground.

"Hi," I said. "I'm actually over here."

The guy raised one eyebrow, but didn't speak.

"I'm just telling you because if you want to shoot me, you'd be better off pointing your gun in my general direction," I said.

He didn't reply.

"My name's David Trevellyan, by the way," I said. "And you're who? Pascoe? Kershaw? Or Reith?"

A smile finally broke out across his face.

"The architects?" he said. "You fell for that? I didn't think anyone would swallow it. But credit to your friend. He told me you would. And he was right."

"I'm a very sociable person," I said. "I have literally several friends. Can you narrow the field a little?"

"Don't try to play me. You know the guy's name. And

anyway, this isn't the time for twenty questions. It's time for you to put down your gun and start talking to us about how we can save your life. And spare you from excruciating pain."

"Let me think. Death. Pain. You paint a very tempting picture. I'm almost inclined to take you up on it. No one's made a serious attempt to kill me for nearly five hours now, which is tedious. It's just the putting down of my gun that I'm struggling with. Remind me why I'd want to do that?"

"See where I'm aiming my gun?"

"At the floor? Are you concerned about dust mites?"

"I'm aiming at the canister."

"Which would kill all four of us if you hit it."

"Actually, it wouldn't. It would only harm you. My friends and I are thorough. We've been immunized. That stuff wouldn't even make us sneeze."

He was bluffing, of course. I was certain of that. There was no way an antidote to this gas existed. And even if one did, he wouldn't use up a third of his arsenal to eliminate a single person. Especially when the gas would inevitably leak out and contaminate the surrounding areas. Keeping their presence secret had to be a vital part of his plan, and that would be pretty difficult if the neighbors all started dropping like flies.

I really should have just shot them all, there and then, and called in some help to gather up the canisters. But every second I delayed, the riskier that prospect became. The first pair of guys was regrouping. I could almost hear the cogs spinning inside their heads. They were weighing their options all over again, watching me, measuring the angles. The older guy's presence seemed to have galvanized them. I was intrigued by him. He had a definite air of authority. I wanted to find out what he knew. How he'd found out. And whether I could use him to get farther up the food chain.

"It's not a good way to go, with the gas," he said. "I've seen it. I wouldn't recommend it."

"What's the alternative?" I said.

"Give me your gun. Then we'll talk."

"Just talk?"

"That depends on what you have to say."

"But you need my gun first, anyway?"

"I do."

I made a show of considering his offer, then spun the Beretta around and handed it to him, grip first.

"Your phone, as well," he said.

"Really?" I said.

He nodded.

I sighed and pulled it back out of my pocket.

"Here," I said. "But take good care of it. And the gun, too. I'll be needing them back, very soon."

One of the other guys laughed.

"Just kill him now," he said.

"No way," the second guy said. "Not in here. He'll make too much mess."

"He won't. And anyway, listen to him. How he talks. He deserves it."

"I know he deserves it. But not here. There's not even

room. He'd break something when he fell. Which we'd end up having to fix."

"Take him upstairs, then. To the observation deck."

"Why? It's crawling with German engineers. Someone will find him."

"No. It's not, anymore. I heard them talking, yesterday. They're waiting for parts. From Stuttgart, or somewhere. Two weeks' delay, minimum. No one will be working up there till then."

"Two weeks?" the older guy said. "Perfect. Plenty of time. No one's ever going to find him."

TWENTY-ONE

According to a report I once read, human beings can suffer from one or more of five hundred and thirty-one recognized phobias.

It's not the number of them that fascinates me, though. It's the different reactions they bring out in nonsufferers. I remember a woman at a data networking company I was sent to work at, once. She was acrophobic. In other words, she had a fear of heights. It was so extreme it even affected her when she was in her car. And unfortunately, her job required her to drive regularly across the Severn Bridge, which spans the river separating England and South Wales.

There were times when her fear was so bad it almost paralyzed her. These became so frequent she was in danger of getting the sack, so one of her friends stepped in to help. He found out whenever she was due to make the journey, and always called her a few minutes before she was likely to reach the bridge. Then he'd talk to her all the way across, keeping her mind off the ordeal and making sure she made it in one piece.

The guy would probably have a bright future in

intelligence work, because looking out for people's fears and phobias is a valuable part of what we do, too.

Only when we spot a weakness, we don't help the victim overcome it.

The regular elevators in the Sears Tower are there to serve the tenants, not the tourists. That means they don't go to the observation deck. To get there we had to return to the basement, cross to the far corner, and take the number one service elevator. And even that only took us as far as the floor two down from the top.

The older guy gestured for me to head up the final flight of emergency stairs ahead of him. I went through the door, and as soon as we were out of the public areas he gave up making any pretense of hiding his gun. I emerged first onto the observation deck, and I have to say I was impressed. It wasn't really a deck, though. As Fothergill had deduced from the architects' model, it was a whole floor. And apart from the square central core, which was covered with displays of information about Chicago, the space was uninterrupted from one wall of glass to the other. With no other people around, it seemed huge. But big as it was, it was completely overshadowed by the view. The lake. The heart of the city. The river. The suburbs. I was spoiled for choice. After a moment I went across to the window on the far side and gazed down, tracing the progress of an El train as it sparked its way around the sharp curves of the central loop. The older guy started to follow, but slowed down and stayed a good fifteen feet away from the glass.

"So why do they need German engineers here?" I said. "And what are these parts they're short of?"

"They're for the Ledge," he said. "To fix it."

"These dangling glass boxes?"

"Yes."

I saw a tiny shiver take hold of him as he gave that last answer.

"Where are they?" I said.

He nodded to his left, toward the far end of the area. It had been closed off with coarse sacklike curtains that were hanging from the ceiling.

"Let's go and look," I said.

"No, let's not," he said. "Let's stay here and talk."

"OK. We can talk. But what about?"

"You could start with your name, and why you're here."

"I could. Or you could, with why you're planning on poisoning the entire building with Spektra gas."

"How do you know what kind of gas it is?"

"Where did you get it from?"

"What's in my right hand?" he said, raising his gun.

"A Walther P38," I said.

"And what's in your right hand?"

There was no need to answer that.

"You have nothing," he said.

"It's one thing to have a gun," I said. "It's another thing to use one."

He shot a hole in the floor, directly between my feet.

"No one can hear us, in this place," he said. "If you're not going to talk, there's no reason for you to keep on breathing. The next bullet will be straight through your skull."

"I know about Spektra gas because it's my job to know," I said. "And I came here to catch the guy who's been selling it to you."

"Who do you work for?"

"Whoever pays me the most. A bit like you, I guess. You're South African?"

"Yes. What of it?"

"Anything to do with the the Republic of Equatorial Myene?"

"Nothing. That's just a chicken-feed piss-pot of a place that happens to be in the same continent I was born on. I'd nuke it, if I could."

"I see. So, if you don't mind me asking, why are a bunch—does three count as a bunch? Anyway, why are South Africans in Chicago trying to poison people?"

"'Cause we work for whoever pays us the most. A bit like you."

"And your employers would be?"

"Even if I knew, I wouldn't tell you. But I don't know. And I don't care. All I want is the money."

"Excellent. I admire a man of principle. In fact, a woman once told me that principles in a man are sexy. Very sexy, were her actual words. She was exceptionally beautiful. And exceptionally smart. I never knew her to be wrong. About anything."

"Stop bullshitting me. Who do you really work for? You're some kind of government agent, right?"

"No. I have issues with rigid authority structures. I'm strictly freelance."

"Oh, so no one knows you're here?"

"Sorry, did I say freelance? I meant to say yes, I am a government agent. Lots of people know I'm here. Including twenty-five of my most violent colleagues who are outside right now, desperate for an excuse to storm the place."

The guy lifted his gun and pointed it at my face.

"You're an idiot," he said. "It's time to say good night."

"I could do that," I said. "And I will. In due course. But in the meantime, just one thing. The guy who's selling the gas to you. What's his name?"

"Do you not get it? You're about to die. The guy's name doesn't matter."

"It matters to me. I'm curious, like a cat."

The guy didn't respond.

"Come on," I said. "You're already measuring my life expectancy in seconds. What harm can it do?"

"He's called Tony McIntyre," he said, rolling his eyes. "And he's English, like you."

"Oh, Tony. I know him, as it happens. He's Scottish, actually. And out of interest, I think telling me his name could do quite a lot of harm. To you, anyway."

"You're in no position to make threats."

"I'm not threatening. I'm just telling you. He doesn't look at all happy, right now. And he seemed fine a moment ago. So I'm thinking, has anything else happened that could have changed his mood so fast? Aside from you blurting out his name?"

"Who are you talking about?"

"Tony Mac. Look at the expression on his face."

The guy didn't react.

"He came in about two minutes after we did," I said. "That's why I stepped over here. To draw you away from him."

He didn't speak, but the muzzle of the Walther betrayed a slight tremble in his hand.

"The thing is, I'm working with Tony," I said. "I'm his loyalty consultant. When he's not sure if he can trust someone, he calls on me. I come in and run a few little tests. How do you think I knew you'd be here?"

Concern was starting to creep into the corner of his eyes.

"We call this Creating a Moment of Truth," I said. "Tony always watches and listens when I'm doing one. That way, he sees and hears everything for himself. The results can't be faked. He's not relying on someone else's interpretation. And he's not left with any worries about false reporting. But right now, I'd say he has major worries about you."

The guy's eyes started to flick to the side. Then his whole head began to twitch. The tendons in his neck joined in. And finally, he couldn't take any more. He turned around to look. Not all the way. And not for very long. But long enough and far enough for what I needed.

Striking someone's brachial plexus in just the right way to knock him out sounds easy, but in reality it's one of the hardest things I had to learn. Go in too high, and the person hardly notices you've touched him. It's the same story if you hit too low. Most of the time a fist or a foot or a knee or an elbow is a much more reliable option. But our instructors insisted that we keep trying. They wouldn't let us move on from the technique until we'd mastered it. All of them were adamant there'd be times when the results would justify the effort. And, as usual, they were right.

I retrieved my phone and Beretta, then hitched the guy's unconscious body over my right shoulder and carried him across to the curtains that divided the space. I couldn't find a join, so in the end I just dumped him back on the floor, lifted up the bottom edge, and rolled him underneath. I followed, and could finally see what all the fuss was about with the glass pods. Only to me, they looked more like giant transparent drawers with open ends. There were three of them, spaced out evenly along the wall. Each one looked capable of holding maybe twelve people in comfort at a time. Two had been retracted, leaving only the right-hand one protruding into fresh air. I moved closer, and saw the source of the problem the engineers had been struggling with. It had to do with the rails in the ceiling that supported the box, and allowed it to slide in and out. Or more specifically, the hydraulic motors that provided the power for that to happen. All three rails had been removed and above them someone had begun to strip down the associated pipes and wires. Most of them had been left dangling, but I could see an empty space in the center of the resulting clump of spaghetti. That's where the part that was being made in Stuttgart would have to be plugged in, I guessed. And then I presumed they'd repeat the procedure with the other two pods.

I retrieved the guy's body, carried it into the right-hand box and laid it facedown on the glass floor, pressed up against the outside wall. He was still out, but when consciousness returned and he opened his eyes, he was going to be looking straight down into the darkness. All that separated him from the sidewalk was three thin layers of laminated glass. And a quarter of a mile of empty air.

I wanted him to get full value for the view, so I went over to where the overhead rails had been piled up and dragged one back into the box. It was heavy. Close up it was more like a small girder, and it wasn't easy to lift one end up and position it on the small of the guy's back. I took a moment to catch my breath, then fetched the second one. That pinned his shoulders. The third, his legs. And with him secured, I sat down to think. I'd let him bring me upstairs because I wanted to know what was inside his head. This would give me the leverage to find out. Only now, there was something else bothering me. Something he'd just said didn't ring true. I couldn't put my finger on what. Not yet. But I had the feeling I wouldn't be able to tie up all the loose ends until I did.

The guy came around with a start. His head jerked back away from the glass floor and when his body didn't follow he began jerking and twisting and struggling to wriggle out from under the metal rails. I let him thrash around in vain for thirty seconds or so, then stepped up to the entrance to the box.

"Good news," I said. "I've figured out what's wrong with these things."

He stopped struggling quite so violently and turned his head to face me, but didn't speak.

"It's the mechanism that keeps the boxes from falling right out of the side of the building," I said. "It's broken. The whole thing could just plummet at any second. It's really unstable. I hope the famous Chicago wind doesn't pick up anytime soon. It's a shame you can't get out, really."

He stopped moving altogether this time, but didn't break his silence.

"How far can you move your neck?" I said. "Can you see those little buttons up there?"

He didn't answer.

"There's a green one," I said. "But I'm not interested in that at all. It makes the box move back inside. I'm thinking more about the red one. 'Cause if I press that, you, and the box, well . . . Let's just say you'd be the first man to try out a glass parachute. And probably the last."

He swallowed loudly, but didn't manage any words.

"It's a good thing the street is closed, down below here," I said. "I'd feel awfully guilty if you pulverized any pedestrians, walking by."

"OK," he said, after another moment. "Enough. You win. What do you want?"

"A little information. Starting with some background."

"I can give you that. Just get these things off my back."

"Questions first, I think. You're planning on murdering what, several thousand people? Why?"

"I told you. Dollars and cents."

"There has to be more to it than that."

"For the people who are paying, maybe. But not for me."

"Who is paying you?"

"That's a stupid question. You know it doesn't work that way. Someone wants a job done. They hire me to do it. Anonymously, through two or three blinds. Afterward, you see their face on TV or the Internet or wherever, claiming responsibility. Sick and cowardly of them, maybe, but it pays the bills."

"OK. Why are they doing it? Did they tell you that much?"

"Yeah, funnily enough. I made it clear I have no moral scruples whatsoever. That's why people hire me. But these guys still wanted me to think they were righteous."

"How, if you weren't in contact?"

"They sent me a load of crap through some intermediaries. And they have vision, I grant them that. The New York guys, in '01—they demolished the Twin Towers. So now, there's nothing left to see. These guys, though, they want this building left intact. What did they call it? A fourteen-hundred-foot-high coffin. A lasting monument to the immorality of Western culture, standing empty and unusable. Something like that. Whatever."

"How would the building be unusable? Spektra gas isn't radioactive. It doesn't seep into the fabric of the place. There shouldn't be any long-term effects."

"That's true. But it's not the point. You're being too

literal. These guys are more like poets. They're thinking about how the whole deal will go down. Starting with every single person in the place being dead. And everyone in the country knowing about it. Hell, they won't even need the TV cameras. People will be tweeting about it while it's still happening. They'll be posting videos of their co-workers twitching and dying. I guarantee it."

I didn't reply. I was too busy thinking about how much I hate Twitter.

"Then the emergency crews will come," he said. "At first they'll stand off, not knowing what to do. Then they'll suit up and charge in. And die, 'cause regular respirators are no good against Spektra. So there'll be delays, waiting for the military. More delays, waiting for body bags, 'cause there won't be enough. So when the bodies do finally come out, they'll be starting to rot and decompose. Are you getting the picture?"

I didn't answer.

"So you see what I mean?" he said. "These guys are like the artists of international terrorism. And after the scene they create, do you think anyone will ever want to work in the building again? Would you?"

I bit my tongue.

"So the building won't be used," he said. "And it'll cost too much to pull it down. So there you go. It'll be like a statue. A sculpture. Call it what you like."

"And you have no problem with that?" I said.

"No. None. It's what I do for a living."

I stood and looked at him.

"Can you move these metal bars now, please?" he said.

"No," I said. "When's all this supposed to happen?"

"Soon, I guess. There's no fixed time or date. Or if there is, they haven't told me. I'm supposed to let them know when everything's ready. Then they'll give me the signal."

"When will it be ready?"

"Later tonight."

"The empty valve, downstairs? You need another canister?"

"Right."

"Where are you getting it from?"

"It's being brought right here, to me."

"Room service?"

"My supplier."

"McIntyre?"

"Right. Normally I meet him somewhere neutral. But tonight, we traded favors. Doorstep delivery, for garbage disposal."

"Garbage, meaning me?"

"Right. Normally he'd take care of you himself, but he's had a couple of bumps and bruises lately. He didn't want to do it, in the circumstances. And I'm beginning to see why."

"What time is he coming?"

"I'll let him know when you're out of the way. Then we'll fix a time."

"How do you contact him?"

"I use this amazing new device called the phone."

"You have his number?"

"Of course."

"OK. Good. Go ahead and call him now. Tell him to be here at eight o'clock."

"You'll have to get these things off me. I can't reach my phone."

"I'll take care of you after you make the call. You reach the phone, or you stay where you are. Your choice."

The guy made a play of straining to get his hand into his pocket, but thirty seconds later he'd produced the phone.

"Wait," I said. "Call up his number. Let me see it."

He prodded a couple of buttons, then passed me the handset. The phone book entry was under McIntyre, and the number matched the one that had sent me the texts just over twenty-four hours ago.

"OK," I said. "That's fine. Make the call. Only tell him nine o'clock, instead."

The guy did as I told him. He only needed six words. The call took less than ten seconds. A relieved smile spread across his face when he hung up the phone. And faded again when he saw the gun that was now in my hand.

"Remind me of something," I said. "Your advice, earlier. Did you tell me to say good morning? Or good night?"

"Good night," he said.

"And remember how I told you I was going to do that? Well, I always keep my word. I'm going to say it to you, first, since it was your idea. And then to your friends, downstairs. I wouldn't want them to miss out."

TWENTY-TWO

There's one word in navy intelligence that no one likes to speak out loud. Traitor.

No one makes jokes on the subject. No one gossips about it. And on the rare occasion that one is unmasked, no one talks about it. The only exception that I ever encountered was a guy in Bermuda. His nerves were still a little shot because he'd just exposed someone he'd worked with for twenty-two years. I hadn't been in the service for twenty-two weeks at that point, so the whole affair made a big impression on me. I sat in a bar on the south side of the island and listened intently as he talked me through what had happened. How he'd first been alerted to his friend's guilt. How he'd double- and triple-checked to make sure there was no mistake. How he'd considered handing the case off to internal security. And how he'd finally hunted the guy down and shot him in the head, leaving his guns in their holsters as an enduring badge of shame.

I could see a pair of plump tears welling up in the corners of his eyes, so I asked him if he regretted what he'd done.

"Absolutely not," he said, without even pausing to blink. "Because this is what you have to understand. A traitor doesn't just betray himself. Or his friends. His family. His country. His queen. He betrays the whole service as well. That means you and me and everyone we're sworn to fight for. So, no. I have no remorse about shooting him. None at all."

I thought he'd finished, but after a long swig of beer he turned back to me and rounded things off.

"Actually, there is one thing I regret," he said. "Killing him once just isn't enough. If I was God for a day, I'd make it so that traitors can die twice. Then I could blow his worthless brains out all over again."

The night-duty receptionist was at the desk when I reached the fourteenth floor of the Wrigley Building, just after seven thirty. She glanced up at me when I came out of the elevator and then gestured vaguely toward the doors that concealed the sniffer machines. I was glad to be able to pick for myself. I wanted the same one that I'd used when I first came to the consulate, four days ago. I always like that kind of symmetry at the start and end of a job. The sense of balance continued when I reached Fothergill's office. He was standing at the same window. And he was wearing the same blue pin-striped suit. There were only two things that were different from the original picture. He had a large pilot's-style briefcase on the floor at his feet. And he was surprised to see me.

"David," he said, spinning around when he saw my

reflection in the glass. "What are you doing here? I thought you were still at the Sears Tower?"

"I was there," I said. "But everything's squared away now, so I thought I'd come over here and tell you about it."

"So what happened? You didn't call. I was worried."

"I had a couple of ups and downs, but nothing to lose sleep over."

"What do you mean? Did you find anything?"

"I dug up a couple of things."

"What things? Tell me."

"Some people that shouldn't have been there, for a start."

"People? Who? How many? Where are they now?"

"Three of them. South Africans. They're still there. And don't fret. They won't be leaving. Not under their own steam, anyway."

"You killed them?"

"It seemed like the thing to do. Seeing as they were trying to flood the building's ventilation system with McIntyre's Spektra V."

Fothergill sagged at the knees, half sitting down on the windowsill.

"They were? Why?"

"The usual. For money. They were mercenaries."

"Who was paying them?"

"They didn't know."

"Didn't know? Or wouldn't say?"

"They didn't know."

"Maybe. But we can't ask them, now, can we? I wish you'd learn to rein yourself in a little, sometimes, David."

"Reining in wasn't the problem. If they'd known, they'd have told me. Believe me. But we've prevented the immediate threat. That's what counts. And the backroom boys can run down the whole network now, as quickly as they like."

"I suppose. But what about the gas itself? Did you find it?"

"All three canisters. Unopened and intact."

"Oh my goodness," Fothergill said, getting back on his feet. "David, do you know what this means? It just occurred to me. We're heroes. Superstars. We just saved countless lives. We stopped the next 9/11."

"I guess we did," I said.

"This is huge. Enormous. I'm thinking, medals. Maybe a trip to the palace. But we're going to have to think very carefully about how we handle things. We want the kudos, but some parts of the story can never see the light of day."

"Well, you worry about milking the glory. I still have work to do."

"We both do. But talking about the gas, where is it now?"

"Still at the Sears Tower."

"What?"

"Don't panic. It's in a safe place."

"You left it in a public building? Are you mad? What were you thinking?"

"Let me finish. I left it because I've got a lead on McIntyre."

"You're not serious? The gas, and Tony? In one night? Really?"

"Why not? I like to be thorough."

"I was beginning to think we'd never get another sniff of him. What did you find? And is it solid, this time? I'd hate for him to give us the slip, again."

"It's beyond solid. I know exactly where he is. My information is accurate to within an inch."

"Then why are we here? Come on. Let's go. We need to grab him before he moves again. You know what he's like. Always one step ahead."

"Oh, I'm going to do more than grab him. Please. Have no doubt. Before nine o'clock tonight, he'll no longer be a problem. To anyone. I guarantee it."

"David, that's excellent. But why nine o'clock? Can't we move now? Holding back makes me nervous."

"We're not holding back. I just need a couple more pieces of background."

"Why? Don't you have enough already?"

"Think of it as setting a trap. The jaws are open. Now we need to oil the hinges. Make sure they're good and ready. I want them to snap shut, all the way."

"Well, OK, I suppose. We could do that. What do you need to know?"

"Come over here. Let's sit."

I took the easy chair on the far side of the coffee table, away from the door. Fothergill didn't move for a moment.

Then he picked up his case and came over to sit next to me, on my right. That was another difference. At our first meeting, we'd been facing each other.

"What are you waiting for?" Fothergill said. "Ask away. Anything."

"Let's start with *A*," I said. "Afghanistan. You told me McIntyre was stationed there."

"He was. That's right."

"What exactly was his job?"

"I don't know."

"Don't be pedantic. I don't literally mean his job title. I want to know what he was doing that brought him into contact with illegal weapons."

"The weapons weren't illegal, actually. Not all of them. Most of them had been given to the Afghans by the Americans, in the first place. Or by us."

"Back in the Soviet era, do you mean?"

"Yes."

"And since then?"

"The game has changed. The people we gave them to have swapped sides. The old good guys are the new bad guys. They're using the weapons against us. So we either need to confiscate them, which is hard. Or get them back another way."

"Was Tony involved in getting them back?"

"Yes. It was a joint operation with the U.S. They put up the money. We did the legwork."

"We were buying them?"

"Yes."

"From the people we gave them to, who used to be our friends, but are now our enemies?"

"David, I hope you're not expecting me to make this sound sane. Because you can cut this or slice this any way you like, and it's still ten kinds of crazy. But you have to be practical. And the thing to remember is that this does work."

"This is something working? McIntyre? The Myenese? The guys in the Sears Tower?"

"Well, it works to an extent. Until people start stealing the weapons and skimming the money, at least. The system struggles a little, then."

"Was that McIntyre's game? Stealing weapons and skimming money?"

"Yes. I believe so. And when he stumbled across the gas, he figured he'd hit the mother lode."

"Wait. You said the weapons were Soviet era, handed out to the Taliban when we were all friends. Spektra gas isn't that old."

"No. It's a couple of years, max."

"So what was it doing there? How did McIntyre get his hands on it?"

"Who knows? This is Afghanistan we're talking about. Nothing makes sense, there. Most likely it was part of a sample batch, sent over for covert evaluation. It doesn't really matter. The point is, all that American cash was like a magnet. It brought all kinds of things out of the woodwork. A lot of it was junk, by all accounts. But if a case of Spektra crossed Tony's path, he'd know enough to see the potential for extra profit. And extra risk."

"Which is why he needed to cover his tracks a little more thoroughly."

"Exactly. And why he tried to frame me."

"You think he was selling to the Myenese?"

"I think that was his original idea, yes. I think he started with a deal to sell to those guys in their own backyard. Then he got a better offer from someone else—the Sears Tower guys, I guess—so he did a runner over here. He could make more money. And lay the blame on me more effectively. Which he needed to do. 'Cause let's face it, dead Americans make bigger headlines than dead Africans."

"So he double-crossed the Myenese, and they chased him here to force him to make good on the deal?"

"Right."

"What evidence have you got for any of that?"

Fothergill was silent for a moment.

"Richard?" I said. "What evidence?"

"Well, no actual evidence," he said. "But that's pretty much what he told me, when he was here. Before he tried to murder me."

"When he spoke to you, how was his accent?"

"What?"

"You told me he was Scottish."

"He was. Is. So what?"

"I noticed Young's Geordie accent was fading a little. He was probably out of the country too long. So how about McIntyre. Did he still sound like he was from north of the border?"

"Goodness, yes. You know what those accents are like.

People never lose them. Not completely. But how is this relevant? If you know where Tony is, what does it matter what he sounded like to talk to?"

"You're right. I'm just curious. Because I was talking to someone who'd spoken to McIntyre on the phone, and they thought he was English."

"That's no big deal. Most foreigners can't tell the difference between English and Scottish, or even Welsh. Someone thought I was Australian the other day, for goodness' sake."

I nodded as if I was thinking about his answer, then shut my eyes for a moment and didn't speak. I started to sway slightly, back and forth. Then I let myself flop forward, nosediving toward the surface of the coffee table. It would have hurt, if I'd made contact. But I didn't, because Fothergill had shot his left arm out to save me. I looked down at his hand. It was pressed against my chest. Palm out, as I'd expected. That only left me with one question, and even though I already knew the answer—or perhaps because I already knew the answer—I was reluctant to ask it.

"David," he said. "My goodness, are you all right?"

"I'm fine," I said. "Really. Thank you. And thanks for saving me from going face-first through your table. That really would have left some broken glass to sweep up."

"Don't mention it. My pleasure. But what happened to you? Are you feeling faint?"

"It's nothing. Something came over me, but I'm OK now."

"Maybe you should go back to your hotel. I told you not to push yourself."

"No. We'll carry on."

"David, you've had a hell of a day. You've just saved thousands of people's lives. It would be OK to have an early night. No one would think badly of you."

"I don't need to, honestly. Let's wrap this thing up, and I'll sleep late tomorrow. I promise."

"It's a deal. And I'll make sure you stick to it. So. Shall we go and close Tony down now, once and for all?"

I waited another moment.

"One last thing, before we do," I said. "What's in the bag?"

He took his time to reply.

"That's none of your business," he said. "I can't tell you, I'm afraid. The contents are classified. You're not the only operative I look after, you know."

"Richard, I need you to open the bag and show me what's inside," I said.

"Don't be crazy. That's never going to happen. Now drop it. Let's go to work."

"This is the last time I'm going to ask nicely. The bag. Open it. Please."

Fothergill didn't answer, and he didn't move.

I reached inside my jacket and took out my phone.

"McIntyre texted me yesterday," I said. "It seemed plausible, because this is actually Young's phone. It was natural that McIntyre should know the number, right?"

Fothergill nodded.

"Only someone else knew the number, too," I said. "You did. Because I'd called you from it."

He didn't respond.

"You knew the conclusion I'd reach when the texts came, because of the phone belonging to Young," I said. "And just remind me—where were you at the time?"

"In here," he said. "With you. I remember when they arrived."

"No. You were out of the room. With the IT guys, allegedly. I wonder if you were really there, that day. I wonder if you were really there at all. I wonder how much they'd know about the Myenese guys' laptop and hard drives, if I went and asked them."

"They'd back me one hundred percent of the way."

"There's an easier way to find out the truth," I said, holding up the phone. "Look. Here's McIntyre's number. The one the texts came from, yesterday. The one the guy from the Sears Tower was supposed to use today, after he'd killed me. Shall I call it now? I wonder if I'd hear ringing from anywhere close by?"

"No."

"What's in the bag, Richard?"

Fothergill didn't answer.

"Let's call him, then, after all," I said. "We could put him on speakerphone and see how Scottish he sounds. Or whether he's suddenly developed an English accent. Like yours."

"David," he said. "Drop this. Don't call that number. Please."

"Open the bag."

He didn't respond.

"Open the bag," I said. "Open it now. My finger's on the call button. You should save yourself the embarrassment."

Fothergill looked me in the eye to see if I was serious, then leaned forward and clumsily unclipped the case's two brass catches with his unbandaged left hand.

"All the way," I said.

He pulled back the lid.

"Take it out," I said.

He waited for a moment, then reached into the case with both hands and lifted out a green metal canister.

"Put it on the table," I said.

"OK," he said, setting it down between us. "There it is. What now?"

"We wait."

Fothergill stared at the floor for a couple of minutes, then his gaze was drawn to the clock on the wall behind his desk. It was ten to eight. The second hand crawled inexorably around, and I noticed that the pulse in Fothergill's neck was jumping twice for every move it made. I remember thinking that kind of heart rate couldn't be healthy for a man of his age, and wondering if nature was going to do my work for me. But he survived fifteen complete revolutions, and then dragged his focus across to my face.

He held my gaze for thirty seconds before licking his lips and starting to speak again.

"There've been lots of questions, tonight," he said. "But here's the big one. This is all down to you, now. And I need to know. Are you going to call London? That's the only thing left that matters."

"That depends," I said. "How many more canisters are there?"

"No more. You have them all. There were always only four."

"There were four all along? Are you sure?"

"Certain. You nearly busted me when I left Gary, remember? When I'd said Tony had sold half the consignment, then found two more canisters? I should have only admitted to one."

"Explain that."

"Tony brought four canisters to Chicago with him. He gave them to me, along with the Myenese guys' details. They wanted all four. I started out letting them have two. I was going to sell them the other two separately, for more money. I asked Tony to set up the meeting, but he caught on. We fought, and he got away with one canister."

"The one you wanted me to retrieve?"

"Yes."

"So you could sell it?"

"Yes."

"And it was you who wanted McIntyre silenced?"

Fothergill looked at the floor and nodded, very slightly.

"What about the hard arrest?" I said. "That was a genuine order. I checked it myself."

"It was," he said. "But it was based on the information I provided. Let's just say I adjusted certain details."

"And the information you provided when you asked

for a team, to back me up? And for a biochem expert? Did you adjust those, too?"

"Perhaps. A little. Couldn't have too many cooks, you know."

"What about the pair of canisters from Gary, in the packing cases? Did you really find them there?"

"Yes. They were the ones I originally sold. Half the consignment, like I let slip."

"But you didn't want to stay in Gary. You tried to talk me out of searching the place."

"I know. I had no idea the canisters were there. Lucky you wouldn't listen or I'd never have got my hands on them."

"But McIntyre didn't really take them back in the car crash?"

"No. I staged that to cover them disappearing."

"And you killed this guy Milton in the process."

"That was an accident. The air bag. The metal thing. It was a fluke."

"It could have been a fluke, I suppose. If you hadn't been holding the metal thing, to make sure it was end-on, ready to stab him."

"No. It was on his lap. I had no part in that."

"You couldn't let him walk away. He'd know you'd stolen the canisters."

Fothergill's head drooped again.

"And your burns were on the wrong side," I said. "They were on the back of your hand. Because you were holding something. If your hand had been empty, it would have been palm out, like a minute ago when you thought I was collapsing."

He didn't respond.

"How did the switch from the Myenese to the Sears guys come about?" I said.

"Oh, that," he said, without looking up. "It was easy. An old friend of mine from South Africa called me. He had big money on hand for anything they could use as a contaminant. I didn't even know they were targeting the Tower, at first."

"They wanted any contaminant? They weren't specific?"

"No. Originally they wanted something with nuclear waste in it. I convinced them that Spektra was better. Safer for them, when they were rigging the place."

"And you used McIntyre's name?"

"Yes."

"Why?"

"Insurance. We'd always used code names before. I figured you'd fall for it, if everything else failed. That's why I lured you to the Sears Tower."

"You wanted me to go to the Sears Tower?"

"Come on, David. Think about the pantomime at the architects' office. I led you by the nose."

"You set me up. Just like you did at the Drake?"

Fothergill shrugged.

"There were no more Myenese left, were there?" I said. "You killed the last two at the Commissariat to stop me talking to them."

"Couldn't have them spilling the beans, now, could I?" he said.

"You burned the entire hotel down."

"That was your fault, really. I tried to talk you out of going once I had things in place with the South Africans, but you wouldn't listen."

"And you killed the rent-a-goons. Why?"

"In case it didn't work, and you escaped. Which you kept doing, you slippery bastard. I thought it would look less suspicious if you weren't the only target."

"So you could try again at the Tower?"

"Right. I was running short of options."

I waited until he raised his eyes again before replying.

"OK, then," I said. "To answer your question. London needs to hear about this. And it might as well be from me."

Fothergill's head dropped until his chin was resting on his chest. His breathing grew heavier, and for a moment I wondered about the state of his heart again. But after thirty seconds he straightened his neck, hauled himself to his feet, and looked me straight in the eye.

"David, I need to ask you for a favor," he said. "A trade, if you like. I have information about the situation with Tony that you should know about. I can tell you all of it, right now."

"OK," I said. "But what do you want in return?"

"We both know what has to be done here. There's no way I can walk away from this one. I'm in absolute disgrace. And there's not much else I can look back on in my life and feel proud of. In fact, there's nothing. Everything I've ever done is tainted in some way. So what I want is the chance to take care of this, myself. To finally do one thing right. To salvage some kind of honor. Some pride, if you like. Will you let me at least have that, before you make the call?"

"What can you tell me about Tony?" I said, after a moment.

"Tony's on the side of the angels," he said. "He always has been. How much do you know about Equatorial Myene?"

"A little. A friend passed on some interesting facts."

"So you've heard about the rebel movement they have there?"

"Are they the idiots talking about a coup? If so, they could use some help with their security."

"They could use some help, all around. Which is why they roped in Tony's buddy, Young. He provides mercenaries. Coups need muscle. It was a natural fit. But things developed. Young started believing in their cause. He talked about it with Tony. And before you know it, they're both converts."

"So Tony was siphoning the money and weapons for the rebels? Not the government?"

"He was. He hated the government. For him it was a case of right place, right time. He felt like he'd found a better use for the guns than melting them down, and more deserving recipients for the money than poppy growers and murderers."

"So what went wrong?"

"It seems they'd been compromised from the start. Only the Myenese government was happy to let them get on with it. They found it easier to keep tabs on them, that way."

"The classic story. If the government clamped down on them, they'd only pop up again somewhere else, and maybe stay underground for a little while longer."

"Exactly. And they weren't too worried about a few old AKs and M-16s kicking around. They weren't threatened by the amount of cash, obviously. But when word spread about a consignment of Spektra suddenly appearing, their ears pricked up for sure."

"They wanted it for themselves."

"Right. But Tony didn't want that to happen. He was worried about the civilians, so he came to me for help."

"Because you're old mates."

"Partly. And partly because I already knew the background. No one does something like that in a vacuum. No one's that stupid. Especially not experienced, serving intelligence officers. So I'd been helping them get the nods and winks lined up that they needed before getting involved."

"What they were doing had official backing?"

"Oh, no. Everything was under the table. Complete plausible deniability was maintained at all times. But no one on our side was going to be counting the beans too carefully, if you know what I mean. And who can tell if a mass of molten metal came from three guns, or only two?"

"So Her Majesty's Government was tacitly helping, but in Tony's hour of need you sold him out for a quick buck?"

"Well, lots of bucks, actually. And the idea was for me to sell the canisters, and have Tony steal them back. That way, we—I—could make lots of money and the gas could be destroyed anyway. No one got hurt apart from the bad guys. It seemed almost poetic. And certainly criminal to let a chance like that go begging."

"But Tony wouldn't play."

"No. We didn't see eye to eye on it at all."

"Which is why you wanted him stopped."

"Don't be so judgmental. I'm not proud of this, you know. Telling the truth is new to me, and I'm beginning to think it's overrated."

"One more question. How did the Myenese know Tony was at that apartment? Did Young tell them?"

"No. You did."

"What?"

"Well, you told me, and I told them. You called me before you went in. But it all boils down to the same thing."

"And you told them that it was Young who killed their guys when they came to snatch Tony?"

"That's right."

"Why?"

"They were mad as hell. I had to give them someone. And I still needed you alive. So in a way, I saved your life."

"Excuse me if I don't thank you."

Fothergill waited, rocking slightly, for another thirty seconds. I had no more questions for him. He seemed to sense this and took a slow, tentative step forward. He took another. Then he turned, stretched out his arm, and picked up the cylinder.

"Stop," I said. "One more thing. The rug. Was it expensive?"

"Very," he said. "I paid for it myself. Take it, if you want it. It's yours."

I waited till both his feet were on the original government-issue, nonabsorbent carpet at the edge of the room before pulling the trigger. But not to save the rug. I never had any intention of keeping it. That wasn't why I'd asked him. I was just thinking it's bad luck to leave a mess behind you, for other people to clear up.